A Widow
Redefined

a novel by
Kim Cano

ISBN-10: 1482791935
ISBN-13: 978-1482791938

To my friend, Kathryn Thumme.
I'm thankful God led me to you.

Chapter 1

Standing in the snow in front of my husband's grave, I came to an unexpected realization. What used to be a romantic tribute had become something disconcerting.

As I kneeled down to lay a pink rose at the base of Justin's headstone, I noticed a bouquet of yellow daffodils in the spot where I planned to place my flower. Daffodils? From whom? I tried to wrap my mind around why they were there, to solve a mystery I hadn't anticipated.

Then a strong gust of Chicago wind slapped across my face. And with it came a new level of comprehension. Today was Valentine's Day. These flowers were fresh.

Confused, I began to look around. I scanned the cemetery for others and saw a lone groundskeeper cleaning near the entrance. I dropped my rose and began running in his direction.

Arriving short of breath, I asked, "Have you been here long? Have you seen anyone else here recently?"

"No," he said, eyeing me with caution. "I just come from break."

Out of frustration I grasped for anything. "Okay, well, is there a log of some kind? Of the people who come and go each day?"

My visitations had never been recorded. I knew this.

The man could see its importance to me, so he gave it some thought before responding.

"No," he said. "No records."

Disappointed, I stood there, staring at him. He gazed back at me, with a polite smile on his face. And after an awkwardly long pause, the groundskeeper's look changed from pleasant to irritated. He mumbled something about being busy and walked away.

My mind began racing and I felt the pulse of a headache starting in the back of my skull. When I left work earlier, I'd been happy to find it wasn't cold and gray. Driving into the cemetery, I had been captured by the particularly brilliant sunset; the sky blazed with pink and purple streaks.

Now, as I stood alone, the sky was dark.

Suddenly, I couldn't leave fast enough. I began running toward my car, somehow managing to not trip or fall, then hopped in and slammed the door shut. A little flustered, I dropped my keys as I went to start the engine. I felt around and finally discovered them jammed between the front seat and center console. I pulled them free, started the car, and peeled out of the parking spot like a teenage drag racer.

As I turned left onto the main road to head home, I considered the possibilities. Maybe Justin's parents were in town and had gone to the cemetery. They popped in from time to time, not always stopping by to say hello. The rare trip to see their grandson was the only reason they ever seemed to bother with me.

I knew it wasn't my mom. After the funeral she never went back, although she was respectful of my visits, which were many over the last two years. Since the funeral, my routine—coming on holidays and his birthday—had always been the same. Only the seasons changed. But today my world tipped slightly off its axis, and I couldn't help but recall what my older co-worker Barb had once told me, that the only constant in life is change.

Something in the pit of my stomach didn't like it.

As I got closer to home, I tried to forget the flowers. I wanted to seem normal to my son, Tyler, and my mom. He's only seven and believed I was out visiting a friend. Mom, on the other hand, is quite perceptive. Nothing gets past her. Stressed out and feeling a migraine coming on, I turned right onto the street where I live.

"Hey, honey. I've got your plate in the microwave," Mom called out, after she heard me come in.

I set my keys and purse on the sofa, took off my coat and hung it up, and walked into the kitchen.

"Amy," Mom said, "You look terrible. Are you okay? You have sweat beads on your forehead."

I wiped my face with the back of my hand. "Oh," I replied, "I'm fine, just a little cold."

She gave me a funny look and put my food on the table. I sat down to eat right away, hoping she wouldn't ask more questions. Then Tyler ran in.

"Mom. Grandma and I went to the library. I got a DVD on bugs of the desert southwest. You wanna watch it with me?"

"Sure, honey." I somehow managed to eat dinner and hold a coherent conversation, but the whole time I felt like I was sinking in quicksand. Luckily, no one seemed to notice. Afterward, Mom returned to her novel, and Tyler and I watched the bug program; at least it appeared like I did. Mostly I just stared at the TV while thinking about the daffodils.

"Scorpions are so cool. Don't you think?" Tyler asked, interrupting my thoughts.

I despised bugs, but I didn't want to disappoint my son. "Yeah, I guess they're pretty neat," I agreed. "You know, it's almost time for bed soon. I'm going to take a bath, and then I'll come and tuck you in."

Tyler frowned but didn't put up a fight. He was well-behaved that way. He put the disc back in its case while I left to go to the bathroom. Once inside, I dimmed the lights and locked the door. I turned the tub faucet on to as hot as I could stand it, added some aromatherapy salts, undressed and climbed in. As the water level grew, I sunk deeper into its protective womb. I closed my eyes and let the warmth slowly relax me. As so often happened when I relaxed, an old memory surfaced—one I try not to remember—of the day my dad moved away, leaving my mom and me for another woman. I was just a kid.

Tears began flowing down my cheeks and into the water. It was a silent sobbing so as not to disturb anyone else. My mind began to race again. *Daffodils!* Soon my head throbbed with unbearable pain. I couldn't allow myself to think about any of it a moment longer, so I released the drain, grabbed a towel and climbed out.

I must have lost track of time, because when I went to tuck Tyler in, he was already in bed, asleep. I leaned over and kissed him on top of his head, then gently closed his door. When I got to my room, I noticed a bottle of Excedrin lying on the dresser, so I took two, without water, and collapsed into bed.

While lying in the dark, I decided to think of something happy. A good memory. A previous Valentine's Day. Justin always took me to Francesca's, our favorite Italian restaurant. I could almost see us sitting at a candlelit table, drinking wine and eating pasta.

Justin raised his glass. "Someday I'm going to take my kitten to Paris."

I flushed. Even after years together, he still had that effect on me.

"We'll eat at the Eiffel Tower restaurant for your birthday, and we'll go on one of those Seine river cruises. What do you think?"

"Say the word and I'm packed," I said.

We spent the night talking, sharing tiramisu. Justin glowed with health and his blue eyes sparkled as he described plans to expand his carpentry business. Soon we'd be financially set. We'd be able to afford to travel the world together, like we always talked about. I don't think I'd ever seen him more excited about anything as he was about this.

People shouldn't die of cancer at thirty.

Every good memory eventually ended up there... in reality. There was no escaping it, no matter how hard I tried. And now there was the mystery of the daffodils. I didn't know what to think, but I desperately needed rest if I wanted to make it to work in the morning, so I shut my eyes and willed my mind to stop racing.

I dreamt of Justin. We floated peacefully together on a lake in a rowboat. The sky was clear and the sun shone bright. He said something funny that made me laugh, causing me to lean over and clutch my belly. When I regained composure and tossed my head back up, still smiling, clouds had filled the sky. They had an ominous look about them, angry. Lightning sparked followed by loud claps of thunder. I looked at Justin, wondering what we should do, but his expression was blank. The waves grew choppy, and all at once, swells the size of skyscrapers surrounded us. One moment we were in their trough, the next we ascended their foamy crest. Terrified, I looked over at Justin, seeking some kind of help. He remained blank-faced and unresponsive. Then, as we began descending back into the dark cavern of the wave, the boat tipped over, and I woke up, choking.

Chapter 2

The next morning, I woke up late. Disoriented, I jumped out of bed and scrambled to check on Tyler before getting ready for work. I found him in the kitchen, eating a bowl of cereal.

"There you are," I said, relieved. "Thank God you're up and ready to go."

"Did you oversleep?"

"Yeah. But I'll be ready in ten minutes, and then I'll take you to school."

I rushed through my morning routine quicker than I ever had, and on the drive to school, remembered promising my son I would take him shopping for colored pencils and paper. Drawing was one of his favorite things.

"We'll stop after dinner to get you those art supplies," I told him, smiling.

He smiled back, and I kissed him goodbye before he got out of the car. I felt so happy, seeing him excited about a hobby and enjoying life again. It had taken a long time—too long, I'd thought, but he was almost back to himself.

I managed to make it to the office, clock in and be at my desk just before my boss, Dave, walked past. He had some new clients scheduled today, so it was important we looked organized. It was a busy time of year for tax accountants, and even though we did well, Dave never stopped drumming up new business. He was a real hustler.

Luckily, Dave never gave me any trouble. He told me once that I accomplished the work of two people. Although I appreciated the compliment, what I really needed was a raise. Things had become pretty tight with only one income.

Fatima walked up to my desk and stood silently for a moment, the way she did when she was about to ask a question. "Did you happen to see *Dancing with the Stars* last night?"

"No," I said. "I went to the cemetery."

The words were out before I could stop them. I had over-shared. Again.

Fatima opened her mouth as if to say something, and then closed it. She shifted her weight—all ninety pounds of it—and finally said, "It was a pretty good episode," and continued on to her seat behind me, next to Barb, the third member of our accounting trio.

"Everything okay?" asked Barb. I thought I detected a tiny bit of exasperation in her voice. I knew they both wished I'd stop reminding them how much I miss Justin. They'd never say it, of course, because even though they were pretty much opposites—Fatima, a just out of college, stick thin beauty, and Barb, a woman who embodied the dictionary definition of "matronly"—they both were much too kind to complain. But they were probably right. Two years is a long time to grieve out loud.

I mumbled, "I'm fine," pressing the words through a forced smile.

"I think this morning needs some music," Barb said. She patted my shoulder as she walked past me to the ancient radio that was balanced on the tallest filing cabinet. She turned the knob in search of a static-free station, but the reception predictably faded in and out. We could only count on two channels: Oldies and a Spanish station. Today she chose the former. On the way back to her desk, Barb smiled warmly at me. Her sweet round face and closely-cropped hairstyle reminded me of a garden gnome. She was the kind of person it felt comfortable and safe to be around.

As the day went on, I cranked out one document after another, working like a machine, but my mind still managed to wander. I decided to take a break and email Justin's mom in Phoenix. I had stopped trying to reach her by phone when she started replying to my voicemail messages with an email. I got the hint that it was her preferred form of communication… at least with me.

I sent her a message asking if she had been in town, and telling her I had been thinking of her recently. I didn't mention the flowers. Since Justin died and they retired and moved away, we hadn't managed to stay close.

Later in the day, I read her reply. She hadn't been in, but would let me know if they planned on coming up to Chicago. No "miss you," no "how've you been?" She was an odd bird that way. Always somewhat distant with me, she was a bundle of sunshine and laughs with her son. A split personality, I thought, but I'd never shared that opinion with my husband. I liked Justin's dad, though. He was sweet. Unfortunately, he never made calls or went on the computer much. He was more of an "in person" charmer. Once you were out of his sight, it was like you didn't exist.

As I drove home from work, I thought about the flowers again. Knowing for certain that Justin's parents hadn't left them stirred an uncomfortable sensation in my gut.

Tyler greeted me at the front door. "Grandma says we're going out tonight. Mexican food." He held up a drawing of an eerily realistic tarantula.

"Sounds good." I eyed his work and nodded approval. "Beautiful picture. I'm afraid it's not gonna make it to the front of the refrigerator, though. It's a bit of an appetite killer."

Tyler giggled, rolled his eyes and took off down the hallway.

The three of us piled into the car and headed to the restaurant. Once seated, the waiter approached us, asking if we would like drinks before ordering our meals.

"I'll have a margarita. On the rocks with salt," I said.

Mom glanced my way, raising an eyebrow. "Letting your hair down?"

I gave a half smile back. "Trying."

I wished the drink were for fun, instead of an attempt to settle my frantic nerves. I no longer knew how to have fun. I had always been the most serious person in the room. It was Justin who had taught me how to laugh. His humor kept us all in stitches.

After he got too sick to work and Mom sold her house and moved in with us, she continued to remark about how funny he was. The complete opposite of my dad.

The drinks arrived and I took a sip. The salt stung an open cut I didn't realize I had on the inside of my mouth. I watched Mom drink her soda and remembered what she always used to say to me: "You're so lucky, Amy. You and Justin have the perfect marriage."

I ignored the brief stab of heartache and took a bigger gulp. Then I turned my attention to Tyler. "How was school today? You have any homework?"

He munched on a chip dipped with salsa. "It was fine. I finished my assignments before you got home."

Of course he had done it. He always did. His teacher had recently spoken with me about the possibility of moving him up a grade. I didn't want to cause him additional stress, so I decided against it.

Soon the waiter showed up with our meals. I took a bite of my chicken enchiladas. "This is delicious."

Mom and Tyler—both with food in their mouths—nodded their agreement. It was nice being out together. We used to do it once a week with Justin. Sometimes Mom would join us; sometimes she'd babysit so we could have a date night.

As I reminisced about Justin, my mind wandered to the daffodils again. I needed to solve that mystery. Alone.

"Hey, Mom. Remember that gym membership I never use?"

She looked up from her meal. "Yeah."

"Well, I was just thinking. I'd like to go swimming. I never do that anymore. They're offering an aqua aerobics class this Sunday, and I can bring a guest. Do you wanna come?"

My mom hadn't been seen in public in a swimsuit in over a decade. She said she felt too old and out of shape; that her days of hitting the beach were over. I thought she was incredibly silly. But I knew she'd decline. The cemetery was on the way to the health club. I still intended to work out, but I also was making secret plans to investigate the mystery of the flowers.

"No. I'd rather not," she said. "I can watch Tyler for you while you're gone though."

Just the response I had hoped for. A big part of me

felt terrible for being so manipulative. Another part of me thought, "How could I tell you something might be wrong with my once perfect marriage?"

I'd have to deal with the guilt in order to find out more.

For the rest of the evening, Mom chatted about her lady friend, Tyler discussed his new teacher, and I weaved in and out of the conversation, listening and responding as appropriate. But a portion of my brain continued to work on solving the problem at hand. Who could have left those damn flowers?

After we left the restaurant, we stopped at the art supply store.

"Gauguin," Mom said, addressing Tyler. "Which colored pencils do you want?"

Tyler loved being called that name ever since he'd seen a program about the South Pacific with Justin and me. We used to sit together watching the Travel Channel, planning future trips we'd hope to take. Tahiti was number one on our list. And once Tyler found out a famous artist had lived there and seen his paintings in a library book, Gauguin became his idol. He wanted to be just like him.

With a serious expression on his face, Tyler replied, "I think these would work best," and handed my mom his selection.

He cracked me up, but I didn't laugh out loud. He was like an old man sometimes. Now and then my mom and I would be discussing a topic, and he'd interject, saying something oddly profound. It never ceased to amaze us.

*****

Saturday night, after our monotonous weekly routine of chores and grocery shopping, we all sat down to play a board game. We chose Monopoly Junior, a simplified version of the regular game. Within an hour my son had kicked our butts. Mom ran out of money, which is technically when the game is supposed to end, but we fight until the last man is standing. Since I only had a few dollars left, I threw in the towel.

"It's getting late," I said. "We should go to bed."

Tyler frowned. He didn't want to sleep, but was up past his bedtime and he knew it.

"What a wonderful idea," Mom agreed. "Let's put an end to this embarrassing defeat."

Once validation came, Tyler stood up and stretched, a proud smirk crossing his face. I wondered if maybe it was time to upgrade to the adult version of Monopoly, to give us half a chance at winning.

"Better luck next time," he joked.

I was surprised I fell right asleep Saturday night. Sunday morning was when the dread set in. I took a shower, dried off and brushed my teeth. While staring at my reflection in the mirror, I noticed something: I looked different. But I didn't know how.

As I blow-dried my hair, I began drifting off, thinking of Justin. I still missed him so much. It hadn't gotten easier with time. But it was something I lived with, something I understood. The flowers, though, they were something new. Their appearance unsettled me. In spite of my fears, I had to find out. I had to know who left them. And why.

I went into my room and stuffed my swimsuit and towel into my gym bag. I was probably overreacting. The flowers could have simply been left by the wrong grave. I decided I was being dramatic and silly over all of this. I'd just go to the health club, workout and come back home.

After eating a small breakfast, I said goodbye to Mom and Tyler.

"Enjoy yourself. Work those muscles," she said to me.

I gave Tyler a quick kiss goodbye, and then found myself driving toward the cemetery anyway. No matter how much I tried to pretend it was nothing, I couldn't deny my curiosity... and concern.

On my way there, my sense of awareness was heightened. I noticed details I hadn't paid attention to before: a for sale sign adorning a neighbor's yard; a new Korean restaurant on the street corner. This wasn't a typical day, grocery shopping in a half hour or less or droning through punching a stack of documents, working on auto-pilot. This was a genuine mystery that needed solving.

And I didn't look forward to it.

When I pulled into the parking lot and got out, I realized I hadn't worn boots. I wore gym shoes. Cursing myself, I stepped into the dirty slush and looked around. Apart from a grieving family gathered on the far side of the cemetery, I was alone.

I began walking around, reading the headstones. There was an equal number of older men and women who had lived a long life. Mixed in were a few middle-aged folks and sadly, some children. And then, of course, there was me, the idiot hanging around with them on my day off. I shook my head, realizing how foolish I was, and I walked over to Justin's grave.

As I got closer, I couldn't believe my eyes. A fresh bouquet of yellow daffodils lay in front of my husband's headstone. I began shaking. From the cold, but also from fear. Anger rose in me. "What's going on here?"

I expected some kind of answer from Justin, in the form of telepathic communication, perhaps, but there was nothing. The only sound was sniffles from my runny nose. I wiped it and inhaled an icy breath before quickly glancing around.

Whoever brought these flowers was gone. But they had shown me one thing; it wasn't a mistake. Someone was putting flowers on my husband's grave. And if I came often enough, accompanied by my good friend—Irish luck, I would find them.

Chapter 3

"Mom. How was swimming?" Tyler asked as I walked in the front door.

I was so upset I'd never gone. But I had to say something. "It was good, honey. I'm on my way to getting into shape." I inwardly cringed as I spoke the words.

White lie upon white lie. They began to compound so quickly, I feared they'd bring some kind of return.

After dinner, Tyler had me critique some of his drawings. He was really getting good. And I had a thought, one that I blurted out before analyzing the affordability factor.

"What would you think of taking a weekly art class? From a private instructor?" I asked.

My son shot me a look filled with wild excitement. I hadn't expected such an intense reaction.

"Can I really take one? Can we afford it?"

The worried look in his eyes broke my heart. He shouldn't know these things. Mom and I would have to take better care to discuss finances in private.

Not sure how it could be done, I responded, "Sure, honey, we'll just find someone who's offering a special deal for new students."

My reply was casual, dismissive of the ins and outs of how it would all come together, but it brought the mood back to where it was supposed to be: positive. And for one classes out of her home, which conveniently happened to be less than a mile away. Her rates were reasonable too. I didn't know how good she would be; no reviews had been posted. But after looking over her qualifications, I noticed she had recently graduated from a prestigious art college in Savannah, Georgia. She'll do, I decided.

*****

Monday morning, I woke up on time, showered, and then dropped Tyler off at school.

"I'll give that art teacher a call tonight. See when you can start," I said, winking at my son.

He smiled. "Thanks, Mom," and gave me a peck goodbye.

After punching in at the office and sitting at my desk, Fatima approached me. I could tell she was upset about something.

"What's up?" I asked. "You look angry."

Her almond-shaped eyes narrowed and her wavy, jet-black hair swished as she shook her head. "Angry is an understatement. You wouldn't believe what I had to deal with this weekend."

Usually, when young people ramble, I zone out, but with Fatima it was different. Her exotic beauty captivated me, and her slight accent made me pay closer attention when she spoke. I listened for a full ten minutes without interrupting to the story of how her supposed best friend

17

was trying to destroy the relationship between Fatima and her boyfriend of two months.

I had just planned to respond when Dave opened the office door. Fatima and I nodded to each other. This would have to wait until later.

As I began working, I noticed Barb wasn't in yet. I worried about her sometimes. She was a senior citizen without any retirement savings. She came back every Monday because she was broke and had no choice; a fate I feared would be my own someday.

At 9:15 a.m., Barb finally walked in. After she sat down and opened her computer, Dave walked past.

"Everything all right?" he asked her.

Noticeably embarrassed, she responded, "Yes, thank you. I just got stuck in traffic."

"I know how that feels," he said, letting it go.

We were lucky to have a boss like Dave. He was easygoing. All that mattered to him was efficiency.

During our lunch hour, the three of us sat in the cafeteria, chatting and eating. Fatima recapped her whole story while Barb and I listened.

"I'm sure you'll get it all straightened out," Barb told her.

If I had made that generic comment it wouldn't have been helpful. But when Barb said it, with that soothing tone she used, the simple words took on real meaning. When she told you something would be fine, you believed it.

"I hope so." Fatima sighed, and then she turned to me. "So what about you? What did you do this weekend?"

They both stared at me, waiting for an answer. I felt like a game show contestant, clueless and wondering what to say. I had to respond, so I told them about my rediscovered love of swimming. I don't know if this lie was white or pathological, but I was thankful they both agreed exercise was a good thing to do in our spare time.

After lunch, I kept busy at work, trying to stop my mind from wandering. Detail-oriented and precise, it wasn't like me to make a lot of punching errors. Today, though, it seemed nothing wanted to balance to zero. I had to pay closer attention. I was losing it. My mind wanted to use its capacity not for work, but for putting pieces together in a puzzle. The only problem being I had too few pieces to work with. I'd have to get more.

In the evening, I called the art teacher. I liked the sound of her voice right away; it had a musical quality to it. She said Tyler could begin this Wednesday. All we needed to do was bring some current drawings so she could assess his education level, and then she'd put together a teaching plan.

Later on, when night fell, I couldn't sleep. I ruminated over the past with Justin, wondering if I had missed anything, maybe not paid attention to some important detail. I thought I had gotten things right. We were happy. I know we were.

Could there have been another woman?

I didn't think Justin would ever disappoint me like that.

I remember him talking about my dad's affair. "He's just a dick," he'd said, while shaking his head in disgust. "Only a fool would leave his beautiful wife and family."

He'd made his opinions on the matter quite clear: I'd never relive my mother's life.

The phrase "history repeats itself" echoed in my mind. And I worried if I didn't find out what was going on soon

I'd go mad. I didn't like secrets. I recognized the irony of that truth—considering the little lies I'd started to tell. But I was in control of my world at all times. At least until God took my husband from me.

I prayed He wouldn't take my perfect memories too.

*****

The next morning, I woke up with bags under my eyes. Not even concealer could cover it up. The evening was more of the same, lying awake, worrying. When I did finally fall asleep, I'd wake up again, thinking some new thought, trying to reinterpret events from the past. I almost preferred the vivid nightmares I struggled with from time to time. At least in them I got some sleep.

Wednesday night, Tyler and I got his drawings together and we headed to his new art class.

"You nervous?" I asked.

He looked at me like I had said the strangest thing. "Nope," he responded, shrugging his shoulders.

Of course, it was only me that created psychosis around simple events. Instead of enjoying them, I stressed out. Luckily, Tyler was different. He enjoyed the opportunity to learn and looked forward to it, without apprehension.

We walked up to the front door and rang the buzzer. The woman from the picture answered, an old yellow Labrador sat behaved at her feet.

"You must be Amy," she said, reaching for my hand. "And this must be Tyler, my new student. I'm Josephine."

Her demeanor was oddly professional for a young girl. It didn't seem to match her eclectic style, which made her look like a modern, hipper version of Mrs. Roper from *Three's Company*. She had long blonde hair and wore barely any make up. She was what they call a natural beauty.

"Hi," Tyler said. "Nice to meet you."

Just then her dog barked, almost in complaint at not being introduced.

"Soleil. Quiet, please. Be a good boy."

She waved us both to step in out of the cold. Tyler couldn't keep his eyes off the dog. He had always wanted one, but we couldn't get a pet because of Justin's allergies.

Josephine offered me a seat on a nearby sofa and handed me a magazine, and she and Tyler went into the next room to get acquainted and begin the lesson. Once seated, I became so comfortable I managed to nod off for a little bit. Luckily, I heard them wrapping up the class and talking about next week's assignment, so I sat up straight, ready to greet them.

They both walked in, grinning.

"We're all done for this week. Your son is further along than I expected for his age. And what a creative spark. We're going to work well together. Seems like the Universe has sent me the perfect student."

I stood up and smiled back at her. I didn't know how to respond to her last comment, so I reached for her check instead, digging it out of my purse.

"Thanks for the compliment," I said, handing it to her. "I'm glad we found you as well."

We said our goodbyes, and Tyler hugged Soleil once before leaving.

"See you next week," Josephine said, waving.

We drove home, and Tyler went right to his grandma, telling her all about his new class. I did the dinner dishes and inwardly smiled.

*****

That night, I hoped to get restorative sleep, but no such luck. My mind still raced. And I began to feel angry that I couldn't have some kind of real control over it.

Hoping to bore myself to sleep, I reached for a fashion magazine Fatima had given me. I thumbed through the pages mindlessly. All I saw were ads upon ads for skin care products, jewelry, purses. I got to the main fashion spread. The first outfit was cute, and I squinted to read the fine print. Floral printed silk blouse—$800.00, trench coat—$1,500.00, flat-front wool slacks... I didn't even bother to read on. If I had, I would've found out what I already knew—just one ensemble costs half as much as my Dodge Neon. Who really wore this stuff?

I woke up in the morning feeling rested. When I rolled over, I realized I had fallen asleep while reading the magazine. It was crumpled between the sheets. I stumbled out of bed, thankful the week was ending soon. I couldn't wait to sleep in on Saturday.

When I got to work, I noticed Barb was already at her desk. She was early. I sat down after saying hi and immediately began working on my own stack of files.

"Amy," she whispered.

"Yeah," I said, turning back to face her.

"I don't know if you'd be interested, but this Sunday we're having an event at my church. There's this nice young man who's right about your age that I've gotten to know—"

"Oh, you know what. I can't. I have that swimming class I signed up for. Thanks for inviting me though."

Barb smiled her famous warm smile. "I understand."

Her gaze lingered just long enough for an unspoken

conversation to occur between us. Then I broke eye contact, returning to my work.

She had good intentions. They all did. It started after the first year and a half. Fatima had a divorced uncle she thought I might like. My boss had a single buddy from his poker game. And now Barb. It was official. They all had tried. Maybe, I thought, they would finally just give up. No one could ever replace Justin.

I continued working, not giving what she had said any further thought. There were a lot of files to be punched, and accurately. I didn't have time to dilly dally. Before I knew it, it was time to leave.

On my way home, I thought about what I had told Barb, about going to the swimming class. Maybe I would do just that.

Saturday morning, I slept in, as I had hoped. When I woke up, I found my family still hanging out in their pajamas.

"Hey, Mom. Did you guys eat?"

"No. Not yet."

"You want me to make some breakfast?"

My mom smirked. "You mean do we want oatmeal?"

I flashed her a smile. "It's like you're psychic."

"Sure," she replied. "That sounds good."

I didn't know what she had against oatmeal. It tasted great, was proven to lower cholesterol, and you never got sick of it. At least *I* didn't.

I poured some water into a pot, and then I stared at it, watching it come to a boil, thinking about our plans for the day. We'd grocery shop, clean, and Tyler would do his homework, both for school and his art class. In the evening, after dinner, we'd play a game or watch a movie. A typical Saturday.

Later on, after Tyler went to bed, I could tell my mom wanted to stay up. She had that anxious look on her face that she sometimes wore. I wasn't sure if it was hormone changes or if she was being haunted by something. Either way, she'd never discuss it with me. But I knew when she wore that expression she needed me and didn't want to be alone.

"Hey, Ma. Why don't you pick a movie? We'll stay up late and watch it."

Her faraway look disappeared and she came back to the present. With the excitement of a youngster she said, "How about *Scarface*?"

We'd seen it I don't know how many times. I was surprised the DVD hadn't cracked. But I knew how much she loved Al Pacino, and how she felt he'd been screwed out of an Oscar for the role, so I said, "Sure, why not."

As I grabbed the disc and took it from its case, I remembered how Justin used to sit with us while we watched it, mimicking the lines in a fake Cuban accent as the scenes unfolded. Somehow it added to the experience.

Mom missed that too. Whenever we watched it now, she also tried to recite some of the better lines along with the actors. I joined in even though my accent stunk. It was fun. Almost like a sport. Plus, I liked making my mom laugh.

*****

The next day was Tyler's friend Sally's birthday party.

In the morning, Mom asked, "Are you going to your swimming class today?"

I gave it a moment's thought. "I'd like to. Tyler has

24

that party in the afternoon. I could drop him off beforehand and pick him up on my way back home. You could finally have some time to yourself."

"Sounds good," she said. "Maybe I'll do a spa day."

After we ate breakfast, I showered and got ready to go to the cemetery. It was a numbers game. That was what I'd told myself.

Lost in thought, I realized I hadn't seen Tyler in a while. I searched the house and found him sitting in his room with a wrapped present on his lap.

"All set," he said.

"Did Grandma wrap your gift?"

"No," he replied. "I did."

I didn't remember showing him how to do that, but I didn't ask questions.

On the drive over, Tyler seemed unusually quiet.

"Something wrong?" I asked.

"No."

Silence lingered. I could tell this would take more work.

"You're not saying much," I noted.

He sat for another minute, unresponsive. Then he blurted out, "Oh… I was just thinking." But he still didn't elaborate.

"About what?" I asked.

"Sally's mom."

He left me hanging again. I decided to wait for him to go on, only if he chose to.

Luckily, he did. "Sally's mom came back from the hospital yesterday, just in time for her birthday party."

I hadn't known she was ill. "What was wrong with her?"

We pulled up to a stoplight and Tyler looked directly

at me. Returning his gaze, I listened as he said, "I don't know… but she came back."

His face was filled with a sadness I hadn't seen in a long time. It broke my heart into a thousand pieces. I wasn't sure what to say. I didn't want to upset him more than he already was and ruin his party.

"Sometimes people get better," I replied. "Thank God for that."

Tyler nodded while holding back tears, determined not to let them spill. Then we walked to the front door and I rang the buzzer. Squeezing his hand in mine, I whispered, "Try to have a good time, okay."

He forced a smile. The door opened to a bunch of screaming kids, and he went in and waved goodbye.

Just when I thought he was doing so well, he revealed a new level of his pain. And there was nothing I could do to take it away.

Saddened, I got back in the car and began driving to the cemetery. On the way there, my mood grew darker. I was glad Sally's mom had recovered, from whatever her ailment had been. But at the same time, I was upset that Justin hadn't made it. Even being under the care of Dr. Friedman—one of the best cancer doctors in the country—wasn't enough to save him.

After pulling in to the parking lot, I got out and looked around and was disappointed to find I was the only visitor. I noticed the original groundskeeper whistling as he worked nearby, the sole moving object in a landscape of gray sky and dirty snow. I ignored him and walked through the frigid air toward Justin's grave.

The closer I got, the more I filled with overwhelming grief. Maybe it was Tyler's reminder that we were still broken, that we only pretended to be fixed. Maybe it was the stress of why I was here. I didn't know.

Once I reached my husband's grave, I sighed. The ground was bare, no yellow flowers. Unsure what to do next, I decided I might as well hang around and look for clues.

I walked the rows, reading the headstones again. Same people as last time. The hilarity of the thought caused me to laugh out loud. At the same moment, the groundskeeper passed by. Once he saw me giggling by myself, he scurried away, muttering something under his breath in Spanish.

I headed back to Justin's grave. I stood there, staring down. "I hope you're not hiding something from me," I whispered. "Remember... no secrets."

In my quest to find the flower bearer, I'd forgotten to bring my own pink rose. All of a sudden the area looked desolate. The only items on the ground were a few pebbles, lying next to a golf-ball sized rock. On impulse, I kicked it, and with unexpected force, it flew through the air and ricocheted off a nearby headstone before smacking back on the ground.

The sound snapped me out of my mood, bringing clarity. I should go. I was destroying the place. Then I glanced back one more time to say goodbye to Justin.

*****

After picking up Tyler from Sally's birthday party, I noticed his sadness appeared to have lifted. He told me about all the fun games they'd played and what kind of cake they ate and about Sally's presents. I was glad one of us was in a better mood.

Once home, I plopped down in a kitchen chair to look

at yesterday's mail. There were catalogs for stores I couldn't afford to shop at, credit offers for cards I didn't need, and one last piece of mail that caught my attention. An envelope from The American Cancer Society.

I ripped the letter open to read its contents. As I did, I felt my stomach drop. They were inviting me to take part in one of their annual programs, something called Daffodil Days.

Chapter 4

Later that night, after everyone had fallen asleep, I dug the envelope out of the kitchen drawer. I'd stashed it away so I could take a closer look at it later, when I was alone. I suspected it had something to do with my dilemma, but couldn't chance reading it and have my mom walk in. She'd sense something was off and ask about it. And I didn't want to share anything with her. Not until I knew more.

I sat down and re-read its contents. The Daffodil Days program happened every spring. And in appreciation for one's donation toward cancer research, daffodils were sent to donors thanking them for their contribution.

I knew this had to be it. A puzzle piece.

I got up and headed to the computer, and sat down and did a search for Daffodil Days. A link popped up for The American Cancer Society, so I clicked on it, and arrived on their home page. It said pretty much the same thing as the mailing I'd received.

I wondered how come I'd never heard of the program before. I'd given money for cancer research in the past. As I continued reading down the page, I discovered there were other opportunities to help, as a volunteer or program coordinator.

A feeling in my gut clicked.

I did a zip code search and tried to find a campaign in my area, but there were no matches within a fifty mile radius. There was a button to search for a coordinator. I punched in my zip code and again, nothing.

I guess I was hoping to find a list of names—of volunteers or coordinators—and recognize one of the people and then everything would make perfect sense. I would tell Mom and we'd laugh about this whole silly situation.

Unfortunately, my browsing led nowhere. All I came away with was the knowledge that there was such a group. And that the daffodil flower represents hope.

*****

Monday morning, I was surprised to see Barb in such a bubbly mood.

"You're extra perky today," I commented.

There was a swagger to her step as she walked past. She wore a silly smirk.

"What gives?" I asked. "You're not yourself."

After she sat down at her desk, I turned to face her. She couldn't hold out on me for too long.

"I went to dinner last night with a man I met at church."

"And?" Fatima asked, raising both eyebrows.

I blushed as if I had been the one on a dinner date, but Barb wasn't the least bit flustered.

"Oh, it was no big deal," she said. "I think he's just looking for a friend. We had a nice time." And then a big smile trickled out—one that she'd obviously been keeping to herself.

"Good for you," I said. And I meant it. But somehow it made me feel a little sad.

After I turned and began working, I remembered the

story of that other young man she'd mentioned.

I dismissed the thought as soon as I had it.

The rest of the day flew by. The only gossip was when I'd overheard Dave on the phone with his wife. From what I could make out, she wanted him to take time off so they could go somewhere for their anniversary, and he was making the "next year" promise. I felt bad for her. Dave never unplugged from his business. He lived and breathed the place.

Later on, when I got home from work, I found Mom standing in the kitchen. "You know what happened to Sally's mom?" she asked.

I shook my head no.

"She had a heart attack. That's why she was in the hospital."

"My God!" I gasped. "Mrs. Pembroke is so young."

"Yeah," Mom replied, nodding her head. "Tyler is taking it very seriously. He spoke to Sally about it at school today. I guess the doctors said she's got to change her diet and start exercising. I think he took the advice to heart, too, because he's been asking me what foods are healthy."

Oh no. This was bad. Not just for Sally's mom, but for us. I knew my son all too well. Once an idea took hold of him, he'd never let it go. I decided I would try to downplay the whole thing.

As soon as I had the thought, Tyler walked into the kitchen.

"Hey, honey. How was your day?"

He reached for an apple and said, "It was fine." After taking a loud bite, he added, "I've been thinking though…"

Mom and I simultaneously glanced at each other.

"… You know how you've been going to the health club, working out and stuff?"

Oh that, I thought. Sure, I remembered it clearly.

"Uh huh," I nodded, feeling awkward.

"Well I've been thinking. I want to come with you and exercise too. Sally said it would be smart to start now."

I wasn't working out at the gym because I was hanging around dead people in my free time. But I needed a reasonable response. And fast. Luckily, I remembered they didn't allow children to exercise there.

"You know what, honey. I think that's a great idea, but the fitness center is only for adults."

Tyler looked genuinely confused. "Well, where am I supposed to get in shape at?"

"I don't know. I think since you're a kid you're supposed to just run and play outside and climb trees and stuff."

Mom giggled.

Tyler let that soak in, then spun on his heel and pushed the curtain aside, gazing out the window. He didn't need to make his case. I could see it. It was freezing cold out there.

"In better weather, perhaps," I told him.

Knowing I'd need to find an alternative, I made a suggestion. "How about we buy some jump ropes and start a routine at home?"

Mom shot me a look that could kill. It was like I had lost my mind.

"Can we, Mom? That sounds awesome."

"Sure," I replied, with reluctance, knowing I couldn't take it back. "We'll stop at the store after we eat and get some ropes."

Throughout dinner, Mom didn't look up from her

meal. I felt bad, because I knew she despised exercising, but what was I to do? I couldn't just leave Tyler hanging. This was important to him.

After dishes, Tyler and I went to the store and bought three red jump ropes. One for each of us. "Grandma," Tyler called out as we walked in. "Look what we got you." He reached into the shopping bag and handed her one of the ropes.

Mom gave me a dirty look, which quickly morphed into a faux smile as she looked down at Tyler. "Thanks, honey," she said in a sugary tone as she accepted his gift.

I think even Tyler knew it was forced, but he didn't care. He wanted us all to be healthy. He wouldn't take a chance on losing anyone else.

That night, while doing the new workout routine together, I remembered that Justin's birthday was right around the corner. As we did sit ups and pushups and skipped rope to all Tyler's favorite songs, I thought about the mystery person. They'd show up for that. I'd bet money on it.

*****

Wednesday night, I had a headache, so Mom offered to take Tyler to his art class. I think she wanted to meet Josephine anyway, so I accepted.

While they were gone, I laid in bed, staring at the calendar. Justin's birthday. He would've been thirty-three. We would've taken the day off work to do something special, maybe visit the Museum of Science and Industry or check out antique stores. He loved seeing how old furniture was constructed and frequently reminded me they didn't make it like that anymore.

Justin used to say it was a sin to work on your birthday, so he never did. I didn't either... until after he died. The last couple of years I just visited him at the cemetery.

This year, his birthday fell on a weekday. I'd have to call in sick. Use a personal day. As I lay there plotting, I heard the front door open.

A few minutes later, Tyler, mindful of my headache, whispered through the bedroom door. "Mom. Can I come in?"

"Sure," I said.

He opened it and began walking toward me. He had some books under his arm.

"Look what Josephine lent us," he said, showing me the stack. "She knows all about eating healthy. They're vegetarian cookbooks."

I sat up, took the pile from him and began looking at the covers. I could almost hear the verbal lashing I would take from Mom. She was a true red meat lover.

"That's great, honey," I replied, patting his shoulder. "We'll give some of the recipes a try."

Tyler left my room psyched. He couldn't wait to get started. I forced myself up and out of the covers. I had to go and find my mom.

She sat curled in a wing chair reading her book from the club.

"Hey... thanks for taking Tyler," I interrupted. I rubbed my scalp and groaned. "My head still hurts."

She set her book down. "Sorry to hear that."

"So how was your visit to Josephine's? Did you like her?"

"I guess she's nice, for a new-age hippie," she said, an edge of sarcasm coloring her tone.

I was prepared for her to go on and on complaining, but she didn't. Maybe she could see that Josephine was only trying to help. And, of course, she was just being herself.

During the week, we tried two of the recipes and were surprised to find they were pretty decent. We didn't plan to alter everything about our lifestyle for Tyler, but we did just enough to make him feel good.

*****

A few days before Justin's birthday, I started planting little hints at work. I began coughing and mentioning my throat felt sore. The night before I planned to call in, I checked the next day's weather forecast. Cold, rainy, gray. I'd need an umbrella.

After everyone went to bed, I rummaged through the closet. While digging, I noticed an old pair of binoculars stashed on top of a box of shoes. I pulled them out and dusted them off, deciding it couldn't hurt to bring them along. I'd add them to my bag, along with lunch.

That evening, I couldn't sleep. I thought of Tyler drawing in his room, and the three of us laughing and jumping rope, trying to get in shape. I thought of my mom. I loved her so much, and it was getting difficult to keep these things from her. I prayed to God if I found out something, that it would be a mistake, a miscommunication of some kind. Then I could write the whole thing off to my own personal craziness, and she'd be immune to it all.

It would be awful for my mom to doubt Justin's integrity.

I felt awful doubting him too.

*****

The next morning, I got ready for work and gathered my lunch, umbrella, and binoculars. After breakfast, I waved goodbye to Mom and dropped Tyler off at school.

Before starting on my journey, I called my boss and got voicemail. "Hey, Dave. It's Amy," I said in a scratchy voice. "I'm not going to be able to make it in today. I've got the flu." I hung up afterward, and began driving the familiar route to the cemetery.

On the way there, my senses were heightened again. Only this time there was one I didn't want to be on high alert. My abdomen began to twist, but I willed myself to ignore it and keep driving. I couldn't deal with something like that—not today. I whistled to take my mind off the pressure, but I only made it a few more miles, then had to give in and pull into a McDonald's parking lot. I raced to the restroom, where I lost my breakfast. Shaking with the chills, I gave myself a moment to take some deep breaths and relax before starting out again.

The closer I got to my destination, the more I managed to calm myself. I was focused when I pulled into the cemetery, parked the car, and looked around.

I didn't see anyone.

I put on my hat and gloves, and stepped outside and landed right in a soggy mud puddle, remnants of yesterday's rain. (This time I was smart enough to wear boots.)

I trekked over to Justin's grave, looking over my shoulder from time to time on the way there, making sure I was still alone. His space looked even lonelier today. No flowers, just dirty ground.

I stood in front of his headstone and sighed. "Happy

Birthday," I said out loud. It came out sounding forced, awkward.

As I continued standing there, I felt anger slowly brewing inside me. This was supposed to be a happy occasion. Now it was ruined. I almost launched into a whole list of complaints, detailing my aggravation and sleepless nights, but then I realized that was not what I came here for. Paranoid, I looked over my shoulder to make sure I was still alone. Then I headed back to my car.

I had parked it in such a way that I could easily see anyone coming or going. The first hour staring across the parking lot wasn't bad. I had my iPod and at least managed to listen to some decent songs. Other than that, there was no movement.

The second hour, someone pulled in and a man and woman got out. I was crouched down in my seat, hidden from view. As they started to walk away, I slid back up to watch them. They were heading in the other direction, but I decided to watch them anyway. They stood close to each other and talked, and the man held the woman, who was visibly upset. Within a short time, they came back toward their car. I don't know why, but I slid back down in my seat again so they wouldn't see me.

After they left, I got out and stretched my legs, moved around a bit. Then it was back in the car for more surveillance. Another hour passed, and I realized the very definition of boredom. Worse still, I felt I might have to go to the bathroom soon. I tried to block it out of my mind, but it began to drizzle outside. I'd have to focus on forgetting about it.

Another hour passed. I was sick of listening to music, my butt hurt from sitting in one spot for too long, and I really had to pee. Since I'd lost my breakfast, I was also beginning to get really hungry.

Just as I was deciding between eating lunch and heading to the restroom, a car pulled in. I slid back down in my seat and looked out the bottom of the window. It was a limousine or luxury car of some kind. They parked, and an older, well-dressed man stepped out and opened the rear passenger door. A woman appeared, and before I could get a good look at her, an umbrella popped open, covering her face from view.

I fumbled for my binoculars and adjusted the focus. The woman was tall, with long, dark hair, and wore a black coat. Her gait was oddly graceful. As she got closer and closer to Justin's grave, I felt my stomach clench. I saw her bend down and set a bunch of yellow flowers on the ground.

Holy Shit! I thought. This is it!

My car was turned off, and the windows had fogged up. I scrambled to wipe the inside of the window with the sleeve of my jacket. Trying to hold the binoculars steady while crouched in my seat, I continued to watch her.

She stood alone, facing his headstone. The old man had returned to the car. With her back to me, I noticed her shoulders moving up and down. She was crying.

Once she turned, I tried to get a good look at her, but I couldn't because her umbrella again blocked her face. As she walked back to her car, it began to downpour.

Panicked, I wasn't sure what to do; I hadn't planned this far. I started my car and turned on the heat and defroster. I watched as the older man stepped out, opened the door for her, and the woman got back in.

Before I knew it, I was following them.

I tailed them from a respectable distance, but almost lost them as a light changed to red and I had to race through it. My heart pounded as I drove faster through the pouring rain, no longer caring if I was detectable. I made sharp lefts and rights and drove close enough so as not to lose them.

Eventually, we arrived in a wealthy North Shore neighborhood. As they turned onto a residential street, I slowed down so I could follow from further away. Within a few minutes, the car turned into a long driveway that led to a house that couldn't be seen from the road.

I stopped and turned off the engine. I sat there—stunned—for a full ten minutes, and then I began to cry. I wanted to think the best of Justin, but instead I assumed the worst. I became furious with him. He'd disappointed me. He'd let me down. Dripping with sweat and nearly hysterical, I struggled with what to do next. Then I realized the best thing to do was to confront her.

I checked my reflection in the rearview mirror. I looked like a monster. My face was puffy and red with black mascara drippings running down it. I took a few deep breaths, and cleaned up my face with McDonald's napkins from the glove box. I brushed my hair, patted on some pressed powder, and re-applied my lip gloss. I looked a little better, but not much. I took a few more deep breaths while adjusting my clothing.

I was terrified. Terrified, then angry.

I opened the car door and stepped outside. It had stopped raining, and I exhaled loudly and smoothed my clothing one more time before I began walking up the driveway.

As I made it up the little hill, the house came into sight. It was a sprawling, beautiful mansion, and the closer I got to it, the more enraged I became. Shaking, I stood in front of the large front door and stared at it.

Then I reached out and knocked.

I heard footsteps coming and then the door opened.

"Hello," the older gentleman from the cemetery said. "How may I assist you?"

"I'm looking for the woman you just came here with," I said.

"Ms. Bergman?"

"If that's her name, that's the person I need to see."

Visibly irritated, he asked, "May I have your name?"

"Tell her I'm Justin's wife."

"One moment," he said, then politely excused himself, closed the door halfway, and began calling the name Sabrina.

All of a sudden, I heard lighter, quicker footsteps approaching, and I went from being angry back to being terrified. I considered leaving, but it was too late. The door flung open and there she stood.

"Hello, Amy," she said with a warm smile, as if I were one of her oldest friends.

Sabrina was beautiful in a way that I wasn't, with long, wavy dark hair that reminded me of a 1940's movie star. Her skin was porcelain; her figure tall and slim. I wasn't prepared to be dealt a blow of this magnitude; it made me lose my balance a bit. After regaining it, I cleared my throat.

"You know my name?" I asked.

"You're Justin's wife."

"But I never said my—"

"My name is Sabrina," she said, extending a hand.

Instinctively, my hand shook hers. She continued smiling like we knew each other. It all seemed surreal and wasn't going according to plan, not that I'd had a plan.

"Why don't you come inside?" she suggested. "We

could chat over a cup of tea."

"No," I responded, a little louder than I should have. "No thank you." Lowering my voice, I asked, "How exactly did you know my husband, Justin?"

She smiled again. "I hired him to renovate this house."

That made sense. And it threw me off. For some reason, I had never considered that.

"And you were at the cemetery leaving him flowers because?"

"Because I knew it was his birthday," she responded defensively. Her expression grew more serious; she could see we weren't going to "chat" over tea.

Standing in the doorway, staring at each other, I decided to come right out and ask the question.

"Did you have an affair with my husband?"

Sabrina looked shocked, and said, "Absolutely not!"

This answer would've been satisfactory, and could've ended the conversation, but I wasn't a fool.

"Well, let me ask you this: Do you think it makes sense to go to a cemetery and give flowers to a contractor on Valentine's Day too?"

This took her by surprise. She fumbled her words. "It's not what you think, Amy. Nothing like that ever happened. You've got it all wrong."

I maintained eye contact without speaking as my frustration grew.

"I was here a lot while he worked," Sabrina added. "I'm afraid I asked him a lot of questions and he was kind enough to answer them," she went on in a syrupy tone.

Her explanation was making me nauseous. Although it sounded believable, and I could picture Justin doing something like that as he often got stuck with chatty clients, I couldn't accept it. Something didn't seem right.

For starters, she wasn't one of his little old ladies who wanted to re-live their life story, talking about how their son went off and fought in the war. This woman looked like a goddess.

My confidence began slipping away, and suddenly I felt a strong desire to flee.

I wasn't prepared for all this.

"I think I'd better be going now," I mumbled while looking down.

Sabrina seemed to understand. No doubt she must've felt uncomfortable too. Then, as I began walking away, she said, "See you next time." Confused, I turned and looked back at her. I said nothing in response to her odd comment, and continued on my path down the drive.

On the way home, I mentally reviewed everything and decided I was satisfied with how the whole thing went down. I had set out to find the person and I'd managed to do it. I'd hoped to confront her, and I did. In the end, I was wrong about my suspicions. She was just a high maintenance client who'd had a crush on my husband.

At least that's what I told myself.

The phrase brought me some comfort and the feeling of closure... for a little while.

Chapter 5

When I came home on time for dinner, Mom looked surprised. She began saying, "I didn't expect you," but didn't finish her sentence. I knew she thought I'd be at the cemetery after work, but didn't want to say it, didn't want to encourage a habit that might be ending.

I felt numb from the experience I'd just had. And I couldn't share anything, so I pushed it from my mind.

"I'm starved," I said. "What are we having?"

"Ratatouille," Mom replied while waving her hand over the pot on the stove. "Tyler saw the recipe in one of Josephine's cookbooks. Since we had just watched the movie, I figured it would be a nice change."

I smiled at her. She was so sweet. She'd gone out of her way and done this for us, to celebrate Justin's birthday.

Once dinner finished, we sat around the kitchen table, stuffed. We'd saved just enough room for crème brulee.

Tyler raised his glass of milk and said, "Happy Birthday, Dad."

"To Justin," Mom chimed in, lifting her glass too.

I raised mine and tapped it against theirs in celebration. I smiled, trying to squash the uneasiness I felt spreading throughout me.

*****

The next morning, I woke up drenched in sweat and had the chills. My throat hurt and my body felt achy. I cursed myself for lying to my boss about having the flu.

That's what I get, I thought.

I tried to get out of bed, but a sinking feeling came over me, the kind that once it hits, makes you long for sleep. I forced myself to get up and change into dry pajamas, and I wandered into the bathroom to take some cold medicine.

Afterward, I went back to my room and collapsed into bed. Remembering work, I reached for my cell phone and called my boss. It was early, so I was guaranteed voicemail. "Hey, Dave. It's me, Amy. I'm still sick and won't be able to make it in."

The next time I woke up it was right before lunchtime. I had no energy and my head was stuffed up. I didn't feel hungry, but figured I should eat something, so I shuffled into the kitchen and ate an orange. The house was empty. I walked around a bit, taking in the abnormal silence but got bored right away and decided to sit down and watch TV. I flipped through a bunch of channels and realized nothing good was on, and then turned it off. Out of the corner of my eye, I spotted a stack of photo albums. I got up and grabbed them, and sat back down on the sofa.

The first was an older one, with pictures of Justin and me at the high school prom. God—we were skinny. And we ate whatever we wanted. As we danced the night away to all our favorite songs, who could have known what the future held? How our lives would turn out?

The next album had vacation shots from Arizona. Although it was pretty, I remember us both dying of heat and feeling like someone was holding a blow-dryer to our faces. Justin's mom and dad were there too. His dad loved the place, and could picture retiring there. He said nothing compared to the beauty of Sedona's red rocks. Justin's mom, on the other hand, had no intention of ever moving away from her only son.

The last album was more recent, with pictures of Tyler as a baby, and Justin holding him in his arms by the Christmas tree surrounded by piles of presents. I stared at that one for a long time. He still looked healthy in those photos. I couldn't find any evidence of what was soon to come.

Looking through the pictures brought back so many good memories. But the sinking feeling came again, and I could barely stay awake, so I decided to take some more medicine and lie down.

While in bed, I thought about how long I'd known Justin, and all the experiences we'd had together, how we had known everything about each other.

But I didn't know about Sabrina.

Maybe nothing happened and she was just a customer, but he never mentioned her. I pictured her at the cemetery with the flowers, how she'd been crying. As I closed my eyes, I heard her voice repeating over and over in my mind, "I hired him to renovate this house."

If Sabrina knew him well enough to deliver flowers to him, like he was a friend, or, God forbid more, how come I didn't even know she was his client?

Though I was beyond exhausted, I decided to get up and go down to the basement. All of Justin's old business records were stored down there.

I slid into my old pair of slippers and made my way down the creaky stairs. Once I found the boxes and separated them from the other stored items, dust began flying around, causing me to launch into a major coughing fit. Gagging on phlegm, I had to sit down to regain composure. Once my breathing returned to normal, I wiped the box with a dirty rag I found nearby, then used every last ounce of remaining strength to carry it up the stairs and into my room, where I let it drop with a loud thunk.

I sat down next to it and pulled out the folders, spreading them across the floor. Each file represented one month. The box held two years' worth of files. I thought it made sense to start at the beginning of the invoices and end with the most recent. Thumbing through them, I saw a bunch of different customer names and lots of job codes (Justin's shorthand) followed by detailed descriptions of the work done. At the bottom was the amount billed.

Looking at the addresses, I realized he drove all over the place for work, wherever clients could be found. I smiled, remembering how motivated he was, a force to be reckoned with. Marveling at all the money he'd made and all the projects he'd done, I came upon the first invoice. "Sabrina Bergman, Lake Forest, Illinois, job code C— consultation on project, two hundred dollars."

A tiny spark of energy I didn't know I had woke me up. This now had my full attention. I continued flipping through the invoices, folder by folder, reading their contents. Each month, there she was. Getting her hardwood floors resurfaced, remodeling her master bathroom and installing a claw-foot Jacuzzi tub.

My interest piqued, but I was sinking again. I couldn't stay awake a moment longer. I had used my last drop of remaining energy and my body was in protest. I left everything spread out on the floor and climbed back into bed. Once my head hit the pillow, I was out.

Hours later, the sound of the garage door opening woke me. I still felt terrible, but forced myself out of the covers and into the kitchen. When my mom and Tyler walked in, I greeted them both and tried to give my son a hug, but he pulled away.

"Mom. Don't give me sick germs."

"Good point," I noted. "How was school? How was last night's lesson?"

"We had testing today and I think I did fine. Last night Josephine gave me an assignment to draw a piece of fruit."

"That sounds easy enough," I said.

"Yep," Tyler replied, then threw his bag down and ran to the family room to watch his favorite show. Mom came in after using the restroom.

"Honey, you look awful. And what's that big mess laying all over the floor in your room?"

Thinking quick on my feet, I replied, "Oh, I was just looking for Mrs. Pembroke's number. I remembered Justin did some work for her."

"Do you need help cleaning that up? I can help you, you know."

"No. No thanks," I said. "I'll deal with it later."

I felt bad saying it, because I knew clutter drove her crazy. She hated disorder and couldn't bear to walk past something and see it out of place. But I didn't mind clutter as much. And those invoices were staying right where I wanted them, until I was done investigating.

She pressed pause on being a neat freak and said, "Why don't you take a bath, and I'll get dinner started."

"All right," I said, realizing I could use one since I smelled bad.

While sitting and soaking, I thought about my tub. It

was your basic, plain Jane tub—no jets, no claw feet. In fact, everything about my house was like that, nice and comfortable, but un-spectacular. Justin and I hoped our next house would be the one with all the options we wanted. He didn't think it made sense to sink a bunch of money into this one.

After relaxing for a long time, and being so tired I almost drowned, I crawled out of the tub, dressed in fresh pajamas and headed back to my bedroom. Once I walked in, I realized it smelled disgusting, a combination of sick and dusty basement. I used a small burst of energy to change the sheets, and I lay back down and passed out.

*****

Friday morning, I still didn't feel well. I decided I'd use another vacation day and hope I'd be recovered by Monday. I felt bad calling Dave, because he was there rain or shine, no matter what. I guessed that's how it was when you owned your own business.

With the house empty, I got up and took the opportunity to look through the rest of the folders.

Each month Sabrina's name was there, either beginning a new project or continuing a previous one. "Looks like she never wanted him to finish," I exclaimed sarcastically.

After looking through two years' worth of files, I realized she was Justin's biggest customer. The majority of his income—our income—came from her. This surprised me, and at the same time made me very uncomfortable.

He'd never mentioned her, yet he was at her house many times over the course of two years.

Hmm.

But it wasn't a "Hmm, that's interesting." It was a "Hmm—now I've got to know more."

Unable to stop myself, I wrote her phone number on a sticky note and put it inside my wallet.

Chapter 6

Monday morning, Fatima approached me before I could sit down. "Oh my God, girl. You totally missed all the action."

Still tired and not ready for much excitement, I asked, "What did I miss?" Meanwhile, a large stack of files that had grown like weeds on my desk competed for my attention.

"Well," Fatima continued, "One of the clients began throwing a fit because he got audited. The guy was flipping out, waving his arms and swearing at Dave, and then Dave threw him out. Can you believe it?"

"Yes. I can." Although Dave was a consummate professional and kept to himself, he didn't take anyone's crap.

It was an interesting story, and I could've gossiped all day about it, but I had to get started on my mountain of work, so I cut the conversation short.

I plowed through my files at a furious pace, trying to get caught up. Each time I glanced at the clock, I had an anxiety attack. Time was slipping by too quickly. I couldn't seem to work fast enough. The only break I took was fifteen minutes to eat a sandwich for lunch. Fatima took hers at the same time and updated me on the rest of the gossip. By the end of the day, I was nowhere near finished with what I needed to get done.

The next few days were more of the same. Work like a madwoman, inhale a sandwich, and race the clock. It wasn't until Thursday that I finally caught up, had a chance to relax, and a chance to think.

My first thoughts were of Sabrina.

As I sat there, tapping my pencil on my desk, spacing out, I couldn't help but zero in on her odd comment as I walked away. "See you next time."

I hadn't planned on there being a next time, but now I thought maybe it was a good idea. Find out what she was all about, do some snooping. If she had lied to me, I'd eventually discover the truth. But, if she suggested seeing each other again, maybe she had nothing to hide?

I shook my head in confusion. None of it made sense.

I threw my pencil down and reached for my purse, then I pulled out the sticky note with her name, address, and phone number out of my wallet.

Should I call her?

On my way home from work, I tossed the idea of contacting her around a bit more. I really didn't want to see her again. I just wanted to let the whole thing go, to believe her explanation, but there was that bothersome little voice in my head whispering, "You never know."

I reached for my cell phone and dialed her number.

"Bergman residence," an older male voice answered, no doubt the same guy who drove her car and answered her front door.

"Um—may I speak to Sabrina, please?"

"May I ask who is calling?"

"This is Amy White," I responded, now unsure of myself and wanting to hang up the phone.

"One moment."

My mind raced back and forth—should I hang up?

Should I stay on the line? Before I could decide, she answered.

"Amy. How lovely to hear from you," Sabrina said in an enthusiastic tone.

Dumbfounded, I didn't know what to say. "Oh, sure. Um—the reason I'm calling is, I was wondering what you meant when you said 'see you next time?'"

"I meant exactly that. You're welcome to stop by anytime."

This was getting weird. I didn't know why she would make that comment. Perhaps there really was more to this story than she'd led me to believe. Gripped by curiosity, I asked, "What are you doing Sunday afternoon?"

"Nothing. I've got the day free. It would be fabulous if you dropped by. How about lunchtime?"

I felt foolish, then replied, "Yeah, that sounds good."

"I'll see you then," she said, then promptly hung up.

How odd it was of her to end the call so abruptly. I mean, what if I had wanted to say more? I guessed she didn't want to give me the opportunity. It would have to wait until Sunday—in person.

As I pulled up to my house and turned off the car, a familiar uneasy mood crept over me. It was just like when I had seen the daffodils for the first time at Justin's grave. The feeling of closure from last week's meeting was gone. Instead, I entered a new portal of disquiet.

*****

Friday and Saturday passed without incident. Tyler was on his "let's get a dog" kick, which I had to admit wasn't a bad idea, but I still wasn't entirely convinced. I told him I'd think about it.

We all watched a movie Saturday night, but I barely took notice because I was too busy worrying about my upcoming meeting with Sabrina.

Sunday morning, I woke up feeling great. A good sign, I thought. After eating breakfast and showering, I got as fixed up as I could without looking like I was going somewhere other than the gym. While applying make-up, I studied myself with a critical eye. I was cute—not beautiful. Blonde hair, blue eyes… yes, but more girl next door type, not blonde bombshell.

I wished I were beautiful.

I let go of that thought and checked my outfit once more in the mirror. I wore purple yoga pants and a white t-shirt, topped with a black sporty jacket. I grabbed my gym bag.

"Mom. You want me to take Tyler to his friend's? I can take him on my way if you want?"

"No," she replied. "I have to run an errand nearby. I'll take him. After that, since no one will be home, I'm going to vegetate."

"Sounds good," I replied. "See you later then."

Before leaving, I checked in on Tyler. He was in his room, reading a book.

"Hey, honey. Have fun at your friend's today, okay."

"I will," he said. I leaned down and gave him a kiss on the cheek.

Tyler looked up at me and beamed. "I think it's cool you're putting in even more exercise time," he said.

My heart sank. I couldn't even form a response. All I could do was fake a smile and wave goodbye.

The journey to Sabrina's house was nerve-wracking. I tried to rehearse some phrases I might say but felt stupid talking out loud while alone in the car. In the end, I decided not to worry about it and trust that things would unfold as they should.

While driving, I recognized some of the places Justin and I used to visit on our trips north. We used to take this route sometimes to admire the beautiful homes. We'd eat at a new restaurant here or there—a romantic lunch while daydreaming about owning one of these mansions. "Not a problem," Justin would say with a smirk. "Just give me a chance to expand the business a bit more."

Within a short time, I was at the base of Sabrina's driveway. I turned in and drove all the way down to the end. Then I froze. It took more effort than I thought I had to climb out of the car, walk forward and ring the bell.

A moment later, the door opened. It was Sabrina.

"Hello, Amy. I'm so glad you could make it. I hope you're hungry?" she asked, "Because lunch is being served."

"I could eat something," I mumbled awkwardly.

She spoke in a formal manner, adding another layer of discomfort to the already bizarre situation.

While following her down the expansive foyer, I noticed she was wearing a floor-length burgundy chiffon gown.

"Excuse me," I said.

Sabrina stopped and turned to face me, giving me her full attention.

"Are you sure you were expecting me? I mean, it looks like you're going somewhere. I don't want to keep you…"

She gave me a confused look. "No. I'm not going anywhere. I was expecting you for lunch. We spoke last week."

"Oh, okay," I replied. "I was just double-checking."

She turned and started walking again. I didn't know many people who spent a lazy Sunday dining in formal wear, but I kept that thought to myself and continued following her.

We ended up in an amazing living room that seemed the size of my whole house. An enormous fireplace dominated the center of the room, which was surrounded by plush velvet sofas and chairs. The walls were adorned with artwork. As I glanced at the paintings, I noticed they were all very similar. The same woman was featured in each one. My gaze was interrupted by a man entering the room.

"Amy, this is Henry," Sabrina said.

It was the man from the cemetery. An employee, I guessed.

"Hello," he said. "Pleased to meet you again."

I immediately thought of how nice it would be to employ someone like him to drive me around, answer my calls and wait on me. Then I changed my mind and decided it would be creepy, that it was only good in theory.

"Please," Sabrina said, motioning to an overstuffed chair, "Have a seat."

I sat down and tried to appear relaxed. I wasn't sure if I should fold my hands over each other or sit cross-legged. I had never felt more out of place in my life. Luckily, within a few moments, Henry reappeared holding a tray of food and set it on the table between the two of us.

"I hope you like Orangina," Sabrina said, breaking the awkward silence.

I looked at the genie-shaped bottle. "I've never had it before."

She reached for hers and took a sip. "I think you'll like it. It's a carbonated fruit beverage popular in Europe. When I'm in Paris, it's all I drink."

"Paris," I blurted out. "Justin and I hoped to make it there someday."

"Yes," she replied. "I know."

Her response made my neck muscles tighten. I wondered what else she knew.

Picking up on the tension, Sabrina added, "I mean Justin had mentioned his plans to take you there after I told him I'd gone."

The comment put me more at ease, but I was still at a loss for what to say next.

"You mentioned every time you're in Paris this is all you drink—which is delicious, by the way—but what brings you over there? If you don't mind me asking?"

"Of course I don't mind," she said. Then she set down her drink. "I go there a few times a year on business. My parents were fashion designers. They're both dead now—plane crash while vacationing in Indonesia—"

"I'm sorry to hear that," I interjected.

"Thank you," she said before continuing. "They left the business to me, and I'm involved with approving what the designers put together for each collection. So I get to travel a bit for work."

I sat in complete awe of what she had just said. It was like I was watching a movie.

"That sounds so glamorous and exciting."

Her expression quietly disagreed. "I guess so," she said in a somber tone. "Paris is the most romantic city in the world, but that fact is amplified when you're there by yourself."

I nibbled at my food, waiting for her to say more.

Reacting to the cue, she continued. "I guess I can be a bit jaded about that, though."

"About what?" I asked.

Sabrina gazed off into her own private space. "About romance, about Paris." Then she looked back at me and said, "I spent my honeymoon there, but we've been divorced for years now."

"Oh, I'm sorry to hear that."

Sabrina shrugged. "Don't be. It was a silly marriage anyway. His family knew my family. It seemed like a good match."

She took a sip of her drink and said, "In the end, it was nothing but a huge disappointment."

"How so?"

Sabrina looked me right in the eyes this time, with intensity. "Because it wasn't true love."

In that moment, I noticed a certain sadness that I hadn't seen before. And it wasn't because of the subject matter, either. The sadness I saw in her eyes ran deep, like a vast ocean, bottomless, endless.

"I mean he loved me," she said. "But he loved every other pretty thing that caught his fancy, too, which was often." She smirked.

I thought my next comment through carefully before speaking.

"I would think someone like you; someone who gets to travel and be involved with the fashion world would be able to meet all kinds of amazing men."

"You'd think that," she joked. "But it's not that way. None of them are really—real."

"I'm confused."

"Well, they're drop-dead gorgeous, that's true, but too many of them are fake. They have nothing more to them than what's on the outside."

"I see what you mean," I said.

And I did. I saw exactly what she meant. Justin wasn't only handsome, he was a regular guy—he was "real." I agreed with her, and that agreement caused my stomach to twist in concern.

Just then, Sabrina asked, "Would you like to see the rest of the house?"

"Sure."

Of course I'd want to see it. I wanted to see all that Justin had done, all he had accomplished. All the things that Sabrina had paid him for. It was all part of the mystery.

Sabrina got up, and I followed her from room to room.

"This was a great house, but it was dated, so I had Justin make it perfect." Her voice was practically giddy as she spoke.

She took me to a gourmet kitchen, with Viking appliances, granite counters, and dark wood cabinets with glass inserts. Dishes were lined neatly inside. There was a large dining room with a beautiful chandelier, and more portrait artwork adorning the walls. There was a good-sized library filled with books from top to bottom, several guest bedrooms and baths, and an over-the-top romantic master bedroom. It had its own matching bath, complete with Jacuzzi claw-foot tub.

As if that weren't enough, Sabrina took me to a sprawling room with an indoor swimming pool. French doors opened to a beautifully furnished patio, with nothing but flowers and trees and land behind it, all impeccably landscaped. It took my breath away. It was enchanting.

"Wow! I'm speechless," I said. "This is such an amazing place. You must love living here."

She offered a polite smile.

"When I first moved here, I didn't like it much. But now that it's been redone, I'm very happy with the results."

I took this as my cue to be more probing.

"Yeah. I looked through Justin's old invoices. It seems like he was here a lot for two years straight."

"He was here often," Sabrina replied with a smile.

It wasn't just a smile, though, it was a glow.

"So were you here the majority of the time? Or were you busy travelling?" I asked.

"I was here while the projects were being done. I wanted to oversee everything."

I'll bet you did. Probably got your money's worth of watching Justin's muscles flex while he worked and broke a sweat. Apparently, the blue-collar guy gets all women, no matter their status.

Just then, Henry walked in the room. "Will you ladies be needing any refreshments, dessert?"

"I'm good. Thanks."

Sabrina shook her head no, and we headed to the living room and sat down. The uncomfortable silence returned for a long moment, until she finally spoke.

"That's how we became friends," she blurted out. "Justin was here so often… well, we talked a lot."

I shifted uncomfortably in my chair and raised an eyebrow.

"We talked about a lot of things," she continued, then, after a long pause, added, "but most of the time I listened to him talk about you."

My jaw almost dropped. "He talked about me?"

"Yes," she replied, obviously happy with the effect her words had on me.

"Well, that must've been really boring."

"Not at all. I actually found it fascinating."

There's no way she could've found it fascinating to hear about the wife of someone she was so obviously interested in. I decided she must be insulting me in a polite way, like how British people tell each other off— no swear words, just a condescending tone.

"I can't possibly imagine what would be fascinating to hear about me."

Sabrina gave me a confused expression. She looked like she was gathering her thoughts. "I guess it wasn't the details of what he said. It was more the way he lit up when he told the stories."

My heart skipped.

"Like how you two first met in high school, or how you planned the best wedding for less than five thousand dollars." Sabrina paused, and said, "Or how happy he was when he discovered you were pregnant."

Oh my God. Justin *was* a talker. I'd imagine if the client kept hanging around all the time, he'd eventually hit every topic.

I was mortified.

"Did you ever talk about anything else? Like maybe your life, for example? I mean, I'm sure that came up."

Sabrina gave it some thought. "Yes, it did. I told him what I did for a living and that I travelled for work." She laughed and added, "He said it seemed like I was from another world."

It was true. She was someone from another world. The kind of person you read about but don't actually know in real life.

"I mentioned the trips to Paris, and he asked me all about it. That's when he said he hoped to take you there."

It made me feel so good when she said that, but I didn't let it show on my face. I was still fishing for information.

"Did you ever mention your honeymoon? Or the divorce?"

I wondered for a moment if I was being rude, but then I remembered this woman was the person who left flowers on my husband's grave. I had a right to be nosy.

"I did," she replied. "In fact, his response was I just hadn't met the right man yet. And not to worry, it would happen."

I could see it in her eyes then—that she'd wished Justin were that man. And who could blame her? He was the best...

"Excuse me," she said. "I need to use the restroom."

While she was gone I looked around and noticed a book on the coffee table. It was an art book containing the works of John William Waterhouse. After picking it up and flipping through it, I realized these were the paintings on the walls. Then I checked my watch. I needed to get going soon. Just then, Sabrina returned.

"I see you found one of my favorite books," she said.

"Yeah. I noticed it had the paintings from the walls."

She let out a laugh. "I wish these were the paintings. They're replicas."

"Oh—they look like the real thing," I said, embarrassed by my stupidity.

"Thanks," she replied. "The real ones, well, the majority of them, at least, are in the hands of Sir Andrew Lloyd Webber."

"The man who composed The Phantom of the Opera?"

"Exactly. And almost every other successful musical I can think of."

"I guess that's the career to have—if I'd only known," I joked.

In that moment, we giggled with each other like we were old friends, but we definitely were not.

I glanced at my watch again. "I have to get going soon and pick up my son," I said. "It was nice to see you."

I got up and set the book back on top the coffee table. Sabrina stepped forward, picked it back up, and handed it to me.

"Why don't you take this with you," she suggested. "You can return it next time."

I accepted her book. And I knew that by doing so, that I would visit Sabrina again.

It was madness.

Chapter 7

Driving back home, I listened to classical music, something I never do, while I thought about our conversation. I had gotten information I was looking for, and a whole lot I hadn't expected. It was as if I'd opened Pandora's Box.

I wasn't sure what to make of it all or how I felt. I was momentarily distracted from these thoughts the moment I walked in the front door and smelled pizza, the good kind—delivery. My mom must've had a very relaxing day.

"Hey, Mom, how's it going?"

"It's good," she said. "I didn't feel like cooking so I picked up pizza for dinner."

"Thanks. It smells delicious." There was nothing like Chicago pizza. I set the table and poured each of us a glass of water.

Tyler came into the kitchen. "Hey, Mom," he said. "We're eating vegetarian tonight. It's healthy."

Mom and I eyed each other. Neither of us wanted to be the one to tell him.

"Well, honey, it's not technically considered a health food even though it's vegetarian."

For a moment, Tyler looked upset. Then he asked, "What is eating healthy, then?"

"One way," I suggested, laughing inwardly at my own genius, "is to eat a lot of vegetables and hardly any candy, cookies, or ice cream."

I got him now.

Tyler kept quiet while chewing his food. When he'd finished, he took a large gulp of water, wiped his mouth with his napkin and announced, "I don't think I'll have dessert tonight."

"Me neither," I agreed. I wanted him to know I was on his side, that we were in this together.

Mom looked at both of us, clearly outnumbered. I could tell she was growing tired of this.

An hour after dinner, Tyler appeared in the family room with his jump rope. He was right on time, like clockwork. That was our cue to get ours and begin working out.

"Mom, you already went to the gym today. Grandma and I could do our routine alone if you want?"

I wanted nothing more than to collapse on the sofa and watch mindless television, but I felt guilty, so I went and put my gym shoes back on and joined them. Afterward, I was exhausted. And my poor mom looked haggard. So much for her supposed relaxing day.

When Tyler left the room to get ready for bed, Mom spoke up. "Jesus! I thought I was going to have a heart attack!" she complained.

"You don't have to do all the reps. Just take it slow."

"That's a good idea. I'll remember that for next time. I'm going to hit the sack, honey. I'm pooped."

"Good night," I said.

Before Tyler went to bed, I checked in on him.

"Brush your teeth?"

"Yep."

"Get all your homework done?"

"Yep."

I grinned at him, "I think we're going to save some

money not buying all those desserty items."

He looked serious. "I'm glad," he replied. "Because I don't plan to eat them anymore."

He meant it, too. Once he set his mind to something, it was done. I was thankful he'd only decided to focus on positive things so far. I'd hate to have to fight that passion in the opposite direction.

After leaving Tyler, I went to my bedroom. I began rummaging through the closet to find something to wear to work the next day, and I noticed the gym bag lying on the floor.

Sabrina's book.

After getting ready for bed, I got the John Waterhouse book out and lay down. As I thumbed through the pages, I saw a brief description next to each photo.

The first one I recognized from the wall at Sabrina's house. It was of a woman—a tortured-looking soul—sitting in a boat. It was called "The Lady of Shallot." The side note said the painting was inspired by a poem written by Lord Tennyson. I stared for a long time into the woman's eyes, then read the caption. It described a lady who lived in a castle surrounded by a river. She had been cursed and couldn't look out at the outside world. She could only see people reflected in a mirror. When a man named Lancelot passed by, she chanced a look at him, leaving her tower. She climbed in a boat and floated down the river, hoping to find him, but died before she could.

Gosh. How depressing.

I glanced at the picture again. The woman was beautiful, haunting. This particular painting wasn't in the hands of Sir Andrew Lloyd Webber; it was at the Tate Gallery in London.

London, I thought. Another place on our list.

I flipped through a few more pages and found the next painting that I recognized from Sabrina's house. It was called "La Belle Dame sans Merci." It was another pretty one, with a lady with long, flowing hair next to a knight. The description said the painting was inspired by a ballad written by the poet, John Keats.

John Waterhouse clearly had a thing for poetry.

I read it, trying to decipher its meaning. Poetry was definitely not my strong point. But from what I could gather, it seemed like this knight met an enchanting fairy woman, and he fell for her, hard. I don't think things ended well, though. It appeared she'd tricked him somehow and really screwed him over—poor guy.

I was beginning to feel drowsy, but as I flipped to one of the last pages, I saw another familiar picture. I had just enough energy to read one more.

The final painting was called "The Danaïdes." It was a scene of several women all pouring bowls of water into a much larger, center bowl, which had holes in it and constantly leaked. I checked the side note for an explanation. The piece was inspired by Greek mythology. It was about women who were forced to wed men they didn't want to marry. Their father instructed them to kill their husbands on their wedding night, and for their crimes, they all end up in Hell, having to pour endless bowls of water into a larger one that will never stay full. They must do hard labor forever.

Enough of this craziness. If I continued reading anymore, I was bound to have nightmares. And I didn't need any help in that department. I'd had it with fairies, Greek mythology, tragedy. I had to get up for work in the morning.

*****

I was surprised to have slept well, dream-free, in fact. I was glad because Mondays were usually busy. I'd need the energy to make it through the day.

Fatima caught me first thing in the morning. "Hey, girl. I've got some good news and some bad news. Which do you wanna hear first?"

"Start with the good," I said.

"Okay," she replied, barely able to contain her excitement. "You're not going to believe this, but I auditioned to be an extra in a Johnny Depp movie, and I got picked!"

"Oh my God—that's awesome!"

"Yeah, I know. It's just for a few crowd scenes, but he's in them," she said. Now she was jumping up and down, and clapping, too.

"So are you going to call in sick? How's that gonna work?"

"Oh, I almost forgot about that." She pouted, but within seconds, her smile returned and she said, "I'll just make something up."

I didn't think that was a good idea, but I didn't want to preach. I was guilty of making up a whole bunch of things myself lately, so I didn't have room to speak.

"So what's the bad news?" I asked.

Fatima frowned. "Oh, it's Barb." She paused as if she felt bad telling me. "You know that man she met, the one she was seeing?"

I nodded.

"Well, I guess he broke up with her. She doesn't want to talk about it, though."

I glanced over at Barb, who was returning from the

restroom. I felt sorry for her, still playing the game and getting hurt in her sixties. I was lucky, I guessed, that I never even had to play. Justin and I met in high school, and we'd always been together. It was easy. I decided not to ask Barb about it. Instead, I delved into my work and minded my own business.

The next few days I did more of the same. Barb didn't mention her situation to me. She kept to herself, but occasionally one of her famous, warm smiles managed to escape.

I wondered who could ever hurt a person as sweet as her?

*****

Wednesday night, I just made it back on time after running an errand to pick up Tyler from his art lesson.

"Mrs. White," Josephine said. "Tyler says you're doing well, enjoying the cookbooks I lent you guys."

"Yeah, we're trying."

She could tell I was just being polite. She'd found a loyal subject in Tyler, though, and she wasn't going to disappoint him.

"If you keep at it, you're gonna feel wonderful," she claimed.

I smiled, then reached into my pocket to pull out her check. "Here you go."

She took it from me. "You know, if you like, I could come by and cook something vegan that isn't in the book. Just let me know. I'd be happy to help."

I nodded. "Thanks. We'll keep that in mind."

When we got in the car, Tyler wore a silly grin.

"How was class this time?" I asked him.

"Good."

He was definitely hiding something.

"What's the big smile for?"

Tyler just shrugged his shoulders and laughed. It wasn't like him to be so silly. Whatever it was, he wasn't sharing. Maybe it was an artist thing. I probably wouldn't understand.

Later on, after homework and our workout routine, Tyler said something that surprised Mom and me.

"I drank some green juice at Josephine's," he said. "It's made of grass."

"Grass!" Mom shouted. "What kind of grass?"

Tyler got spooked by her reaction. "Wheat grass," he answered.

I'd heard of it, and there was no way it was making an appearance in our home. At least, I had no intention of drinking it. Not a single drop.

"What did it taste like?" I asked him.

Tyler's face contorted. "It was gross."

"But did you tell Josephine you liked it?"

He shook his head no.

Good, I thought. At least my son was honest, not like me lately—queen of the white lie.

I really liked Josephine. She had a good heart and I knew she was just trying to help. I'm sure she knows all about Tyler's quest for long life and his desire to not lose anyone else. In the end, I thought it was kind of sweet.

That night, I had trouble falling asleep. I lay in bed, thinking about my visit with Sabrina. I thought about how she had honeymooned in Paris, and how she had gotten a divorce. I felt sad for her that the marriage hadn't worked out. "It wasn't true love," she had said.

My thoughts drifted to Justin. I couldn't believe all the

things he'd told her about us. Yet, it was nice to hear her describe how he lit up when he talked about me. Something about the way she had said that, it was like… I don't know. I had to hear more, and soon. As I lay there, I realized she didn't have my phone number, only Justin's old one, which had been long since disconnected. I decided I'd call her tomorrow to make plans to return.

I waited until my way home from work to give her a buzz. After I dialed her number, I got voicemail.

"Hi, Sabrina. It's Amy," I told her I'd finished with her book and left my number, asking her to call back and let me know if I should drop it by or mail it.

I didn't want to mail it, but I thought it appropriate to offer, just in case she was being polite by having me over in the first place.

All of a sudden the lunacy of the moment hit me, and I began laughing. The whole situation was odd. Me hanging around her, trying to see if she was hiding something, if she really had an affair with my late husband. I decided if I didn't hear from her soon, I'd just mail the book back and be done with it. End of story.

*****

The next day, on my way home from work, I checked voicemail. There were two messages. The first one was from my mom, saying Josephine was stopping by. She'd called and offered to make us dinner, which blindsided me. I appreciated her enthusiasm, but wasn't sure I liked another woman in my kitchen telling me what to eat.

The second message was a bit more interesting. "Hello, Amy. This is Henry, Sabrina's assistant. Sabrina is in Europe right now and will return in a week. She asked that you not mail the book back, that you bring it in person. She will contact you when she comes home to make plans."

She hadn't mentioned going overseas. But why should she? I wasn't her keeper, and we weren't friends. I suspect we were curiosities to each other at best.

I wanted to see her again, that was true. And she wanted me to come back in person as well. I knew my reasons but didn't know hers.

More than ever, I couldn't wait to discover what secrets Sabrina held from me. I was like my son; nothing could stop me once I'd focused on something. And I had no one to monitor which direction my passions went— good or bad—because no one in my world knew Sabrina existed but me.

Chapter 8

When I walked in the door I was greeted by the sound of rapid chopping and the smell of onions and garlic and some other spice I couldn't quite place.

Josephine was in my kitchen. She was wearing an apron and in the middle of creating something surprisingly colorful for us to eat.

"Hi, there," I said, smiling.

"Hi," Josephine said back. She threw some raw vegetables into the skillet, and I heard them sizzle.

"How nice of you to come by and cook for us. It's so unexpected. A wonderful surprise."

Josephine looked confused. "Well, Tyler was nice enough to invite me."

I stole a glance at my son, who sat reading a book at the kitchen table.

He looked up at me and grinned.

Josephine was in on his mission of better health for us. And she seemed like she couldn't be happier. She pushed the vegetarian lifestyle like a bible-banger pushed Jesus Christ.

I'd have to find a polite way to put the brakes on this.

Mom walked in and began setting the table, and I grabbed everyone something to drink.

"Coke?" I asked.

I already knew my mom's answer—yes.

"I'll have water," Josephine said.

I looked at Tyler. "Water for me too."

My son never drank water. But I poured him a glass and set it in front of him before Josephine served us dinner, and we sat down to eat.

I took a bite and puzzled over the strange texture and odd flavor. I felt Josephine's expectant eyes waiting on me. "Different," I said.

"Good different?" she asked.

Tyler cut in. "I love it."

Josephine smiled at Tyler. She'd found herself a little convert.

Mom took a big swig of her soda to wash her food down. I couldn't chance eye contact with her though, because she'd probably say something embarrassing.

"I'm glad to be here," Josephine said. "I love that Tyler is so focused on health at such a young age."

I smiled, but inside I wondered if she knew the reason why. I hadn't told her. And I didn't know if Tyler had. I decided I wouldn't say anything. It would be up to Tyler if he wanted to bring up his dad and share that experience with her.

"Tell us about yourself?" Mom chimed in, putting the poor girl on the spot.

"What would you like to know?"

"Tell us about your family," she said.

Josephine nodded. "Okay. Let's see. My mom is a registered dietician. My dad's a Philosophy professor, and I used to have a little brother, but he died when we were kids, of cancer."

Josephine and Tyler made eye contact, sharing an unspoken connection, and it was then I knew they'd talked.

Josephine cut into her food and continued. "My

parents are what normal people call weird. You can't imagine the kinds of debates I witnessed in our living room as a child. My dad loved talking with others about their spiritual beliefs, sometimes a little too loudly."

My mom and I laughed, and I glanced over at my son. He sat glued to her every word. I'd never seen him so enchanted by another adult. It was sweet, and at the same time it saddened me somehow.

I wondered what Tyler had said to Josephine about Justin. I wondered if he shared his feelings more freely with her than he did with me. Then I laughed at myself for even having such a silly thought. I was glad he had someone to talk to. I don't think we could've asked for a better person.

As our meal drew to a close, I stretched and rubbed my belly. "I'm stuffed. Thank you so much for stopping by and doing this."

"My pleasure," Josephine said.

After we finished cleaning up, she stood. "Well, I should get going. I don't want to take up your whole night. One more thing though…" Josephine reached into her bag and pulled out an index card. "Here's the recipe for what we just ate, in case you'd like to have it again."

I smiled at her and said, "Thank you." Then I walked her to the front door to say goodbye. Tyler was right behind me.

"See you at class," she told him, then winked.

Tyler nodded and wore that big, dopey smile he'd had on before.

I giggled as she walked away.

*****

Friday night, Tyler acted even weirder. "I've got a lot of homework this weekend," he blurted out. "Maybe I can work on it tonight, and you and Grandma can watch a grown-up movie."

This sent up my mom antennae. It wasn't like my son to blow off movie night.

After Mom and I watched a scary movie, I went in to check on my son. He was in his room, drawing, all done with his homework.

"Hey, Mom. What are we doing this weekend?" he asked in his voice that always preceded a favor.

"Nothing. Why?"

"Well, last time I was at Josephine's she was talking about the Art Institute downtown, asking me if I'd ever gone."

He didn't have to butter me up with my own movie night to go on an excursion. "Do you want to go there this weekend?"

"Can we?" he asked.

"Of course," I said. "We can all go down on the train, make a day of it."

Tyler sprung to his feet. "Cool!"

With plans made and everyone off to bed, I decided to go online and map our route and find out what the museum entrance fees were. I spent a little time on the site and was ecstatic to discover they had nine paintings by Gauguin on display. Tyler will be psyched.

I browsed the web mindlessly for a few more minutes. Then, just because, I Googled Sabrina Bergman.

I was surprised by how much information came up. The majority was connected to her family's fashion business: The Bergman Collection. I checked a few links, but most were reviews of what someone of importance in the industry thought about the clothing. I clicked a link to the company website. There were pictures of skinny models wearing outfits, shots of them walking down the runway. If I hit the right arrow button, I could see photos of the show for the current season, which I did.

Each outfit was beautiful. There weren't any prices listed, but I guess if you have to ask... Heck, what did I know, I shopped at Target. I checked the link on where to buy. Boutiques I'd never heard of popped up, and Neiman Marcus. Yikes! I knew that one, the most expensive department store in the mall.

I noticed an "about us" button. I clicked on it, and there was a picture of Sabrina. I let out a sigh. She looked better than ever.

I thought of Justin. Why had he never mentioned her name? Not even once? He often talked about his other clients.

I read what was written in the "about us" section. Instead of providing juicy details about Sabrina, it was a statement describing the company's artistic vision. Boring.

I scanned down to the end of the page. There was one interesting nugget. It said Sabrina was carrying on where her parents, Don and Monique, left off.

Out of morbid curiosity, I Googled their names. Again, a bunch of links popped up. The one that caught my eye was "Fashion Industry's Tragic Loss." The article went on to describe the untimely death of Don and Monique Bergman. While vacationing in Indonesia, their privately rented plane went down after leaving Bali. The wreckage was found between Bali and Java. The cause of the crash was unknown.

After reading the article, I felt sad. And a little

ashamed. I was behaving like a nosy old lady. Disgusted with myself, I logged off the computer and went to bed.

*****

Sunday morning, we got up early, ate breakfast and headed to the train station. On the ride there, Tyler talked non-stop about Josephine.

"Did I tell you she went to a special college for art?" he said.

My mom and I glanced at each other and grinned. Of course we knew that.

"No, honey," I replied with interest, "you didn't."

I let him rattle on as we bounced around in our seats. The benches weren't very comfortable on Metra. And, of course, our train hit every single stop.

"Did I tell you she went on vacation with her friends for a whole summer to Europe?"

"Nope." I figured he was going to tell me, though, and that story would cover the rest of the trip downtown. I sat there nodding and responding in all the right spots as he spilled the details.

As I listened, I felt bad we'd never taken Tyler on a vacation. I know he heard Justin and I dream out loud about our travel plans, but they never materialized. I hoped travel would be in my son's future. Justin would like that.

I heard them call the final stop, and we gathered our belongings and caught a cab to the Art Institute. Tyler loved the big stone lions out front, so we took some pictures there, before heading inside.

We wandered aimlessly for a while. Then we found ourselves in the modern art section. Mom liked the paintings, but I didn't. I know they're supposed to evoke a feeling instead of be about something, but I didn't care. I thought they were ugly. All I could think was how could paint be randomly splattered around and end up in a museum?

"What do you think, T.?" Mom asked Tyler.

He gave it some thought. "I like it," he said. "It makes me feel happy."

"See, he gets it," Mom ribbed me.

"It must be me," I said. "I'm not in touch with my emotions."

After I spoke the words, I realized they were true. I hardly felt anything anymore.

"Where to next?" I asked, switching the subject.

"The restrooms," Mom replied.

After hitting the bathroom, we located the Gauguin section. It was filled with pieces bursting with vivid colors and tranquil scenes. Tyler was in Heaven. He walked around slowly, taking them all in.

"These are my favorites," he said.

"I thought you might say that," I replied.

Tyler kept going back to one painting. "I think this is the best one."

I walked over and read the plaque. The piece was called "Day of the God." It depicted a Polynesian beach scene with some kind of religious ceremony.

"You've got expensive taste," I joked. "Maybe they have a poster in the gift shop."

Tyler smiled back. He was having a great time.

We walked until our feet throbbed. Then we stopped at the museum cafe for lunch. Once we sat down, it made getting back up almost impossible.

Our last stop before leaving was the gift shop. They

sold posters, even the one Tyler wanted, but he stumbled onto a sale section with last year's Gauguin calendar. That was a better deal, because he got a bunch of pictures for the same price as a single poster.

We took a cab to the train station, and once we boarded, we fell silent. On the ride home, we all had our eyes closed, waiting for the conductor to call out our stop.

Chapter 9

Back at work Monday, I was restless. I couldn't concentrate. When I punched out at the end of the day, I checked voicemail and was excited to find a message from Henry. He was calling on behalf of Sabrina, inviting me to come this Sunday. I could return the book, have lunch, and go swimming.

What irony. Finally I would be swimming after all. Just not at the gym. I wondered why I didn't just tell the truth, at least to my own mother. Then I remembered the awful situation with my dad, and I decided I couldn't do that. Not yet. Not until I was sure about everything.

Throughout the week, I put more focus on the family workout routine because I'd have to wear a bathing suit in front of Sabrina soon. I knew it was childish, but I felt every abdominal crunch was a tiny boost to my fragile ego.

Once the time came to try on my swimwear, I was bummed. It was worn-looking and plain, and I didn't have the cash to buy another one, so I'd have to just deal with it. On a mission, I rummaged through my entire closet to see what else I had that made me look cute. After digging for twenty minutes, I found nothing. I hadn't bought new clothes in a long time. I guess I stopped trying once Justin was gone.

I thought about what Barb had said to me, that I was

depressed. I studied my reflection in the mirror and sighed. I used to look nice. Justin always complimented me. But I had let myself go.

Saturday night, before bed, I thumbed through Sabrina's John Waterhouse book again. I wondered what feelings these pieces evoked. As I turned the pages, I got a sense of them. Romantic, mysterious, and tragic. I closed the book and looked at the art in my room. They were Tyler's drawings. Islands, bugs, pieces of fruit. He sure was coming along as an artist. It gave me a warm, fuzzy feeling inside. I let that feeling usher me into a deep sleep.

When I arrived at Sabrina's on Sunday, she answered the door herself and was dressed down, like a normal person. Maybe she'd realized how nutty she looked in the chiffon gown.

I pulled her book out of my bag and handed it to her. "Thanks," I said. "I really enjoyed it."

She took it from me and reached for my coat and bag. I looked around and wondered where Henry was. Maybe it was his day off. Surely servants got a day off. Then I realized I was being politically incorrect and made a mental note to switch the phrase to hired help.

"Follow me," Sabrina said, interrupting my inner dialogue. "I have a surprise for you."

She turned, and I began walking behind her down the hallway. I hesitated for a split second when I realized we were alone. I don't know why, but I got a little frightened.

We arrived in her bedroom, where I glimpsed a bouquet of yellow daffodils sitting in a vase on the dresser.

A familiar ping gripped my gut. A reminder to stay alert, to remember why I was here.

Sabrina reached into her closet and pulled out a hanging bag. "This is for you," she said.

I reached out and took the bag from her. When I unzipped it and revealed its contents, I saw two brand new designer outfits.

"I thought you might enjoy these," she said. "I know you work in an office, and I think these pieces will be just right."

"Thank you," I replied, finally getting words to form in my mouth, "but I can't accept these. They're too expensive."

"No, they're not," she said, waving them off like it was no big deal. "They're samples left over from the show."

I'm smart enough to know (from watching *Sex and the City*) that runway samples were a size two. These were a six—my size. How the hell did she know my size? Something about this felt terribly wrong.

"What do you think?" she asked.

My first thought was "you're giving me a present because you're guilty about something, and you're trying to make up for it." My second thought was maybe rich people just did stuff like this; maybe it was normal, like giving half your sandwich to a co-worker who forgot to pack lunch. I'd have to decide on a correct answer to continue this charade, so I broke down and gave in to the truth. An embarrassingly selfish truth.

"I love them," I replied. "I was just thinking I needed to get out there and buy some new clothes."

We smiled at each other, and I took another glance at the daffodils sitting on Sabrina's dresser. When my gaze returned to her, she wore a poker face.

"Would you like to eat lunch first or go swimming?"

The thought of eating and then putting on my suit

didn't appeal to me. "Let's swim first."

I followed Sabrina back into the foyer, where she reached for my bag and showed me to the guest bathroom. Once inside, I changed and surveyed myself in the mirror.

I was still average. None of the workouts had made a visible difference.

Oh well, I thought, then slipped on my flip-flops, put my hair in a ponytail and stuffed my clothes back in the bag.

When I stepped out of the bathroom, Sabrina wasn't there, so I hovered in the hallway, mentally squashing my desire to meander about and snoop. Part of me feared Henry would show up— out of nowhere—with a Coke or Sprite in tow.

"Looks like we're all set then," I heard Sabrina say.

I turned and was stunned by what I saw. There she was in a black one-piece swimsuit with plunging neckline. Her long, dark hair was pulled up and wrapped in a salon-worthy twist. I looked down. She wore black kitten heels, too.

A wave of depression hit me as I realized I could never compete with her. She was a Chanel ad; I was a soccer mom.

"Yep," I said. "All set."

We walked to the indoor pool area, kicked off our shoes and got in. The water was perfect, room temperature.

"This is refreshing," I said. "And a lot quieter than the pool I usually go to."

"Which pool is that?" she asked.

"There's an indoor pool at the health club, which I've been to only a few times, and there's the outdoor community pool I take Tyler to in summer."

"That sounds like fun," she said. "I'd love to have a child to go places and do things with."

Now we were getting somewhere, getting into her brain.

"It's fun, but it can be exhausting," I admitted. "When there's two of you to share the parenting, it's easier."

"It must be difficult for you," she said.

We had stopped swimming and were just standing in the water, talking.

"My mom moved in with us and helps out a lot. Plus, Tyler is like a thirty-year-old man in a child's body."

Sabrina let out a laugh. "I remember Justin saying that."

Her familiarity with Justin was beginning to get on my nerves.

"That's my husband," I said, "always the bragger."

Did I overemphasize the word "my?"

"Yes," Sabrina quickly added. "He always spoke very highly of both you and your son."

I decided to take the conversation back to where I wanted it to go. I was here to learn her secrets.

"So you mentioned the outfits you gave me were leftover from a show?"

"Yes," she said. "We just had a show in Paris. It went well, but I'm actually rather glad to be back home."

"Why?" I asked, thinking her insane.

"Oh... it's silly, really, but I had a run-in with my ex-husband." Her expression grew strained. "He was with his new wife and baby."

"Wow. That's awful. How strange that you'd bump into him there."

"Oh, it's not strange. He's originally from France (like

my mother) and after the divorce, he moved back home. My mom enjoyed living in the U.S., but he didn't; he'd always grumble on about everything. Nothing was ever good enough for him."

I felt sorry for her. I couldn't imagine being in her shoes. Having made it through a terrible marriage, getting divorced, and then running into the jerk down the road, with his new, French wife, and worse yet, baby. She'd mentioned wanting a child, so I guessed this chance visit was especially painful.

"Looks like you're the lucky one," I told her.

"How so?"

"Because you didn't get stuck with him."

Something about the comment caused Sabrina to burst into laughter. "I guess you're right," she agreed, then began treading water.

"Plus," I added, "Who wants to be with a guy for whom nothing is ever good enough? It sounds exhausting."

Sabrina looked at me, her expression a sad mix of "I've already lived it and you just wouldn't understand."

No, I thought, answering her in my mind, I wouldn't.

"Justin would've told you to not even bother trying, to just be yourself."

Sabrina gazed off into nowhere for a while, then looked back at me. "We talked about it," she said, "while he was working on the bathroom, I think." She paused, no doubt remembering their time together. "He listened patiently while I rambled on and on about our brief courtship, and the roller-coaster marriage with all its nasty little events."

"And what did he say?"

"He didn't say anything then, just worked and listened, poor guy."

I smirked.

"Since I was full of steam, I continued complaining about my ex's every indiscretion, leaving no hurtful detail untold."

"You were really that transparent?"

Sabrina shrugged. "Well, I hadn't meant to be. But Justin was patient. After I was done, he got up, wiped his hands with his work towel, and told me he was going to have to charge me extra for therapy."

She shot me a smile, which was contagious, and I smiled, too.

"How did you respond to that?"

"At first I was stunned, but then I erupted into uncontrollable laughter, and Justin said, 'Mission accomplished, made you smile.'"

Was my husband flirting or just being nice?

Sabrina went on, "He told me he was sorry to hear about my bad experience, and that, unfortunately, these stories were becoming more and more common, but that it didn't have to be that way. Love could be a simple thing."

I listened with equal measures of curiosity and concern.

"He said he'd met you in high school. You shared a few classes together, went to prom. After graduation, you moved out and got married."

"Wow," I groaned, "Could we have been anymore simpleton? We're positive bores."

Sabrina gave me a stern look. "You're not simpletons," she stated. "It's how it's supposed to be... easy."

Then, without getting her hair wet, she dove forward like a dolphin and began swimming a lap. I began swimming too. As I did, I thought about what she'd just said. How things are supposed to be easy. I wasn't sure if that's how it had always been for us, or if we just stuck together more than the average couple. Gliding through the warm water, without either of us speaking for a full ten minutes, I got lost in my memories.

Sabrina stopped. "I'm sorry, Amy. I'm a terrible hostess. Are you getting hungry?"

"Sure," I said. "I could eat."

With the grace of a ballerina, she climbed out of the pool. I couldn't help but notice her perfect posture. Maybe she had taken dance lessons or practiced yoga. My posture was horrible, with shoulders curved forward, the unfortunate result of working at a desk for over a decade. I'd have to try harder to sit up straight from now on.

After getting out of the water, I expected a towel, even a beach towel would've sufficed. Instead, Sabrina handed me a fluffy spa robe with matching head wrap. I needed it as I had gotten my hair wet. She only needed a robe. Her updo stayed neatly pinned in place.

"Shall we?" she asked, motioning to leave the area and change.

I followed her through the house to the guest bathroom. I dried off and put my clothes back on, then ran a brush through my hair. I pulled it into a ponytail with a rubber band, which made me look like a high school cheerleader.

I stayed in the bathroom longer than necessary, thinking. I felt so uncomfortable around Sabrina. Maybe it was the odd, formal phrases she used. Maybe it was the situation.

I liked hearing about Justin, though. Hearing him talk about us, about me and Tyler. It made me feel alive again. Oddly enough, I'd also enjoyed hearing the conversations he'd had with Sabrina. His sage advice and off the wall humor… I hadn't expected that.

I wrung my swimsuit out in the sink and put it in the plastic bag I'd brought. Then I stuffed it in my gym bag and went into the hallway. Sabrina was waiting there.

"All set?"

"Sure," I replied.

We went into the kitchen, and I sat in the offered chair.

"Can I help with anything?"

"Oh, no," she said. "It's all been taken care of. I made part of it yesterday and part today."

She took a pot out of the fridge and set it on top the stove. Then she pulled out a tray and added it to the oven. She seemed to know her way around the kitchen pretty well.

"I just bought a new vegetarian cookbook, so I thought I'd try one of the recipes today," she said.

My God. I was in a recurring nightmare from which there was no escape.

"Sounds good," I said as politely as I could muster. "We've been doing some of that at our house lately, too—Tyler's idea."

"Really?" she asked, looking suspicious. "A child's suggestion?"

"A thirty-year-old man-child… remember?"

"Oh, yeah," she giggled, but this time her familiarity didn't get on my nerves.

"He's obsessed with eating healthy and exercising," I said. "It all began recently, after a birthday party."

Sabrina stirred the contents of the pot and looked back at me, "Go on."

"His friend's mom had heart surgery, and after she recovered, the doctor ordered dietary changes and exercise. Tyler took the story very seriously. He's got us all working out together every night."

"That's adorable," Sabrina said. "But how did the vegetarian come in?"

"Oh, I forgot to say. That was a suggestion from his art instructor. He started talking about it to her, and she lent him, or should I say *us*, some cookbooks."

Sabrina smiled. "Well, you'll like this then."

She came over and poured us each a glass of iced tea and added a pre-cut lemon wedge to the side. She served butternut squash soup with grilled vegetable sandwiches, and she was right. It was delicious.

She was a better cook than me.

"Tyler would like this," I said.

"It's heartbreaking to hear of a young child so focused on that sort of thing."

Her eyes were filled with compassion as she spoke. It caused me to get a little choked up inside.

Damn it! I wasn't going to cry in front of this woman—my presumed adversary, my unusual friend. I willed the tears back into my eyes and cleared my throat.

"Yeah, well, he's been through a lot."

"I'm sure he has," she said in a soothing tone.

I managed to regain composure and was chewing a bite of my sandwich when Sabrina decided to press a little further.

"Has he had any counseling?" she asked.

"No. Our insurance plan doesn't cover mental health. He draws now. That's his therapy."

I didn't know if what I said made sense. But I understood how it helped Tyler, how he enjoyed having his creative time alone.

"Art can definitely be a form of therapy, that's so true."

She stirred her iced tea, looking inside her glass. "You mentioned he has an instructor?"

"Yeah. My mom and I found someone reasonably-priced and signed him up for lessons. She's a younger girl, just graduated from Savannah College of Art and Design."

"That's a prestigious school. You're lucky she's reasonable."

"I know," I said. "Once she finds a job, I'm sure she'll be gone, and art classes will be out of the budget, just like everything else. I'm trying to get out of my gym membership, because I could save some money there, but it's on a contract. Once that ends, I could probably get back to saving for Tyler's college…"

I stopped myself. I was saying way too much. I was carrying on with her like she was Barb or Fatima.

Even though I'd trailed off, Sabrina politely ignored it. "So does your son enjoy his lessons?"

"Yes. He loves them. Actually, I think he has a crush on his teacher, Josephine."

Sabrina grinned. "That's cute." Apparently she couldn't get enough of hearing about him.

"I know. It's his first crush, and he talks about her non-stop. He's eating like her, telling us all her travel stories. Plus, she's got a dog. Tyler's always wanted a dog but—"

"But Justin was allergic," she said, finishing my sentence. "I remember. He told me."

It became uncomfortable again. And I wondered what else Justin had told her.

"Well, yeah… then you know," I replied awkwardly.

"So Josephine, in addition to graduating from such a fine institution, has travelled extensively as well. What a nice thing to hear. Do you know where she's been?"

Sabrina was a master at smoothing out ripples of tension. I was grateful she'd re-directed the conversation. I was only too happy to share. "I guess she's been to most of Europe and part of South America. She hasn't been to Tahiti, though. Tyler asked."

Sabrina tilted her head and smiled. "Ah, Tahiti—that glorious place."

"You've been there?"

"No," she said. "My sister has been. She went for her honeymoon. I saw the pictures."

I was surprised she hadn't gone. If I was even half as rich as she was I'd have gone by now.

"Tell me about your sister," I said.

"Oh, let's see. She's younger. She's married and has a daughter. She lives in California with her husband, a film executive. They went to Bora Bora for their honeymoon, and all I got was a few pictures and a t-shirt."

Her joke made me laugh, like we were on the same level. Of course, we weren't. She could travel whenever she wanted, wherever she wanted. And all I ever wanted was to go to that special island with my husband.

"Justin talked a lot about Bora Bora," Sabrina said.

"Yeah."

"He planned to take you."

"Yeah, I know."

"He said he wanted to renew your wedding vows there, for your fifteen-year anniversary."

Suddenly, I lost all capacity to breathe. I hadn't known that specific plan, and hearing it knocked the wind out of me. My eyes erupted into a waterfall.

Embarrassed, wiping tears from my face, I said, "Excuse me." Then I ran off to the guest bathroom.

Once alone, I sobbed freely. I leaned over the sink and cried harder than I had in a long time, eventually collapsing on the floor.

This is worse than the funeral, I thought. At least then, at the end of the day after everyone had gone, I'd been able to break down alone. My mom had taken Tyler for a walk in the park. Poor T., I thought. No father to play with, no counselor to talk to. He rarely spoke to me about his feelings, only danced around them, the way he did with Sally's mom and her heart surgery. His response to getting sick and dying was simple: Eat right and exercise. Problem. Solution. I formed a half-smile at the thought. He was already on his way to becoming the action-oriented, logical man. His emotions went into his artwork.

I sat in a blubbering heap on the bathroom floor. I had been in here for too long. Worse yet, I'd have to face Sabrina, something I didn't look forward to.

I managed to climb up and check my reflection in the mirror. My face was a red, swollen mess. My eyes glowed green. I turned on the faucet and splashed my skin with cold water, then took some deep breaths.

When I slipped into the hallway, Sabrina wasn't there. Sheepishly, I walked back toward the kitchen. I wanted nothing more than to escape.

I poked my head into the room and saw Sabrina seated, looking frantic.

"I'm so sorry, Amy. I didn't mean to—"

"No. Don't apologize," I said. "You did nothing wrong, really. It's me. I didn't know about the vow renewal, and it just took me by surprise."

Sabrina looked uncomfortable. "I thought you knew. I'm so sorry. I didn't know it was meant to be a surprise. I mean, he never said—"

"Please," I said, interrupting her. "Don't apologize. You haven't done anything wrong. I mean it."

She accepted this time and got up and began straightening the dishes, an obvious attempt to distract herself from the awkwardness of the moment. I wanted to leave, but didn't want to be rude, so I asked, "Can I help with anything?"

"Oh no," she said. "I was just clearing these out of the way so I can serve dessert."

I couldn't eat another bite of food if I tried. My stomach was a knot. "Sabrina, I apologize, but I don't think I'll be able to have any."

She turned, her expression softened, and she said in a low voice, "I understand."

I looked at my watch, wondering if it was time for my mom to pick up Tyler. Sabrina noticed I was antsy, too.

"Let me get your things," she said, and walked toward the closet by the front door.

I followed her and took my coat and gym bag. I saw the hanging bag with the clothes she'd given me. I felt terrible accepting them now. Sabrina handed them to me anyway.

"Here you go," she said. "Enjoy."

I stood in the foyer feeling horrible, not knowing what to say.

"Thank you," I replied. "This was... fun."

Sabrina broke into a nervous laugh. "Part of it was,"

she said in a genuine tone. "See you next time."

And there it was, that odd phrase she'd spoken after the first time we met. Those words haunted me. Because, unlike Justin, who was paid to come back again and again, I could no longer comprehend the real reason for my own visits.

Like the siren's song to the sailor, her "see you next time" would continue to pull me, as the tides control the sea.

Chapter 10

I hopped into my car and started the engine, anxious to get home. After I checked my watch, I realized it would be perfect timing; I'd make it back just as Tyler and my mom were getting there. I hoped by then it wouldn't look like I'd been crying.

When I walked in, no one was home. So I took the opportunity to hide the bag Sabrina had given me in the back of my closet. I took my swimsuit out and began rinsing it in the sink, and I heard the garage door open.

"Hey, Mom," Tyler said, poking his head into the bathroom.

I waved, then dried my hands on a towel.

Later on, after dinner, I let my guard down. I felt compelled to talk, even if all I could share was a partial truth. "So I met this lady at the gym today, and she invited me to swim at her house."

Mom's curiosity peaked. She wasn't accustomed to me hanging out with my old friends, let alone meeting someone new.

"What lady?" she asked.

I knew I shouldn't have said anything, but I'd already begun. I felt a sudden pressure in my chest.

"Well, it ends up—if you can believe it—that she was a customer of Justin's. Somehow she recognized me and introduced herself."

Mom looked confused. Tyler seemed interested. The inquiring looks on both their faces made me wish I hadn't brought it up.

"How did she recognize you?" Mom asked.

I was weaving a tale now, and I didn't have any idea where I was going with it. "Umm, that's a good question," I said. "I don't know. She just came up to me and asked if I was Amy White. Then she introduced herself, and we got to talking."

My mom didn't say anything, but I could tell she sensed the story was false. Her posture wasn't relaxed enough to be buying it. And there was too much unevenness in my voice. She had a questioning look in her eyes that asked, "What really happened?"

I hated disappointing her, but I couldn't provide an answer to that. I didn't even know myself. But I had to say something about it all, to share this secret or I'd simply burst. It was becoming too much for me to hide.

"So," Mom continued, "She invited you to her place to swim?"

"Yeah. She's got a pool in her house. She lives on the North Shore. She was one of Justin's best customers."

My mom gave me a long, speculative glance. "Well, I guess you were meant to make a new friend," she said. It didn't sound like she meant it.

She would be snide if I wasn't going to be truthful. I felt terrible now that I'd brought it up.

"I think it's nice you made a friend," Tyler chimed in. "Sometimes the Universe is speaking to you."

"What?" Mom barked.

"You know—The Universe," Tyler repeated, this time with more emphasis. He looked at us both like we were clueless and should know these things.

"Honey, where did you get an idea like that?" I asked.

"Josephine."

Of course—Josephine. The hippie, vegetarian art instructor. Now there was a stereotype if there ever was one.

"Tell me what she told you," I said.

Tyler looked eager to discuss the topic. Anything Josephine-related held special interest for him.

He sat up straight and clasped his hands together, like a guest speaker at an event. "Well," he began, "she said the Universe is always working its magic, always speaking to us, and that everything happens for a reason."

His serious expression amused me. I spent a moment considering what he just said. It actually sounded acceptable, not too crazy.

I smiled at Tyler and put my hand on his shoulder. "That sounds good, honey. That sounds real good."

Mom just walked out of the room, shaking her head, muttering inaudible words.

*****

The next morning, I woke up, showered, and dressed in one of my new designer outfits. I felt great, reborn almost.

When I got to the office and sat at my desk, Fatima came by. "Hey. Nice threads. Where'd you get them?"

Good question. And one I didn't really want to answer. Fatima reached down the back of my blouse and pulled out the tag.

"Bergman Collection!" she shouted. "What'd you do, rob a bank?"

"No," I said defensively. "It's from Target."

97

She gave me a surprised look. "I didn't know they had a collection at Target."

"I guess they do now," I said, hoping she'd just let it go. I loved her—I did—but sometimes young people got on my nerves.

My day improved as we got busier. Everyone pretty much kept to themselves while we listened to the Spanish channel, the only station that seemed to come in lately.

When I clocked out at 5:00 p.m., the weather was wonderful. No more cold, rainy, gray skies. It was a fine spring day, so I rolled down the window and let the fresh air rush in.

I was happy. I hadn't felt that emotion in a long time.

When I got home, I could tell Mom had noticed the shift in my mood, too. She didn't comment on it, though. We shared that unspoken mother/daughter connection.

After dinner, Mom had plans with one of her friends, so Tyler and I decided to go for a walk outside. We both wore jackets, because it was still colder than it looked. Blue sky could be deceptive in Chicagoland.

"How was school today?" I asked.

"Good."

"Any homework you could use help with?"

"No. I'm pretty caught up," he said. "I did it in class."

Sometimes I felt so unneeded. My son seemed to have everything in his life under control.

"How's Sally's mom doing? Is she feeling better?"

"Yeah. Sally said she's doing good."

Our feet hit the pavement while our arms swished back and forth in unison, the coat fabric making rubbing sounds. I was out of ideas on how to create conversation that went beyond mere question and answer. Usually my son talked more. I wasn't sure what was up with him. But then I remembered Sabrina's idea, about the counseling.

"Hey, T."

"Yeah."

"Do you ever feel like you wish you had someone to talk to? Someone other than me?"

He kept walking. "I talk to all kinds of people."

It was a general statement. One he made to avoid the topic at hand. I knew he discussed something about it with Josephine, but that wasn't what I meant.

"No, honey. That's not what I mean," I articulated. "I mean maybe talking to someone about problems."

Tyler halted. "What are you saying? That I should go to a psycho doctor?"

I paused, carefully choosing my next words. "No, honey. I'm not saying you need to go to a psychologist. I'm just asking if you would like to, to have someone to talk to."

I had offended him. He took great pride in his child-like ability to hold everything together. I felt bad I'd mentioned it.

"No," he said. "I don't think so."

He began walking again, and I did, too, striding at his side.

He was quiet for a while, then said, "I don't need to see a doctor about Dad, if that's what you mean."

I let silence fill the air, hoping he might fill the space with more conversation about his dad.

We continued walking in silence for a while, and he finally spoke.

"Dad's just gone," he said. "That's the way it is. There's nothing I can do about it."

"Honey, I understand those are the facts, but what I was suggesting is maybe you'd like to discuss your *feelings* with someone."

Tyler stopped again. "I *am* discussing it with someone. I'm telling you—right now—it makes me sad."

With that out, he turned and changed direction, heading back toward home. He'd stated the obvious. And right then, I realized my son was growing up. He was already becoming like most men, where the obvious is all there is. They didn't see the need to go past it.

I still had a lot to learn about raising a boy. Luckily, he was such a good one, I didn't mind.

Helping me out of an uncomfortable moment, Tyler spoke again. "Before Dad died, he told me I needed to be strong." His face composed, he said, "He told me everything would be okay."

"He told me it was normal to feel sad, and to cry. And he said if I wanted to talk to him, all I'd have to do is talk to him the way I've always done, and he'd be there, listening."

"And do you?" I asked, somewhat surprised.

"Sure," he said. "All the time. Not out loud, of course. In my head."

We were approaching the house now, so I fished the keys out of my pocket.

"I told him about Josephine and my art lessons. I told him about her dog, Soleil, and how I'm hoping we could get a dog, too."

I looked down at him and smiled. He was right. It was time for my son to experience the unconditional love of an animal. I'd have to look into it soon.

We walked inside and took off our shoes and jackets.

"I asked Dad to send happiness your way," Tyler said.

"And look—it worked. You've already got a new friend."

I nodded and smiled at Tyler. A new friend. Yes, but that was the outer facade. Inside, I was free-falling through the Twilight Zone, spinning and disoriented.

Something about what he'd just said, and the way he said it rang true, but I wasn't ready to accept it.

I pushed the concept from my mind, trying to regain mental balance as I did the dishes. Somehow I managed to wash the whole stack without breaking any. It was miraculous.

After Tyler went to bed, I decided to switch my focus. I went online to research dogs. How to pick the right one for us, how much did food and vet bills run. I quickly learned that millions of dogs and cats were euthanized each year because they weren't adopted. That settled it. We'd get a shelter dog as soon as the gym membership ended.

The next day at work, I told Barb my plan. "I'm planning to adopt a dog soon. You have any idea how much vet bills might be?"

She looked perplexed. "That depends, sweetie. It varies so much, depending on what health issues the animal has. With Shadow, for instance, and the cancer…"

Barb stopped mid-sentence, and began fidgeting with her hands. "Well, what you need to do is buy pet insurance. They have policies with three levels: basic, regular, and deluxe."

"Okay," I said, truly appreciating her advice. "I'll do that."

As Barb walked away, I felt terrible. She couldn't even talk about her *dog* having cancer in front of me. I was growing tired of making people uncomfortable. Although I was still struggling with depression, I didn't want to appear pitiful. I made a mental note to try and be more of my old self again, which I might be able to do, if only I could remember who she was.

That night, I curled up in bed, wearing my comfiest pajamas. As I lay in the dark, I wondered: Do I pity myself?

I considered the way I interacted with others. I didn't think so. I was unhappy to be a widow, to be in this position, but I wasn't aware of anything I was doing to appear pitiful.

I turned over and fluffed my pillow. I guess if I really wanted to be honest with myself, I'd have to admit I was doing one thing that invited pity. I was grieving too long, or at least longer than what my friends and co-workers thought was appropriate. Part of me felt angry at them. I mean, I didn't know there was a time limit on these things. Was I supposed to just pretend I'm okay when I'm not?

They didn't have a clue.

Sadly, my friends were the first to go after Justin's death. After the cheering up campaign was unsuccessful, they began calling less and less. Sometimes I went along with them, because I felt I should. But there's nothing lamer than hanging out with a single mom who's also a widow. Add broke to the mix and you've got yourself a genuine friend deflector—I couldn't blame them.

My co-workers were a bit more patient with me. Or maybe they had to be, since they had to sit next to me each day to receive their paychecks. It wasn't like we hung out in our free time. They'd invited me, though. And in time, tried to ease me back into life with casual mentions of single men they knew.

My family, on the other hand, was always there for me.

I never felt judged for going to the cemetery. They never tried fixing me up with someone else. They just let me be. I guess since Tyler didn't know I still visited Justin, what it really meant was that my mom was there for me. She was amazing.

I felt terrible not confiding in her about Sabrina.

As the evening went on, I lay awake, thinking about Tyler talking to his dad, how he'd wished happiness for me. My sad life must be obvious if even a child could notice.

Of course, there was Sabrina, my new "friend" bringing me happiness. I looked over at the alarm clock. Even at one in the morning I could be a smartass. She wasn't a real friend. When you're friends with someone, it's supposed to be fun, not filled with a general sense of foreboding.

Maybe I was pitiful.

I pulled the comforter over my head, trying to make it all go away.

It didn't. And I couldn't sleep. I went to the kitchen, poured myself a glass of orange juice, and sat down at the computer to research pet insurance.

I settled on ASPCA pet insurance. I knew the prices, and had all the info on pet food. Soon we would be dog owners.

The next morning, I decided to spill the good news to Tyler as he got ready for school.

"So I've thought about your request to get a dog."

My son's eyes popped open, and he stopped brushing his teeth.

"And I think it's a good idea," I told him.

Tyler began jumping up and down, then attempted to speak, but choked on a mouthful of paste. He quickly spit it out and rinsed.

"We're really gonna get one?"

The look on his face could have made any problem in the world melt away.

"Yes," I replied. "But there's a minor glitch."

He stared at me, without blinking.

"We have to wait a little bit to be able to afford it. Then we can go to the shelter and adopt any dog you choose."

Tyler threw his arms around me and hugged me tighter than he ever had. After letting go, I felt the urge to jump up and down, too. We both started hooting and hurray-ing.

Mom walked past. "What's going on here?"

"Grandma. We're getting a dog!"

A smile broke out and stretched the length of my mom's face. Not only would she like a dog, she'd prefer a whole pack of them, maybe even a cat or bird, too. We'd always had a pet in the home while I was growing up.

"This is good news, honey," she said, rubbing Tyler's head.

It felt wonderful to start the day off that way. I knew Tyler would be anxious to tell Josephine. Luckily, he would only have to wait until tonight.

I ate breakfast and hopped into the shower. I rummaged through the closet, looking for something to wear, and my eyes caught sight of the hanging bag Sabrina had given me.

I still had one new outfit left, so I took it out and tried it on, admiring my reflection in the mirror.

I looked nice. Even my figure looked better. Must be the cut and quality of the fabric, I thought.

My mind drifted off, wondering what the true cost

was. I ran my fingers through my hair, and promised myself no matter what it took, I'd find out.

*****

Driving to work, I felt confident and happy. I didn't know if it was the new wardrobe, or if it was the anticipation of getting a family pet, but I felt good.

I clocked in and noticed Dave was having a meeting with one of our top clients. I quickly sat down, and Fatima passed by with a cup of coffee.

"Amy, you look hot," she said.

I blushed. Okay, I'll admit it, sometimes young people were kind of fun, too.

"Thanks," I whispered, trying to keep it down.

Fatima leaned forward to talk. "You know, I went to Target and I couldn't find any of the pieces you bought."

I got nervous, remembering the white lie. "No? Well, I'll bet they sold out. You know how those things are."

"It's cool," she said. "But hey, since you're so lucky lately, maybe I should start shopping with you?"

I beamed at her, realizing what a large compliment she had just paid me. I remembered my plan to be more outgoing.

"I'd be happy to help you shop," I told her. "Just let me know when."

Dave opened his office door and was saying his goodbyes. Fatima didn't want to get in trouble, so she gave me a thumbs up while back-tracking to her desk.

Would we ever go to the mall together? I doubted it. But it felt good to be asked.

Once I got home, we rushed through dinner. I packed Tyler in the car afterward, and we went to Josephine's. It was pouring rain, so I held out an umbrella to try and cover both Tyler and I as he clutched his homework, neatly stowed in his carrying case. After we rang the doorbell, Soleil began barking.

"Hey, you two," Josephine said. "Come on in."

Mom or I usually dropped Tyler off, then left to run an errand or hit the grocery store, but with the inclement weather, I decided to stick around.

"Hope you don't mind," I said.

"Not at all, Mrs. W. Let me get your coat."

"Thanks. I'll just sit over here, out of the way."

"Whoa, whoa… wait," she said. "Let me check you out."

I struck a pose.

"Looking good. Looking good. You want a cup of tea and a magazine?"

I felt silly. I was never very good with receiving praise. "Tea would be fine, any kind," I said. After a brief hesitation, I added, "And thanks for the compliment."

I sat down on the sofa and watched her walk away. Then I noticed Tyler in the other room, checking out his hair in a mirror. Oh my God! This was going to be cute.

While waiting for my tea, I continued studying my son. As he unpacked his bag, Josephine passed him, and I was amazed by the sudden transformation. Instead of giggling or being bashful, as most children who have a crush are, he stood tall and confident. He wore a cool, James Dean-esque expression.

"Here's your tea. It's chamomile," Josephine said, interrupting my reverie.

"Thank you," I said, and grabbed a nearby magazine so I'd appear busy. Soleil wandered over and lay down near my feet.

Josephine returned to the room with Tyler, and they began talking and reviewing the lesson. I couldn't hear what they were saying, but I sat, transfixed, gazing over the top of my magazine like I was watching a movie in slow motion. There they were, moving about, conversing back and forth, my son acting like a completely different person.

Check this out, Justin. Our baby is growing up.

*****

The sound of someone clearing their throat woke me.

"Mom. You fell asleep."

I sat up, embarrassed.

"Don't worry," Josephine said, trying to make light of the situation. "It was probably the chamomile tea. It makes people sleepy."

I had no idea how I could've dozed off. The nap had felt good though. I got up and smoothed my clothes, and reached in my purse to give Josephine this week's check.

"Thanks," she said. "I'll get your jacket."

We said goodbye and piled into the car to head home. The rain had slowed and visibility was much better. Mom greeted us at the door.

"Hey, guys. Guess what? I checked out a few library books on dogs."

"Cool!" Tyler said, his demeanor suddenly child-like again.

They both took off and plopped down on the couch together.

I followed them into the family room. "I don't know what's gotten into me," I admitted, yawning, "but I'm beat."

"Yeah, she fell asleep at Josephine's."

My mom gave me a look.

"Kind of embarrassing, I know. But at least I didn't snore," I said. "If you two don't mind, I think I'm going to lie down, but I definitely want to look through those books later."

"Sure, hon," Mom said. "Goodnight."

"Night, T.," I said, and kissed the top of his head.

I managed to wash my face and brush my teeth before passing out, and within a few minutes, I drifted into the most peculiar dream.

Everywhere I looked I saw the color yellow. I walked alone, in an expansive, never-ending field of daffodils. There was a light wind blowing the flower tops, causing the landscape to ripple like a gentle wave. Someone walked toward me. It was Justin. Instead of running to him, like they do in the movies, I kept the same pace, taking him in slowly.

He was perfect.

As he drew closer, he began to change. His face went from suntanned to grayish-white. His eyes grew dim.

"Justin. Are you okay?" I asked.

He kept walking toward me, growing skinnier, paler.

"No!" I screamed. Then I began to run to him.

Out of nowhere, an angel appeared and caught him as he was falling. I tried to get to them both, but my legs were moving too slowly.

The winged creature gazed up at me, and it was Sabrina.

I came to a stop, and, to my horror, Justin began disintegrating in her arms. She tried to grasp some of the particles as they fell but couldn't. The warm breeze blew them away in an instant.

The angel lowered her head into her hands. Then she morphed into a giant raven, glanced up at me, and flew away.

I woke up, terrified. Reeling with fear in my dark room, I managed to jump up and flip on the light. I wiped the sweat from my forehead before climbing back into bed.

I hated dreaming of Justin dying. It didn't happen often, but when it did, each time it was painful in its own, unique way.

Chapter 11

The next morning, on my way to work, I thought about calling Sabrina. But remembering how I'd left in an excited state last time, after crying hysterically in her guest bathroom, gave me pause. I felt like such a fool. Maybe I'd call on the way home.

At work, I began spacing out. I was exhausted from the terrible night's sleep, and I began playing with my calculator, hitting random numbers, watching the tape grow. What I needed, I decided, was a better way to interact with Sabrina. I'd hoped our visits would help me uncover what I wanted to find out about her and Justin. Turns out it wasn't so easy.

On the drive home at the end of the day, I had a flash of insight and dialed her number.

"You've reached the Bergman residence," the recorded voice said. Henry's voice.

Damn it. I should hang up. But I didn't.

"Hi, Sabrina. It's Amy. I'm calling to see if you want to get together this weekend? I feel terrible about last time and was thinking maybe we could do something else. Maybe go to my health club?"

After I hung up, I felt like a moron. Whenever I called her I sounded like a green telemarketer reading from a script. I shook my head in disgust and stashed the phone in my purse.

I turned on the radio and flipped through the

channels. I couldn't find a single song to listen to, so I switched it to NPR. I could always count on them to make the drive home bearable.

"We're talking to author Brittany Hyatt," the interviewer said. "We're so glad to have you with us today."

"Glad to be here."

"Your book is called *Dating Again, Life Goes on After Death.* Tell us a little bit about it and yourself."

"The book addresses the topic of widows/widowers and their often different approaches to getting back into a relationship again. Often, after a spouse dies, a man will go through a grieving process, but within a few years will usually re-marry. Women, on the other hand, will often spend many years alone, not dating anyone."

"What do you think is the cause of these differences between the sexes?"

"Well," Brittany said, "My book isn't a scientific study, per se. It's coming from my own personal viewpoint, based on hundreds of interviews I've done throughout the country."

"Go on."

"It all has to do with one's perception of love. Men viewed marriage in a healthier light. They enjoyed sharing their lives with someone."

"I like this," the interviewer said. "A book written by a woman who's telling us we're doing things right."

They both giggled.

Brittany continued. "Women, on the other hand, tend to have higher expectations. They share a more idealistic view of love, mainly romantic love, and this, I suggest, is from their upbringing." She cleared her throat and went on. "Young girls are told fairytales. There's always some version of the Prince Charming character. Then when they grow up and become women, they watch lots of romantic comedies."

"But how does that translate into women not dating after a spouse passes away?"

"Well, women tend to idealize a lost partner more than men do. And this causes them to get stuck."

"So in your book you have suggestions to help both sexes, particularly women, to move forward and into a relationship again."

"Yes," Brittany replied.

Loud honking interrupted the interview, and I realized I was stopped at a light that had already turned green. I looked in the rear view mirror at the person behind me honking and waving his hands. I couldn't read lips, but it seemed like he was screaming obscenities. I hit the gas, the action of pressing the pedal knocking me back to the present moment.

The interviewer went on. "So, Brittany, you yourself are not a widow. What got you interested in writing about this topic?"

"I noticed a trend in my own family's life and the lives of my friends. My grandmother's husband died and she outlived him by 25 years, never going on a single date. My best friend's aunt…"

I pressed the off button. I was sure I had a good CD somewhere in the glove box. While digging, I heard my phone beep. I took it out of my purse and was going to check voicemail when I realized I was barely paying attention to the road. I set it aside and decided it could wait until later.

I drove the rest of the way in numbing silence.

Once I got home and changed into a t-shirt and

sweatpants, I remembered the voicemail and checked it.

"Hi, Amy. It's Sabrina, returning your call. Thanks for the invite to the health club. Ordinarily, I'd say yes, but I have a facial appointment this Sunday at Northbrook Court. If you're interested, we could meet afterward and spend the day at the Chicago Botanic Garden. I'm a member, so we'll get in free, as long as we take my car with the member sticker. Give me a call if you'd like to go."

I let out a sigh. Once again, I was not in control of the meeting place, which meant I was not in control of the situation. I desperately wanted control, the upper hand—something to give me the confidence to uncover the information I needed.

I dialed her number and was surprised when she answered.

"Hello, Amy. How are you?"

"I'm... I didn't expect to catch you. I'm doing well. I just got your message, and, yeah, that sounds good. I can meet you and we can drive in one car."

"Wonderful," she replied. "Can you meet me outside Red Door Spa at noon?"

"Sure," I answered, having no idea where it was. Then I added, "I'll bring lunch for us this time."

"Sounds great," she said.

"I'll see you then."

"Okay," she replied. "Have a good evening."

*****

While clearing the table after dinner, I decided to mention the upcoming outing.

"I'm going to the Botanic Garden this Sunday with my

new friend from the health club."

Tension instantly filled the room. Was it real or only in my imagination? I turned to find my mom studying me.

"Justin's old customer?" she asked, the look on her face suspicious.

"Yeah," I replied. I looked away and set a dish in the sink.

"That sounds like fun, Mom," Tyler said. He went on to tell me about a fight someone had gotten into at school. Over another little girl, no less.

I listened to his story and as I did, Mom gave me her "I feel left out" face, which I pretended not to see. I couldn't tell her anything about Sabrina, not until the time was right.

"Should we walk to Redbox and rent a new release?" Tyler suggested, now done with his tale.

I wouldn't mind skipping our workout. I wasn't in the mood. But I noted the walking part, and realized we'd still be exercising. Somehow I'd gotten scammed. "Okay," I agreed.

"You two go," Mom said. "I'm too full."

As I finished drying the dishes, I noticed Mom was pouting. Why did she have to act like this? Did she expect me to tell her every little detail of my life? I felt bad hiding this from her, but that was just how it had to be for now.

"Is there a particular movie you want to see?" I asked.

"No. I'm going to read my novel tonight. Pick out whatever you like."

"Are you sure?" There was no budging her out of this mode. I knew that but asked anyway.

"I'm sure," she replied. "Oh, and I'm not busy Sunday if you want me to watch Tyler while you visit your friend."

Now I felt even more awful. I hadn't even asked her if she was free.

I was a terrible daughter.

I finished the last dish and watched my mom disappear to her room. Eventually, I'd be honest with her. But not yet.

Tyler had to go to the bathroom before we went to rent the movie, so I plopped onto the couch to give my food a chance to digest. With my eyes closed, I began thinking about the author on the radio. Were men really healthier than women when it came to love? If I'd been the one who died, would Justin have been dating someone else by now? Or be re-married? The thought was so alien I could barely wrap my mind around it.

And what about Sabrina? Why didn't she get hitched again? She was still young and beautiful. Wealthy, too. She could have anyone she wanted. What the hell was her problem? I continued analyzing her, because it was much easier than trying to analyze myself.

"Hey, Mom," Tyler said, interrupting my mental jabbering. "I'm ready to go."

I wasn't, but I pushed myself up and off the sofa, and we both put on light jackets and headed to the store.

"So T., how was this week's lesson with Josephine? You know, the one I slept through."

He laughed. "It was good. I told her about us getting a dog soon, and she was excited for us. You know what? I think when I grow up, I might become a teacher."

I liked this. He was more the normal Tyler today, chatting me up, jumping from topic to topic. I was surprised, though. I hadn't realized he'd thought much about his future.

"Planning that far ahead already?"

"No," he said. "But Josephine asked me what I wanted to be when I grow up, so I thought about it."

"And is that your only interest?"

As we walked he gave it some thought. "No. I'd like to be an artist. That's what I said first. Then I told her I'd like to be a teacher, like her."

I looked down at him and grinned. He had charisma. "You've got plenty of time to do both," I assured him.

Once we got to Redbox, Tyler picked out *Kung Fu Panda 2*. We watched it together when we got home, and Mom stayed in her room, true to form. She was an expert martyr.

*****

Saturday flew by. Tyler and I played Checkers and exercised. I even posed for a portrait. We looked through dog books, narrowing it down to his top three favorites: pug, boxer, and Pomeranian.

I knew we'd get a dog from animal control. I doubted he'd be purebred, but you never know. I figured a little research couldn't hurt. And slowly, my mom became a little more involved in the process again, getting Tyler's opinion on breeds and asking him questions.

Sunday morning, I woke up and made breakfast for everyone. Tyler was going to spend the day with his friend, Sam. They were going to watch Sam's older brother practice some new sport called parkour.

"It's so cool, Mom," Tyler said. "We saw him doing some of it. He runs, he flips, and you're not going to believe it. He can climb walls like a ninja!"

"And you're going to watch or participate?"

"I'm going to watch, but Sam said he could show us some beginner moves."

His eyes pleaded with me not to shoot this down. I didn't want to say no, and frankly, it made sense he'd eventually outgrow exercising with me and his grandma.

"Okay," I said. "Just be careful."

He looked at me like I was nuts, like he was born careful. "I will," he replied.

Mom took Tyler to Sam's, and I mapped out how to get to the mall in Northbrook. It was halfway between my house and Sabrina's. After showering and getting ready, I realized it would be polite to wear one of the new outfits she had given me.

On the way to the mall, I stopped and picked up sandwiches and bottled water. I had decided Corner Bakery would be much better than bologna and yellow mustard on white bread. I didn't want Sabrina to find out I was a plain Jane in the kitchen too.

I found Red Door Spa and waited outside. Some very put together ladies were going in and out. Just after noon, I saw Sabrina.

"Hey, Amy. You look fabulous."

"Thanks," I replied. "I wore this to work last week, too. Lots of compliments. My co-worker looked at the tag and asked me about it. I don't know why, but I told her it was from Target. Sorry about that. I don't know what I was thinking."

Why was I talking about this? I wondered. When I was nervous complete bumbling took me over.

"Actually, that's not a bad thought. Lots of big name designers are partnering with them."

Great. Now I was giving her ideas to add to her vast fortune. I had to stop blabbering and stay focused.

"Where did you park?" she asked.

"In the upper-level Macy's lot."

"I'm there too."

We walked through the store and out to the cars. She pressed a button to turn off her alarm, and we got into her two door silver Mercedes. It wasn't the same car I'd seen her in before, the one Henry drove her around in. I wondered what he was up to today. Then I stopped myself. Focus, Amy.

Sabrina pulled out of the mall and we drove a few short blocks, arriving at our destination. We hadn't even made meaningless small talk along the way. She slowed to greet the entrance attendant, who waved us through after seeing the member sticker on her windshield.

After we walked in, Sabrina eyed the Corner Bakery bag. "There are tables right here if you want to eat first."

I nodded. We found a spot, and I unpacked the sandwiches and handed one to her, along with a bottle of water. We sat in awkward silence, eating our food.

I was doing a lot of thinking, that was my deal. But I didn't know what she was up to. It definitely felt like a mental showdown, though. Maybe she didn't want to say the wrong thing and have me lose it again. I was keeping quiet and chewing, trying to figure out the best way to maneuver our upcoming conversation to my advantage.

"We're lucky," she blurted out. "It's a sunny day. My favorite way to see this place."

The weather was a safe enough topic.

"I've never been here," I admitted. This was a major Chicago attraction, and I'd lived here all my life. I wondered how Justin and I could've missed it.

"I come here often," she said. "Every season it's different. Sometimes it can even change from day to day."

"How's that?" I asked.

"How can I describe it," she said, mulling it over. "Well, for example, the same garden will transform from one look in the sunlight to a completely different place in the rain."

Sabrina gazed around as she spoke, an intense expression coming over her face. She seemed to be remembering other visits here, memories that weren't easily hidden behind a placid exterior.

So she wasn't always one hundred percent poised and in control after all. She had little breaks from time to time, too. Or maybe our visits were wearing her down.

"Seems like the perfect place to spend a day," I said.

I had decided I would remain calm and avoid rambling on about nonsense the way I often do. I wanted to get her to talk more. That was the only way to get somewhere in this odd situation.

We finished eating, and Sabrina got up and led the way, beginning our garden tour. I noticed other people were using maps to find their way around. She didn't appear to need one.

"So you're a member here, huh?" I asked.

A sly smile crossed her face as we walked. "Yeah. Me and the Botanic go way back."

I kept pace next to her, wondering what she meant.

"My mom was on the board of directors here when I was a kid," she explained. "My sister and I would come along when she had a meeting sometimes. We'd run and play hide and seek in the English Walled Garden."

"That sounds like fun," I said. I meant it, too. I was an only child and had often dreamed of what it might be like

119

to have siblings to play with.

"It was more than fun," Sabrina said. "It was magic, you know?"

As I looked to my right I noticed the way the sun glinted off the lake and cast a warm glow on the surrounding plants. A fountain in its center shot water into the air, sending spray out in a 360-degree radius. Ducks quacked happily in the background, and then, in the next moment Sabrina and I walked under a leafy trellis, emerging into another beautiful spot.

This place was magic.

She continued. "When you're small, it's larger than life here. It's like a whole new world. My sister and I would really get into it. We'd talk with fake English accents. We'd pretend we were running from dragons."

Sabrina laughed out loud, reliving a memory, and clapped her hands together.

"Sounds like good times," I said.

"They were some of the best."

I had wanted her to talk more, and she was doing just that. She was even sharing personal things about herself. But somehow, I felt guilty. While I was listening to her and enjoying it, I had this ugly interior motive, and it felt wrong. Could I just let go of my worry? My fears about her relationship with Justin? I wanted to, I really did. It would have been so nice to just enjoy her friendship. But something continued to nag at me, and I couldn't let it go. Just because she was interesting didn't mean she was good. Still, it was difficult to reconcile the two conflicting feelings.

"We're coming up on the Enabling Garden," she said. "It's one of the nicest."

So far, she'd been a great guide. She let us walk and

talk and take it all in without going on and on about every single flower. I was thankful she wasn't spewing their Latin names.

"Isn't it great?" she said. "Notice the layout."

I looked around. It was pretty, but I didn't see anything unique in its design.

"It's laid out so anyone can work and plant in it, even if they're confined to a wheelchair."

I took a second, closer look. Now I could see what she meant. The flowers and plants were at hip level. There were pots hanging from the wall, all within reach.

"It's amazing," I said.

"It's a lot of work, but what I love about it is how it shows anything is possible despite one's limitations."

I listened to the way she spoke. It was how successful people talked. I remember Justin always saying things like that. From attempting a stunt on his skateboard as a teenager, until he was in the hospital fighting cancer, telling me not to worry, he had this beat. He never let doctors quote him outcomes in percentages based on past success. He just knew his surgeries and treatments would work. I had a hard time understanding how he could be so positive.

"So far this is my favorite garden," I told her. "Which one is your favorite?"

Sabrina's pace slowed while she considered my question.

"I don't know," she responded, looking perplexed. "Each one has its own special meaning for me. The whole place reminds me of my mom. I still really miss her." She paused and said, "The English Garden takes me back to simpler times, to being a kid. But I think right now I enjoy the Japanese Garden most. I use it as a place of quiet reflection."

We continued walking, taking in the contrasting yet complimentary colors in the landscape around us. Part of me wished I could get inside that brain of hers and see what she was thinking, remembering, but part of me was just enjoying her company. And who couldn't help but fall in love with this place? I felt like I had been transported to another country. Everywhere I looked there was one display of flowers more beautiful than the last.

Sabrina stopped walking. "Here's another spot that has meaning for me," she said.

I looked around. All I saw was a lake surrounded by a concrete area with tables and chairs. It seemed like no big deal so I glanced back at her for an explanation.

"This is where I got married," she said.

Just one sentence. That was all it took for me to give the area a closer look. As we strolled together in silence, the spot gained new significance. I could almost feel regret hanging in the air, like a rain-filled cloud before a storm.

"We could move on, if you'd like," I said. "I don't need to see this one."

Unlike me, Sabrina didn't break down crying in front of people when upset. She appeared cool and controlled.

"No. It's fine," she said. "I told you I'd show you the place. I wouldn't want you to miss any of it."

She turned to me and smiled. I couldn't tell if she was reining in her emotion… or if she'd simply moved on. If it was me, though, I'd never want to visit that garden again. And if I had to come back, I'd probably do something terrible, like take it out on the plants and then run away before getting arrested.

"I'm sure it was a beautiful wedding," I said.

"It was." There was a long pause, and she added, "I guess we all hope it will last forever."

I walked beside her, unsure of what to say.

Sabrina continued. "I think I even knew at the wedding that it wouldn't last. I didn't admit it to myself out loud, but I knew on an unconscious level."

"How?"

"I wish I could tell you. It was just a gut feeling, you know? That he didn't love me enough."

I felt terrible hearing Sabrina say that. Everyone deserved to be loved completely by their spouse.

"I'm sorry," I said.

"Thank you. That's very kind."

Sabrina was still cool and composed. I don't know what came over me, but right then, I wanted to puncture that exterior.

"Do you think you'll ever re-marry?" I asked.

The question super-charged the air around us. She didn't have an immediate response.

"I think I'd like to," she finally replied.

Much smarter than saying, "Yes. I wanted to steal your spouse from you and marry him."

"How about you?" she asked. "Do you think you'll re-marry?"

I was so busy thinking poisonous thoughts of her I hadn't seen that one coming. I was blindsided. How dare she even have the nerve to ask?

"I haven't given any thought to the matter." My voice sounded even, but I was enraged. I know I didn't really have a right to be since I'd asked her the very same question. But it made me angry. She seemed to sense it, too, and we continued strolling for a long time in silence.

"Here's the English Walled Garden," she announced, with a renewed sense of enthusiasm.

I didn't know why I was so pissed. I guess I was one of those people who could dish it out but not take it. I had no one to blame but myself.

Exhaling and tucking the emotion away, I saw the entrance to the English Garden. A high wall of reddish-colored bricks formed a large square, hiding what lay inside. The way in was through a doorway held open by a blue wooden gate, which provided a glimpse of the beauty within.

As we walked in, I was taken by the wildness of the flowers. They seemed to have a mind of their own, growing in all directions yet coming together somehow. To my right, there were two white benches, placed on opposite sides of a trickling fountain, the perfect spot to contemplate or have a photograph taken.

This was by far the best garden I'd ever seen. I could visualize Sabrina as a child, running around here, playing with her little sister.

Some of my inner fury dissipated.

"There are six walled rooms," she said. "I'll show you."

I followed her, in awe at the beauty that surrounded me. I was enclosed in a real secret garden, right out of a Jane Austen novel. There were more than just wild flowers, though. Vines twisted and crawled up lattices. Manicured hedges separated areas and created order where there seemed to be none. Unique sculptures popped up in the most unexpected locations, adding to the enchantment.

Sabrina found a black wrought-iron bench and took a

seat. I sat opposite her in a matching chair. I felt like a child at a tea party. I used to love playing with those plastic tea sets as a kid. I filled the cups with Kool-Aid and served crackers on plates to my mom and stuffed animals.

"Amy," Sabrina said. "There's something I'd like to tell you."

I looked over at her, wondering if it could really be this easy.

"I'm not sure how to word this," she said.

This was the moment I'd been waiting for. I was sure.

"What I'm trying to say is," she continued, "that toward the end, when Justin was really sick, well... he made a point of telling me that he hoped someday you would re-marry."

I stared at Sabrina, unable to comprehend what she had said.

I continued staring, like someone who had undergone a lobotomy, unable to speak. Some petals fell off a tree overhead and landed on my lap. I didn't brush them away. A couple strolled past, hand in hand, and still I stared at her, transfixed.

"Amy," Sabrina asked. "Are you all right?"

I heard her call out my name, but she sounded far away. I knew I should speak, that I should say something, but my mouth didn't want to move; it wouldn't listen to my brain. I saw her get up and come toward me. She kneeled in front of me and reached out.

"Are you okay?" she asked, now holding my hand in hers.

The physical contact worked. I could feel myself returning to my body. I was able to blink a few times and clear my throat.

"I'm okay," I said, while slowly pulling my hand free and clasping both of them together in my lap.

How could I respond to such a statement? A concept so foreign to my mind I couldn't comprehend it. I couldn't believe it was true; I wouldn't let myself. There must have been some kind of mistake.

"I'm sorry, but is it possible for you to repeat what you just said?" I asked, still disoriented.

Sabrina got up from her kneeling position and sat in the chair next to me. She no longer appeared cool and collected. Her expression showed genuine concern.

I listened as she repeated the same phrase she had said before. Then I swallowed the lump that had begun to form in my throat.

There was no mistake. I had heard her right the first time. I didn't cry, though. I couldn't. I was too stunned.

"I'm sorry that didn't come out well," Sabrina said. "We were on the subject, and since I had spoken to Justin about it, it just felt right to say. Maybe I shouldn't have."

Sabrina's face was a mix of compassion and terror. I responded, to my surprise, a little more like her. I remained calm.

"I guess I'm just in a state of shock," I said. "Justin and I never discussed that, not once."

I wondered how the two of them had. Why he would tell her something like that? Something that's meant for a friend. I stared at her, and all at once comprehension sunk in. Sabrina and Justin were friends.

I barely had a moment to get used to the idea before she began talking again.

"He said he'd never tell you, that he didn't want to diminish what you two had, but that he hoped, in time, you would find someone else to share your life with."

I listened, wide-eyed and present, taking in every word. As the phrases made sense, my brain began clicking, making new connections. I realized if they had these types of conversations, that Justin must've accepted the possibility of death, had been getting his mind around the idea.

He'd never shown this side to me. All I'd heard was never-ending positivity. "Gonna get chemo today, take a few days off, then I'm back on the Vibbert kitchen remodel." And, "After recovering from this surgery, we should take a weekend family trip. Where does my kitten want to go?"

He'd always make it seem like he was stopping off at the dentist to have a filling done. He never acted like cancer was serious. Half the time, he'd have the doctors and nurses wailing with laughter at one of his off-color jokes. I'd arrive to find them leaning over, wiping tears from their eyes, telling me I'd married a comedian.

I only saw Justin smiling and laughing. He hid his pain from me. He continued to make plans for our future, like we had one. I guess a big part of me believed we did. His optimism was contagious, especially when it was something I so desperately wanted to catch.

"This is a bit overwhelming," I said. "I'm still trying to take it all in. I mean, he never... we never talked like that. He acted like every procedure was routine, that he'd be home in no time."

She listened as I rambled on, nodding her head in understanding.

"Justin wanted to have a life with you," she said. "That's why he still made plans. It makes sense to act in accordance with one's wishes."

I looked at Sabrina, still confused about their

friendship. "I don't understand why he would make plans with me, and then discuss alternate futures for my life with someone else, with you?"

A look of careful consideration crossed her face.

"I think, and, obviously I cannot speak for him, but I think he just wanted someone to talk to. A person he could confide in and didn't have to be strong for. Someone he didn't have to worry about hurting."

Was my Justin foolish enough to think he had found that person in Sabrina? Did he think his client-turned-friend, this odd, otherworldly woman could be a buddy to confide in and not hurt? Could he not see the light shining in her eyes, the glow on her face when she spoke of him?

Justin was strong for me, not showing fear while being eaten from within by a vicious monster that plotted his death. And Sabrina, this porcelain lady sitting next to me, had listened to his plans for our future—his plans for my future, all while pretending to be a casual friend who couldn't be hurt.

I studied her carefully, wondering why she had done it. Why she put herself through all that. Maybe she felt she had no choice, that it was her fate or her destiny. Her expression answered none of those questions.

The only thing I knew for sure is that she loved him. She hadn't told me, of course, but this I was certain of. I couldn't imagine how it must've felt to be in her position, what kind of exquisite pain that might be.

The cool woman at my side suddenly appeared very fragile.

"Sabrina," I said, carefully phrasing my words. "I appreciate you telling me all of this. We were on the subject and it *was* right of you to say. I'm just trying to digest it all, you know?"

She nodded, and I stood up and brushed the flower petals off my pants. She got up too, and we began strolling again, continuing the tour.

As we headed toward the Japanese Garden, I found myself wondering why she would want to spend any time with me.

Our first visit was not her choice. I had shown up unannounced to confront her. She had answered my questions and that should have been enough. Why would she say, "See you next time?" Why would she want there to be a next time?

I knew my own motives but couldn't understand hers.

When we arrived in the Japanese Garden, I could see why it was Sabrina's favorite. Acres of brilliant green sprawled between waterways connected by bridges, one in the shape of a zigzag. Waterfalls spilled down from rocks creating a tranquil, constant hum. The air smelled fresh, a byproduct of the pruned pine trees throughout.

The garden had an overall coolness to it. A lot like my tour guide. It felt controlled and formal, yet peaceful. It was not a place for kids to run wild and play; the children I did see were walking politely, transformed by their environment. I stood a little straighter, too.

Sabrina said she often came here to think, and I could see why; it was the ultimate spot for quiet reflection. She hadn't uttered a single word since we arrived. Maybe it was on purpose, to give me the full Zen-like experience.

"Look there," she said, pointing across the lake. "It's the Island of Everlasting Happiness."

I looked across the water to see a small, peanut-shaped green island.

"How do we get there?" I asked. "There's no bridge."

Sabrina pointed to a plaque that read: The Island of Everlasting Happiness cannot be reached by mortals. It is meant to be contemplated from a distance.

I broke into a fit of laughter—probably not the usual reaction—and Sabrina stared at me, surprised.

"I'm sorry," I said, gasping for air. "I just found it funny to see it in writing, a declaration of how messed up a species we are."

"You think so?"

"Yes. I do," I admitted. "I mean, we're all given this life to enjoy, but we supposedly can't find everlasting happiness until after we're gone?"

"Maybe we find it in our next life," she suggested.

"I'm not buying that," I replied. "I'm Irish Catholic."

"Me, neither," she agreed. "I'm Jewish."

Now Sabrina burst into laughter, and I began giggling again, too. It felt nice to lighten the serious atmosphere, even if it wasn't appropriate. An elderly woman who appeared to be meditating nearby got up and walked past, visually scolding us.

"We'd better lower our voices," Sabrina said, while regaining composure.

I shut myself down like I was in a library trying to show some respect. I don't know what had gotten into me. Most people would've read the plaque and sighed, appreciating its deeper meaning. For me, it was like one of Justin's off the wall jokes. They'd come out of nowhere and knock you with their hilarity. That was some of the happiness I missed most.

"That lady was upset," I said. "I think she was meditating."

"She'll get over it."

I wasn't used to this side of Sabrina. Her down-to-earth response made me comfortable somehow.

"Is that what you do when you come here?" I asked.

"No. Not really. I sit and think, but I don't meditate."

I followed her to an area near the waterfall where we took a seat on a smoothed rock.

"I sit here a lot and watch the ducks," she said. "I read somewhere that they mate for life."

"Really?" I replied. "I didn't know that. Maybe if we were more like ducks we'd be able to get on that island."

"Yeah. It said no mortals, it didn't say anything about birds."

Sabrina smiled at me, then returned to gazing at the lake. The sun was high in the sky and shining bright. Sabrina pulled a straw hat from her bag and put it on her head. I closed my eyes and let the repetitive splash of the waterfall relax me. I could have fallen asleep.

"Do you think we're meant to find it?" she asked.

I opened my eyes and looked confused, and she added, "Everlasting happiness?"

I sat up straight and gave it some real thought. "No," I decided. "I don't think so. I mean, we have chances at happiness, but it comes and goes. It never stays."

Sabrina continued gazing at the lake, at the little curved island sitting in the center.

"I wonder why we have to wait until we're gone to experience it?" Sabrina asked out loud, but not directed at me.

I took a shot at answering. "I haven't a clue, but I think I may have just gotten a migraine trying to find out."

Sabrina laughed. Maybe Justin's wacky sense of humor had rubbed off on me. Maybe that's why she wanted to be my friend, because, in some small way, I was a link to him.

"You've probably got a headache because the sun is beating on your head," she said while getting up. "Let's go to the Rose Garden. It will be our final stop."

I stood up and stretched my legs. I was beat. I looked forward to finishing our tour soon.

We both walked as slow as possible on the way there, conserving our last bit of energy. But once I saw the circular promenade with lush roses in the center and even more lining the outer path, I came alive again. Everywhere I looked, there were rose bushes, all bursting with color. The scent was intoxicating.

Sabrina and I began walking the rounded path. I was so engrossed with reading the signs and smelling the flowers, I forgot all about my headache as she excused herself to get a drink of water at a nearby fountain.

I came upon a bush of soft pink roses and paused. They looked just like the ones from my wedding bouquet. I remember that day like it just happened. It was summer, and it could've been too hot or humid, but it wasn't. It was perfect. Even my blonde hair, which is usually limp and lifeless, cooperated, like it knew better.

My dress fit perfectly, and I didn't stumble as I walked down the aisle. I could see Justin's blue eyes getting closer with each step. I remember the flowers being unusually heavy. I hadn't expected roses to weigh that much. As I inched closer to my future husband, I felt my arm muscles flex, trying not to lose hold of the bouquet.

"I see you've found your flower," a voice said.

Cut short from my reverie, I looked up and saw Sabrina.

The pink rose held special meaning for Justin and me,

always had. Even after he was gone, it was what I brought to his gravesite to tell him I loved him.

"Yeah," I replied. "These are just like the ones from my wedding bouquet."

"I didn't know that," she said. "I was thinking of the flower you leave for Justin at the cemetery."

I suddenly felt like my privacy had been violated.

I wondered how she knew that, and why she was bringing this subject up now. Then it occurred to me that this was just the topic I'd wanted to discuss with her all this time, ever since I saw her standing in front of my husband's grave.

I took a cautious look at Sabrina, unsure of what to say next. I never felt on even ground with this woman. I'd come with an agenda: to uncover her lies. Instead she'd shared information about my personal life that unhinged me. Then, after spending the day together, I'd decided she was all right. I had let my guard down.

"I saw you leave one of those roses at Justin's grave, in case you're confused."

"I'm still confused," I admitted.

Sabrina stepped back. She took a deep breath and continued. "The Christmas after Justin died, I went to the cemetery to wish a friend Happy Holidays."

I listened, warily.

"And I saw you standing there, with a pink rose in your hand."

Sabrina cleared her throat and continued. "I realized that it would be wrong for me to intrude on your private moment, that it wouldn't look right, so I left."

That explained how she knew who I was when I came to her house. Justin never carried a picture in his wallet. He wasn't the type.

Now was my chance to launch into the questions I'd been holding inside. I wanted answers. I'd accept nothing less.

"So you're saying you left and returned later so we can each have our own *private moment*?"

There was no mistaking the sarcasm in my voice.

"Yes and no," she responded. "Let me explain."

I felt the spark ignite on my Irish temper. Once it started, it was difficult to cool down. I wasn't sure I had it in me to maintain self-control a second time. Whatever came out of her mouth next would be the deciding factor.

"I didn't want to intrude on your time with your husband," she said. "That would be rude and disrespectful."

Yeah—you think?

"All the same," she continued, "I wanted to be alone with my thoughts, and I didn't want to run into you for fear it would look all wrong, me being there."

I crossed my arms in front of my chest, in an attempt to contain the breathing bull trying to bust out from within.

"And what's with the daffodils?" I asked. "Why are you leaving my husband flowers?"

Sabrina looked alarmed. "The daffodils are because of my involvement with the American Cancer Society. But the flowers aren't important. It's what I'm trying to accomplish with them that has meaning."

"What are you trying to accomplish by leaving Justin flowers? I don't understand what you're talking about."

Sabrina let out a heavy sigh. No doubt whatever madness she had tucked away in her skull was going to be difficult to put into words. My patience was growing thin.

"This is hard to explain," she said. "But I visited Justin

because he was my friend. The flowers were a symbol for a wish. I did the same ritual each time. I came to say hello, thanked him for being such a good friend. Then I requested his assistance."

While staring at her, I realized just how eccentric she truly was, like the day she was hanging out at home in her burgundy formal gown.

Finding another ounce of patience, I managed to ask, "What kind of assistance?"

Sabrina locked eyes with me. The intensity I saw in them frightened me. She looked positively wired. "You may find this odd," she said, "but I request Justin's spiritual assistance in important matters in my life."

Somehow, that made sense coming from her.

"I'm still listening."

"All the time he was working on the house and we were talking, all I could see was what a wonderful husband he was, how much he truly loved you."

I uncrossed my arms and let them hang at my side.

"Justin possessed all the qualities I was looking for in a partner but had never found for myself. And now that he's gone, I request his help. I repeatedly ask him to send me someone like that to share my life with, a future husband."

Her description of how good Justin was to me, and how she admired him, made me feel proud. Proud that he was mine, and sad that he was gone. I believe my husband would, if he could, send her the perfect partner if it was in his power to do so. Since she was still single and it hadn't happened after a few years, I guessed he wasn't able to help. Yet she continued to ask, her confidence in him unshaken.

I remembered back to the day I saw her at the

cemetery, crying. And how I felt compelled to follow and confront her. Knowing what I know now, I realize there was no way she could've told me something like this. I wouldn't have believed her. Maybe she said "see you next time" because she wanted to explain; she knew she would have to someday.

All at once, my fears and apprehension dissipated. The angry bull in my chest lay down and went to sleep. I looked over at Sabrina and felt an overwhelming sadness fill my heart. There she stood, like an old-time movie star. Successful, intelligent, kind… but still alone. She'd lost her parents in an accident and was married to a philandering imbecile whom she divorced. Then she met Justin, the perfect man. It would be so easy to fall in love with him.

I wondered how it would feel to live in her shoes. The unrequited love, the casual befriending, and then watching the man deteriorate right in front of you, unable to stop it.

I looked into Sabrina's eyes. I wanted to cry, but didn't. Instead, I watched her look at me, seeming anxious for my reaction.

"I'm sorry Justin couldn't be of more help," I said with sincerity. "He would do anything for a good friend."

"I know," she said.

The sun hung low in the sky and the garden began to clear out. Most of the people were probably heading to dinner. I was getting pretty hungry myself. But I still had one more question.

"When I saw you that day at the cemetery, you were crying. Why?"

Sabrina turned her head to the side, trying to recall the memory.

"I was crying because I was desperate. I felt so alone and was begging Justin to do something to help me. Then a half hour later you showed up at my door."

"Not exactly what you were looking for, huh?" I joked.

Sabrina smiled and threw her hands in the air. "Definitely not what I was expecting," she said. "But there's one thing I do know."

"What's that?" I asked.

"I know Justin is the one that sent you."

Chapter 12

Driving back home, I thought about Sabrina's comment. Instinctively, I knew it was true. Justin was involved somehow. I could feel it.

When I walked in the door, Tyler was waiting there, super-psyched to see me.

"Hey, T.," I said, and gave him a kiss. "You look like a water balloon that's ready to burst. What gives?"

"Mom. Check this out."

Tyler began running toward the patio and into the yard, so I followed him. Then he stopped, and seemed to be in some form of deep concentration. He took a few breaths and stretched from side to side. And, without warning, he ran at full speed up to the side of the house, appeared to climb it somehow, then flipped over in midair and landed back on his feet.

A reservoir of adrenalin I didn't know I had rushed through me and I gasped. "Oh, my God! Are you all right?"

Cracking up, Tyler replied, "Of course."

"What just happened? What was that?"

Tyler was only too happy to provide the answer. "It's that sport, parkour, that Sam's older brother does. I told you he was going to show us some moves."

I thought he said it was a sport, like basketball. This looked more like super hero stuff, like Spider-Man.

"Wow, honey. That was amazing! Did you learn all that in one day?"

"Kinda," he said. "We did some easier stuff that led to that, but I've been really practicing that one."

"Very impressive." It looked like he'd been practicing for more than a day. That stunt didn't look easy at all, but I didn't call him out on it. I was too proud of him.

Tyler straightened his shoulders and stood a little taller. He wore a smirk on his face that reminded me of Justin's, the same expression he used to make as a teenager when he pulled off a really cool skateboard stunt.

"Sam lent me a DVD so I could keep practicing," he said.

"Sounds good," I replied, nodding. "Keep it up."

I was thankful Tyler found another hobby he enjoyed, and that he was becoming more involved with his friends. He'd been withdrawn for too long. Now, between school, his art lessons, this new sport and the workouts with us, Tyler's life was becoming full again. The void left by Justin didn't seem as large.

Mom called to us from inside the house. "You guys interested in leftovers?"

"Sure," we said in unison, and walked back in.

We nuked some meatloaf and mashed potatoes and put together a quick salad, and we sat down to eat.

"Have you seen this one, with the back flips?" Mom asked me.

"I sure did."

Tyler sat at the dinner table eating, but he appeared larger somehow, like a peacock with its feathers spread out.

"T. claims it's a sport from France."

"Cool," I replied.

We munched for a while, not talking.

Mom turned her attention to me. "So how was the Botanic Garden?"

"Very nice," I said. "We had a good time."

The less said the better, I thought. I still didn't feel ready to share.

"What's your friend's name again?" she asked.

All I'd said was that she was one of Justin's old customers. But I decided there was no harm in answering.

"Her name is Sabrina."

Tyler seemed to take an interest, too. After shoving a large serving of mashed potatoes in his mouth, he asked, "Isn't that the lady with the pool in her house?"

"Yes," I replied.

"Cool," he said back.

We continued eating, and after a few minutes of not talking about it, I assumed we were done.

"This Sabrina," Mom continued. "What does she do for a living?"

"She owns a clothing design company," I said.

Tyler and Mom stared at me. Both of them had stopped eating and were holding their forks, looking at me as if I spoke in tongues.

"She's a designer?" Mom asked.

"I don't think so. She said her parents were, but they died, and now she runs the business. She said she goes to Paris to oversee things, to approve the new collections. I think it's more like she is the CEO."

They both continued to stare at me like I was talking about a Martian from outer space. That had been my initial reaction, too. It was funny, I thought, how over time she became less and less alien and more of an ordinary human being. Okay, maybe not ordinary, that was pushing it.

"So did you like the gardens?" Tyler asked, changing the subject.

"They were gorgeous. We walked all day long."

Mom winked at me. "Sounds like we've all had quite a workout today." (She never missed an opportunity to wiggle out of the evening exercise routine.)

Tyler caught on quickly. "I guess we'll start back tomorrow night then," he said, sounding a little sad.

After dinner and dishes, Tyler still found strength to go into the backyard and practice his jumps. "I wish I had half of his energy," I said aloud.

Mom replied, "I wish I had one-fourth."

That night, after climbing into bed, I thought about the day's events. So much had happened; it felt like a week had passed. I was so happy I'd found out I was wrong about Sabrina. That she wasn't lying to me, that she posed no threat. The nagging voice in my head, although usually helpful, had been mistaken.

I curled into a fetal position and hugged my pillows. Once again, I was beat. I would've fallen asleep in an instant, but I ended up thinking about Justin. I wondered, *What are you up to?*

Sabrina believed Justin had sent me to her. I believed it too. But before I could figure out the reason why, I fell asleep.

*****

The next morning, I arrived at work ten minutes late. Dave was irritated because Fatima had called in sick. I remembered her acting gig and realized that's where she was. She had told me to keep tight-lipped about it, so I busied myself with paperwork.

When Dave left for lunch, Barb spoke up, "Hey, Amy."

"Yeah."

"Just so you know, Fatima isn't sick. She's downtown, working as an extra in a movie."

I laughed. I guess I wasn't the only one who knew the secret. Just as long as Dave didn't find out, everything would be okay.

Fatima punched in the following morning looking positively radiant. She tried to control her bubbling enthusiasm but wasn't successful.

Dave walked past. "You're looking well," he said, then dropped a heavy stack of files onto her desk. Of course, he wasn't fooled, and he was going to get back at her by doubling her workload.

When he stepped out a few hours later, Fatima turned to Barb and me. "Oh, my God! You have no idea," she said.

We both looked at her with anticipation.

"I was there, in the crowd scene with Johnny Depp!"

"Isn't he a little old for you?" Barb asked.

Fatima shot her a "how dare you speak such nonsense" look and continued. "So I was in the crowd, and then he pushed his way through and delivered his lines to the other actor. It was so awesome. We repeated it a bunch of times. They even filmed it from different angles."

Just as she was spilling the details, Dave opened the office door, and I cut her off mid-sentence. "I think I can find those files you're looking for. Let me take a look in this cabinet."

Fatima looked confused, then heard the door shut behind her.

"Okay," she said, playing along. "I appreciate it. I can't find them anywhere."

I got up and looked around to make it seem legit, and I sat back down, empty-handed. Fatima turned and slapped a yellow sticky note on my desk. "Thanks," it said. "I made $75.00 for the day, too."

I grinned at her, then I crumpled the note and threw it in the garbage can. We were acting like children. Like sisters, even. It was fun.

*****

When I got home from work, Mom told me, "You have mail from your friend. It's on the counter." As I walked over to look at it, she added, "Oh, and I'm going out after dinner, to my new book club."

Half-listening to her, I mumbled, "Sounds good."

I flipped through the stack of mail looking for the letter. But it wasn't a letter; it was a card. An invitation. I ripped it open and read it over.

I had been invited to a cocktail party at the Bergman residence—formal attire required. Please RSVP by phone or email if you can attend, it said.

I laughed out loud. *Me.* At a cocktail party. I don't think so. I put the invitation back in the envelope and set it aside.

Tyler came barreling in from the back yard. "Hi, Mom," he said, passing me by and disappearing in his room.

Later on, my mom's curiosity got the best of her. "Your friend have anything interesting to say?"

"No," I said. "It's just an invitation to a party."

I turned and headed to the refrigerator to get a glass of water. I thought if I kept busy enough, conversations I didn't want to have would go away.

"What day is it?" she asked. "You need me to watch Tyler?"

"Nah. I don't think I'm going to go, but I appreciate your offer to babysit."

The room grew quiet. This was the sound of my mom's mind trying to figure out what to say next without seeming nosy.

"But I thought you liked this lady?" she finally said.

"I do. But I don't think I'd feel comfortable around her other friends. Plus, it's a cocktail party, the kind where you have to dress up."

"Oh," she said, looking alarmed. This was as foreign a concept to her as it was to me. "Well, if you change your mind, and need me to watch Tyler, let me know."

"What about me?" Tyler asked as he came into the kitchen.

"Nothing, honey," I replied. "Grandma was just saying she could babysit if I went to the party I got invited to."

My son gave me a look. I didn't need him to utter a word to know what he was thinking. He wanted happiness for me, and he liked that I had a new friend to hang out with, but a party? This may be going too far.

Tyler was unusually quiet the rest of the evening. While my mom was gone at her book club, he wandered off to his room to finish his homework. Then, when he didn't come get me at the usual time for our workout, like he always does, I went to find him.

Opening his bedroom door, I said, "Hey, T. I'm all set to exercise."

He was sitting on his bed, reading a book. He held it in front of his face so I couldn't see him.

"Do you want to exercise inside or outside?" he asked.

"Whatever you prefer."

Without responding, he set the book down and began putting on his gym shoes. He went toward the foyer, so I followed.

I guessed we were going outside.

"Everything okay?" I asked.

"Yep," was all he said.

The weather was pretty warm, and after doing a few stretches and walking a block or two, sweat beads formed on my forehead.

"Hey. How's Sally's mom doing?" I asked.

Tyler, disguised behind his kid sunglasses replied, "She's doing good. Much better."

I wasn't in the mood to dig stuff out of him this time, so I switched the subject to something I knew he'd like.

"Grandma tells me that parkour is a French sport."

"Yep."

Even his new, favorite topic didn't provoke conversation.

We continued walking.

"It's hot," Tyler finally commented.

"I know. Must be 100% humidity. We should've gone to the pool. I think it's open now."

"Your friend, Sabrina, is her pool indoor or outdoor?"

"Indoor."

I was glad he wanted to talk about her. I figured he must be curious and I wanted to answer whatever questions he had, to make him feel comfortable. The last thing I wanted was for Tyler to feel threatened. For the longest time, it was just the three of us, our little family. I hadn't spent much time with friends.

Tyler wiped his forehead and took off his sunglasses. Squinting, he asked, "Was Dad the one who set up her pool? When he worked there?"

"No," I said. "I think the pool came with the house. He may have put in some new tiles, though."

Tyler smiled. "Yeah. I'll bet they look good." Then he asked, "Could you tell Dad had been there?"

My heart sank. No. I couldn't tell Justin had been there, apart from the evidence in all the invoices I'd found. But when I looked into my son's eyes, his whole face awaiting a positive response, I said, "You know, I think I could. Everything did look pretty cool. I'll bet Dad picked out a lot of that stuff."

Tyler's face lit up. I had spoken another white lie. But perhaps it was true. Justin wasn't just a good carpenter, he had a good eye for design. Surely Sabrina would've listened to his suggestions.

We turned around and began walking back home. It was way too hot now.

"Are you going to your friend's birthday party?" he asked.

I looked down at him, realizing why he'd assume that. When you're a kid, those are the only parties you're invited to.

"No. It's not her birthday. It's a grown-up thing. A cocktail party."

"What's that?" he asked, making a face like he'd just bitten into a lemon.

I laughed. My reaction was similar after I'd opened the invite. Going out to do something like that went against the very grain of my being. I prefer to keep to myself.

"Basically, it's a party for people to dress fancy and eat

tiny snacks," I replied.

"Sounds boring."

I nodded, "My thoughts exactly."

"But you have to go, right? Otherwise, your friend will get mad?"

Surely, I couldn't be expected to go. Sabrina would understand if I declined. Heck, I didn't even own formal attire.

"I'm sure she won't mind," I said.

Tyler shot me a look like I was a bad friend. I ignored it, even though a small part of me knew he was right.

After enduring the heat and humidity, then being greeted by ice cold air-conditioning, I decided to take a shower. Afterward, I changed into fresh clothes, and I sat down in the kitchen, exhausted. I wished some of these workouts would start to show on my actual figure. But so far, nothing. I looked the same.

I reached out and grabbed the mail, and pulled the party invitation out of its envelope. Sabrina had included an email address to respond. Good. I wouldn't have to call to say I wasn't going to come.

I took the invite to the family room and fired up the computer. After logging into my email, I got a case of writer's block. I couldn't figure out what to say that wouldn't sound rude.

After mulling it over, I decided honesty was the best policy.

"Sabrina," I wrote, "Thanks for inviting me to your cocktail party. I don't think I'll be able to make it. I'm not a formal attire type of girl. Thanks for understanding, Amy."

I proofread it and hit send. Then I deleted all my junk messages and logged off.

Tyler walked in wearing pajamas and holding his parkour DVD. "You wanna watch this?" he asked.

I nodded yes, and we got comfortable on the sofa. Then I proceeded to watch a group of the healthiest people I'd ever seen do things I didn't know humans were capable of. I thought stunts like that were special effects in kung fu movies. I didn't know people could really do such things.

I glanced over at Tyler. He was completely engrossed. His eyes followed their every movement.

It put a smile on my face.

*****

Wednesday night, Mom offered to take Tyler to his art lesson. While alone, I decided to check my email. I hoped Sabrina wouldn't be angry at me for blowing off her party.

She had responded.

"Amy," the email said, "You simply must come to my party. I have it every year and it's mostly business associates. I could really use a friend there this time. Oh, and don't worry about the clothes. I'll send some dresses over in your size. You can borrow one for the night."

I sighed. I was out of excuses, short of a real emergency coming up. I had a wardrobe for the night. I had free time. And Sabrina had mentioned she could really use a friend there. There was no way I could get out of this now, so I succumbed.

I hit reply and typed: "Sabrina, I guess I'll see you then. And thanks for the wardrobe help." Then I logged off.

I was so dreading this thing, it's hard to put into

words. It ranked about as high on my list of fun things to do as getting a root canal.

I heard Mom and Tyler come in. "Hey, Mom. Can I take you up on your offer to watch Tyler for that party?"

Her face lit up. I didn't know what the big deal was, why she seemed so happy. "Sure. I can do it. What got you to change your mind?"

"You really wanna know?"

She nodded.

"Good old-fashioned guilt," I replied.

My mom grinned and said, "Whatever works."

Chapter 13

During the week, Tyler's friend Sam came over to visit. He tried to convince my mom and me he could teach us some parkour moves. We both declined. Mom wasn't particularly interested in breaking a hip. It was entertaining enough watching them practice.

One night, after coming home from work, I noticed a box sitting next to the mail. I checked the label and saw it was from Sabrina. My costumes, I mean dresses, had arrived. I would open it later.

Tyler's curiosity got the best of him during dinner, "What's in that box?"

"Just some dresses my friend sent over. She said I could borrow one for her party."

"Good," Tyler said with conviction. "I'm glad you're going to go."

"Why are you so glad?"

"Because," he said. "She's your friend. She invited you. It wouldn't be nice not to go."

I glanced over at Mom to see if she had anything to add, as she usually did. Tonight, she kept quiet.

After we cleaned up, she said, "If you want a second opinion on those outfits, I could give you some input."

"Sure."

I put away the last plate, and went to the counter and opened the box. There was a hand-written note inside. It said: "Amy, Here's a few options. Any one of them would be fabulous on you. I'm curious to see your choice. Sabrina."

Each dress was on its own hanger and covered in a clear plastic bag. I pulled out all three. One was an emerald green satin get up, with a v-neck and feminine, capped sleeves. The second was a black sleeveless silk cowl neck with an open back. The last one was different. It was a platinum gray one-shoulder silk dress. It looked sleek and modern.

"Wow," I gasped. "All of them are beautiful."

I checked the tags and didn't recognize the names. They weren't Bergman Collection.

"They look brand new," Mom commented.

I had noticed that, too. I fished around, trying to locate price tags, but couldn't find any. I sure hoped she hadn't bought them just for me. She said I could borrow one, so I assumed she was sending clothes that had already been worn.

I was mortified.

"Why don't we take them to your room, so you can try them on? I'll zip."

I slung the dresses over my shoulder, and we went to my bedroom. I hung them up on a nearby hook.

"What shoes are you going to wear?" Mom asked.

My choices were limited. I had flats, which I wore every day, one black pair, one brown. I owned a pair of gym shoes, and one pair of black heels. I found them in the back of the closet and dusted them off with a t-shirt from the laundry basket.

"How about these?" I asked. They were my only option.

"Perfect," my mom replied.

I was so full from dinner. It couldn't have been a worse time to try on dresses. But, I figured, I'd probably eat at her party. Better to see how each one fit while full.

I got undressed and slipped on the emerald green gown. I put on the heels, and Mom zipped the back.

"What do you think?" I asked while turning.

Mom's expression told me she wasn't sold. "It's pretty," she replied. "Has a vintage feel to it."

I walked to the full-length mirror that stood next to my bed and took a look. She was right. It had an old Hollywood feel to it, Sabrina's style, not mine. I laughed to myself about how defensive I got over my "look," like I even had one.

I changed out of the green dress and into the black one. I liked the cowl neck a lot, but the open back bothered me. It was too revealing. I felt exposed.

"I think it's beautiful," Mom said.

It was beautiful, for someone else. I wasn't the kind of woman to show off her back. I mean, what if I had an itch and I scratched it and it left red marks on my skin? There was too much to worry about.

I took the black dress off and hung it on the hook. I reached for the gray one. Since it only had one shoulder, I wasn't sure what kind of bra I'd be able to wear with it. After looking at it closer, I noticed it had a built-in bra.

Mom saw it too. "Don't they just think of everything," she said.

I took off my own bra and shimmied into the dress. It was more form-fitting than it appeared on the hanger. It had a side-zip, which I did myself. I turned to look in the mirror, expecting disappointment, because I don't look good in body-conscious clothing. To my surprise, I looked great. Maybe it was the cut, or the fabric.

"Oh, honey, you look amazing!" Mom said. "It really complements your blonde hair."

She was right. This was the best choice. I never would've picked something like it myself, yet, somehow it was perfect.

"Third one's the charm," I said, then began unzipping and changed back into sweats.

Mom agreed, and left the room smiling, happy she was able to help.

*****

Since Tuesday night was a scorcher, I offered to take Tyler to the community pool. My mom declined as she was off to her book club.

Tyler was thrilled to get out of the house. He packed his things, and we arrived at the pool just as it was clearing out. I saw two available lounge chairs and threw our towels over them. Afterward, we ran and jumped into the water. Tyler was the first one to hit, creating a massive splash.

We did some laps back and forth, and got out to rest in the sun. We lay side by side, on our backs, letting the now cooler air dry us. I was just about to nod off when I heard someone call Tyler's name.

"Hey, Tyler, Mrs. White. It's Josephine."

Tyler and I both sat up, squinting into direct sunlight to see her. She wasn't alone.

"Hey, guys. This is my boyfriend, Mark."

He waved to us and smiled.

Mark's teeth were perfectly straight and white. A nice contrast to his bronzed skin. His hair was jet black and wavy, somewhat messy. His eyes were electric blue. He reminded me of one of those male models on the Abercrombie shopping bags.

"Hi," we both said back.

"This is one of my best students," she said, pointing to Tyler. "And this is Amy, his mom."

Mark continued to smile and nod his head. I couldn't help staring at him. He looked like a Roman statue.

"Well, see you tomorrow night," Josephine said, and they walked off, hand in hand.

I glanced at Tyler. He wore a sourpuss expression and let out a loud sigh before turning to lie on his stomach.

Within a few minutes, Tyler got up and threw his towel aside, then jumped into the pool. He began swimming laps at a furious pace. I thought of joining him, but something told me not to. Instead, I turned over and caught some rays on my back.

"I think I'd like to go now," I heard Tyler say. "I'm pretty tired."

"Okay."

I got up, gathered our things, and we drove home. Once we got back, Tyler ran straight to his room and slammed the door. I decided it was best to give him space, so I didn't follow.

Within an hour, Mom came home. She plopped on the sofa and joined me, and out of nowhere, Tyler whizzed past, wearing his workout clothing and earphones. He got situated on the other side of the room and began doing push-ups.

"What's his deal?" she asked.

Even though Tyler couldn't hear us under his headphones, I whispered, explaining how we'd bumped into Josephine at the pool, with her incredibly hot boyfriend.

A sorrowful expression came over my mom's face. "His first heart break."

I frowned and nodded in agreement. It was bound to happen. I continued to sit on the couch and read after my mom left. The room was quiet, other than the huffing and puffing coming from my son's direction.

Half an hour passed, and after checking my watch, I realized it was past Tyler's bedtime. I set my book aside and got up to interrupt him. He was in the middle of an abdominal crunch but stopped when he saw me coming.

I didn't want to treat him like a child, even though he was one, and tell him it was time for bed. He already knew that. Out of compassion, I did something else.

"Why don't you turn off the lights when you're done," I said. "I'm going to hit the sack."

I left the room, knowing he'd both turn off the lights and remember to brush his teeth. I wanted him to know I thought he was more "grown up."

The next morning, I woke to an unpleasant surprise. Tyler had fallen asleep in the family room on the sofa and he'd left all the lights on. The television was still on too, and he'd managed to knock a few knick knacks off the coffee table.

"What's going on here?" I asked, waking him.

Tyler jumped. "Huh, what?"

Once he realized where he was he knew he'd blown it. "Uh, I stayed up and practiced some parkour moves, and I couldn't sleep so I watched TV."

I gave him a stern look. "You could've broken Grandma's collection."

Tyler got up and started checking the figurines, then returned them to their places and turned off the TV. "Sorry," he said.

I was aggravated, but I let it go. He was allowed to act up once and a while, but I wouldn't be foolish enough to let him stay up without me anymore. He wasn't grown up enough, no matter how old he seemed.

That evening, I decided to take Tyler to his art lesson. He was in the bathroom for an awfully long time, and if he didn't hurry up we were going to be late.

"You almost done, T.?" I called through the bathroom door.

Within a moment, he opened it and stepped out. His hair looked messy, like he'd put some gel in it. "All set," he said.

I giggled to myself. It was impossible to stay mad at him. My son might've taken a jab to the heart, but he was no quitter.

When we got to Josephine's, she offered us lemonade.

"No, thanks," I said. "I've got to run some errands. Tyler might like some, though, if it doesn't conflict with his healthy diet/workout routine."

Josephine looked at Tyler. "You're in great shape. Indulge a little," she said, while handing him a glass.

Tyler took the lemonade from her and smiled. I walked out the door, my heart filled with happiness. That was just the kind of comment he needed to hear.

*****

Throughout the remainder of the week, I thought about the upcoming party. I wondered why Sabrina was so intent on having me come. And I was embarrassed she'd sent those dresses over. I wasn't sure if I could ever be comfortable having such a wealthy friend.

Saturday morning, I wasn't really motivated to go

anywhere, especially to a party. I lounged around all day doing nothing, and as the time to leave drew nearer, the more disinterested I became. When I couldn't waste a single minute more, I forced myself to get up and take a shower.

I dried my hair and curled it, inwardly cursing because it took so long to style. I hadn't bothered with a curling iron since Justin was gone. I didn't see a reason. Now I was forced to look nice. Okay, not forced. But it was expected.

As I put on my make-up, I wondered why I was such a complainer, why I didn't enjoy being out, surrounded by groups of people. I didn't know. I guess I liked to keep my circle small.

I finished my hair and make-up, put on the control-top hose I'd bought, and slipped on my one-shoulder gray dress and stepped into the heels. I was officially in costume.

I came out of the bathroom and found Mom and Tyler standing there. They'd been waiting, like I was Cinderella or something.

"You look pretty, Mom."

I did a twirl to indulge them.

"You look beautiful," Mom agreed.

The looks on both their faces. They both seemed so happy, eager. It was sad, I thought, how they were making a silly cocktail party into a big deal.

"Now you go and have yourself a good time," Mom said. "Tyler is going to use me as a model for his next homework assignment."

"I have to draw a human hand," he explained.

I smiled. "Now *that* actually sounds fun."

Tyler rolled his eyes, then waved goodbye. I grabbed

my purse and dug out my car keys. I walked outside and paused to study my little Dodge Neon. It was dirty and its red paint was faded. It looked like a stale tomato. Oh, well. Too late to worry about it now.

I climbed in, continuing to think along the Cinderella line. My car resembled a pumpkin. I started the engine and willed my coach to take me to Sabrina's party. After hitting the gas, I was thrown back in my seat. My pumpkin had torque. That's why Justin had picked it.

I thought of him all the way there. How if he were alive, we'd have spent the night together as a family, doing something fun. We would've played Battleship or worked on a puzzle. He might've even been bold enough to try some parkour moves with Tyler and Sam. All that could've been seemed endless.

As my mind wandered, time went by quickly. Before I knew it, I was at Sabrina's, pulling into the long drive that led to her home. I parked behind an Audi. After I got out and looked around, I noticed there were several Audi's parked together, a little cluster of German engineering. I smirked as I walked away from my own car.

I smoothed my dress and rang the buzzer.

Henry answered. "Welcome," he said. "Please come in."

Henry was dressed up as well, smiling and wearing his game face. His expression seemed genuine. Either he was that good, or he was one of those rare individuals who actually enjoyed their job. I smiled back at him and stepped inside.

Once in the foyer, I noticed a larger than expected crowd of guests. A wave of discomfort came over me and a knot tightened in my stomach. It was at times like these I wished I had Harry Potter's invisibility cloak. All I wanted was to disappear.

Sabrina poked her head out of the crowd and made eye contact with me. She must've noticed my reluctance.

As she walked toward me, I was struck by her beauty. She had never looked better. Her hair was finger-waved and smooth. She wore a dark purple vintage gown that was fitted yet feminine. She was pure glamour.

"Amy. You look absolutely gorgeous!" she said.

"Thanks."

"I knew you'd choose that one. It complements your blonde hair."

I smiled. That was exactly why I had picked it over the others.

I whispered to her. "What do I do now?"

A devilish expression overtook her facial features—a bad girl face—and she said, "Follow me."

I walked behind Sabrina, momentarily wishing that I could turn back, but then it was too late. She was introducing me to someone.

"Kathy, this is Amy," she said to a larger, red-headed woman. "She's Irish, like you. You two will adore each other."

"Hello," Kathy said, with a heavy Gaelic accent. "Nice to meet you."

"Hi," I replied, and became terrified as I watched Sabrina prance away into the milling crowd.

Henry offered me a martini, something I don't usually drink, but I took it from him, happily. At least I had something to hold onto.

Somehow, I managed to have a conversation with a boisterous woman I could barely understand. All while holding a cocktail and sipping without spilling. Sabrina was right. I did like Kathy, a computer consultant who handled all things technical for the Bergman Collection. I could only catch every third word she spoke, and I had to piece sentences together, but I liked her.

My drive up north had been long, and after standing a while and having a drink, I needed to use the restroom. I excused myself and started in the already familiar direction.

On my way there, I noticed an attractive Hispanic man standing in a corner, staring at me. I quickly turned my eyes away.

In the bathroom, I rediscovered what a nuisance control-top nylons were. Taking them on and off was like wrestling a tiger, for God's sake. I broke a sweat doing it, and when I checked my face in the mirror, I noticed my cheeks were pink. I didn't know if it was from the alcohol or the hosiery struggle. Either way, I was ready to go home.

I opened the door, and no sooner than I turned the corner, Sabrina appeared.

"There you are," she said. "There's someone I'd like to introduce you to."

I followed obediently, like a circus animal in a travelling show. We walked past a group of people, all of whom laughed at the same time, startling me.

"Amy," Sabrina said, getting my attention away from the rowdy guests, "This is my friend, Miguel."

It was him. The handsome Hispanic man I'd intentionally broken eye contact with. He extended his hand and I shook it. Instant tension.

Sabrina scampered off like a little mouse. Damn her! I thought.

"It's very nice to meet you," Miguel said. He had an accent, but it was much easier to understand than

Kathy's. His face was kind. It had an honest quality to it.

"Nice to meet you too," I said, feeling terribly uncomfortable.

Miguel had dark hair and hazel green eyes. He wasn't overly tall, but still as tall as me with heels on. He smiled. That's when I noticed his teeth were perfectly white and straight. He exuded genuine warmth… and it made me want to run away as fast as I possibly could.

"So," he began, "how do you know Ms. Bergman?"

It was too weird to explain.

"She used to do business with my husband," I said.

Miguel looked at my hand and saw my wedding ring. "Ah, you are married," he said, sounding disappointed.

"I *was* married," I corrected him. "He passed away a few years ago."

I fidgeted with my hands, and then dropped them to my sides. People often asked me why I still wore the ring. I hoped I wouldn't have to explain it now, and to a stranger.

"I'm so sorry," he replied.

We stood there for a few moments, and I figured it was my turn to say something.

"How about you? How do you know Sabrina?" I asked.

"I'm her lawyer."

Lawyer? Aren't lawyers supposed to look threatening and aggressive? This man seemed none of those things. He seemed like a regular guy.

For lack of a better follow-up comment, I asked, "What do you help her with?"

Miguel shrugged. "I do a little bit of everything. I mainly help with international business, but if personal matters arise, I handle that, too."

I was surprised. He was kind of a hot shot without being full of himself. He seemed down to Earth. Normal.

"And you?" he asked. "What do you do?"

I felt a wall go up. I didn't like talking about myself.

"I'm a mom to a seven-year-old son, Tyler. And I work at a desk during the day, processing paperwork."

I was sure this would be his exit cue. Men always found a way to politely excuse themselves at the mere mention of children. That would be fine with me. I was ready to go home.

"You speak of your job like it's not important. Do you think this way?"

He hadn't left. I didn't know how to respond.

"I guess not," I stammered. "It's just, compared to other people's work, it seems trivial."

He fixed his hazel eyes on me. "I see," he said, nodding. "But you are a mother, too. That is the most difficult job. No?"

I smiled at him. It was a nice compliment.

"How about you?" I asked him. "Do you have children?"

"No. No children. Never married, either."

This surprised me, but I didn't say anything.

"You see. I am always working," he said. "So many hours, all the time. There was a woman I loved once, back home in my country, Argentina, but she didn't love me back. She ran off and married a bum."

"I'm sorry to hear that."

"Thank you," he replied.

I guessed he was the type of guy who cured heartbreak by drowning himself in his work. And, as the years go by, he'd find himself married to his career. I felt sad for him. But I wasn't really sure what to say next. I wished Sabrina would rescue me, but of course, she didn't.

"So how are you enjoying this party?" Miguel asked, lightening the mood. He wore an expression that hinted of mockery, which confused me a bit.

"It's okay, I guess. But I'm going to be honest here. This is my first real cocktail party."

That didn't come out right. A grin appeared on his face.

"What I mean is, I usually only attend kids' birthday parties. And my other friends don't have things like this, and get all dressed up."

The more I said the worse it got. I sounded like the boring person I truly was.

"I never would've guessed," Miguel said, flashing a warm smile. "You're so beautiful and glamorous. You seem completely at ease."

I let out a nervous giggle. I'd never been complimented like that by anyone other than Justin. And I definitely was not at ease. I could feel my cheeks turning pink again.

"Thanks for the vote of confidence," I replied. "This glamour," I said, while pointing to my outfit, "is all on loan from our mutual friend, Sabrina."

Miguel laughed. "That's Ms. Bergman," he said. "Clothing is her life. Any chance she gets to plan things like this, she does." Then he shook his head and made a tsking sound. "I don't like wearing suits outside of work, but I did, because the invite said formal attire."

"Sounds like you're perpetually in costume," I said.

He laughed again. "Sometimes it feels like that. But, soon enough I'll be back home, relaxing and playing my guitar with Gordito."

I thought he must have a roommate, a fellow musician.

"Gordito is my cat," Miguel explained. "He's very fat, and he loves music. Whenever I'm playing, he comes by and meows, like he's singing. I'm happy to have him join in."

I formed a mental picture and was struck by its silliness. "Maybe you two could compose something together. The YouTube crowd can't get enough cats."

He smiled, and all of a sudden looked rather serious. "Maybe I will compose a song for you," he said.

Maybe this was meant to knock me off my feet or something. And yes, it was nice, but I wasn't going there.

"That must get a lot of women," I replied, straightening my stance and taking an unconscious step back.

Miguel didn't move. He looked unsure of himself. No doubt he wasn't used to ladies who were so abrupt. They probably fell at his feet on a regular basis.

"No. It doesn't," he joked, "But it doesn't hurt to try if I meet a woman as exceptional as you."

I wasn't exceptional and the poor man was wasting his time.

"Tell me about your family," he said, quickly changing the subject.

I wanted to bolt, but it would've been rude, so I obliged him in conversation.

"Let's see. My son is seven. My mom lives with us now. And my husband, Justin, passed away a few years ago from cancer. We were high school sweethearts."

"I see," Miguel sighed. He seemed to become more of a listener and less of a flirt.

I relaxed a little.

"Well, my family lives in South America," he added. "Luckily, I get to see them pretty often. My closest relative here is furry with four paws."

I laughed. "Gordito."

"Yes. My cat, my musical partner. The best friend a man could ever ask for."

I raised an eyebrow. "I thought that was a dog."

Miguel smiled. "No, my dear. A cat is a man's true best friend. Plus," he added. "I don't have to walk him."

I giggled and was just starting to relax when my stomach growled. Miguel acted like he didn't hear it.

"Well, I better go and find Sabrina. I've got to get going soon," I told him. "It was nice to meet you."

"It was very nice to meet you too," Miguel said. He reached for my hand and gently kissed the top of it.

A riot of conflicting emotions ran through me all at once. I pulled my hand free and waved. Then I flew out of that corner as fast as I could in high heels and made a beeline for the kitchen.

I got there moments later, and found elegant appetizers arranged next to fine china and napkins. Starving, I took a plate and loaded it with a few highly-styled snacks before hiding in a corner so I could relax and eat, alone.

I was a little disappointed Sabrina hadn't spent any time with me yet. Hadn't she been the one insisting she could use a friend at this party? I figured I'd better find her soon, and visit for a little while, otherwise it wouldn't be polite of me to leave.

I devoured my small meal and washed it down with sparkling water. As I sat in the chair, I closed my eyes. I was starting to feel stressed. I patted my lips with a napkin and got up, ready to find Sabrina.

While walking through the crowd, I made no eye contact with anyone. I scanned the room for a purple gown, for the hostess. Once I spotted her, I snuck up on her left-hand side, not wanting to interrupt her conversation.

Sabrina kept talking to the little group while I watched her. She oozed charm and captivated her listeners, with both her witty conversation and sense of style. She had a magnetic quality. She clearly didn't need me here. Everyone was already fascinated by her.

I wondered if Justin had been.

"Amy," Sabrina said, turning to me. "This is Tatiana and this is Magda."

She identified the tall, goddess-like women she'd been talking to.

"Hello," I said, raising my hand up in a little wave.

Sabrina continued. "These two ladies model for us in runway shows and print ads."

Of course they were models. People in real life just didn't look that good.

"Nice to meet both of you. Sounds like fun, what you two do," I added.

They both smiled and looked down at me like I was insignificant. Under other circumstances, they probably wouldn't even have acknowledged me, but since their boss was standing right there, they behaved. Still, they didn't ask me what I did for a living, or engage in any further conversation like the other guests I'd met. A polite smile was all they had to give. Then they excused themselves and walked away.

"So how are you doing?" Sabrina asked. "Are you having a good time?"

I answered with the best I could come up with. "Yeah,

I'm having fun. The food's delicious."

Sabrina gave me an inquisitive look.

I wore my blank face and asked, "How are you doing? Is everything turning out well?"

She surveyed the room and said, "I think so. It's mostly business associates. I try to get them all together from time to time, to get to know each other."

I nodded. She was doing a fine job, I thought.

"Sabrina," I said. "I'm having a great time, but it's a long ride back to my side of town. And I'm sure my mom and Tyler are up waiting for me. Would you be offended if I left a little early?"

She sighed. I could tell she was disappointed. "No. Of course, I understand. It was good of you to come."

I was relieved. I didn't think I could handle anymore mingling. "Thanks for inviting me," I told her. "I had fun. I'll have the dress cleaned and return it with the others."

"Don't worry about it," she said, waving her hand. "Here, let me walk you to the door."

Sabrina and I began heading toward the foyer, and someone called out to her.

"Don't worry about me," I said. "I know my way."

I waved goodbye as she went back toward her business associates, some of whom were now intoxicated enough to shout to her from across the room.

I did a quick scan for her friend, Miguel, but he was nowhere in sight.

I shut the front door and inhaled a breath of fresh, evening air. On the exhale, I let go of all the tension I'd built up about going to the party. I'd done it. And now I was heading home. It was a comforting feeling.

After taking a few steps, I heard a car door slam shut and someone talking. I recognized the man's voice. He was alone, so he must've been on his cell phone. As he drew nearer, I discovered who it was.

"Doctor Friedman?"

"Yes," he answered, stowing his phone in his suit jacket pocket. He looked confused. I could tell he recognized me, but couldn't figure out from where.

"It's Amy White," I said. "You were my husband Justin's oncologist."

As he stared at me I could almost hear the gears turning in his head. Then they clicked.

"Yes. Of course," he said, extending his hand. "How are you doing?"

"I'm hanging in there."

He looked at me with his professional compassion, and then put his hand on my shoulder. "I want you to know I did everything I could," he said.

My heart ached. The old pain felt as fresh as the day he'd first spoken those words.

"I know," I replied.

I wanted to disappear, to do anything to stop that memory from advancing. I quickly changed the subject.

"So Dr. Friedman, what brings you to this party?"

He grinned and said, "I was in town and wanted to surprise my cousin. Sabrina will be shocked to see me."

With that, he waved and strode past me. I walked over to my car, climbed in, and shut the door. I couldn't believe what I'd just heard. *Dr. Friedman is Sabrina's cousin?*

I repeated the phrase over and over in my mind on the way home. Then I came to a realization. Dr. Friedman wasn't from the Chicago area. He was from Minnesota. He practiced at the Mayo Clinic.

I remembered a head nurse telling me how lucky I was that a specialist like Dr. Friedman was in town helping

Justin, that he was one of the top cancer doctors in the country.

The oncoming light turned red. I slowed and came to a stop. I remembered something else. I'd never received a bill from Dr. Friedman. In all the shuffle of papers and insurance claims, I assumed it had somehow been taken care of. But the more I thought about it, the more I realized I had never received an invoice with his name on it. Of course, I never went in search of medical bills that didn't arrive. And here I'd thought it was a fluke, or just plain Irish luck… but it wasn't. This was Sabrina's doing.

A well of emotions overflowed inside me, and I began to cry. There was no stopping it. I lost all control. I sobbed, wondering why Justin had to die when he had one of the best doctors in the nation. I wondered for the thousandth time why he couldn't be cured. I continued thinking these thoughts, feeling hopeless, while at the same time trying to pay attention to the road.

My sadness was soon replaced with something else—gratitude. I was so thankful Justin had a friend like Sabrina. Someone who cared enough to help, someone who knew important people. I wondered if she'd paid Dr. Friedman. Or if he'd done it as a favor to her.

I pulled up to my house and turned off the car. I wiped my eyes dry and sincerely hoped my mom and Tyler weren't waiting up for me. I didn't want them to get the wrong idea, to think I'd had a bad time.

Once I walked in, Mom came from down the hall to greet me. She could see I'd been crying. "Honey, are you okay? Did something happen?"

"No," I said. "I'm fine. I just heard a song on the radio and it set me off. Must be PMS."

She nodded.

"I had a good time," I said. "I'll tell you both about it tomorrow."

I walked to my room and kicked my shoes off, and they landed in a heap of undone laundry. I carefully unzipped and hung up my borrowed gown. Then, with all my might I pulled down the control-top nylons and flung those to the ground before putting on a t-shirt and sweatpants. After washing my face and brushing my teeth, I was finally in my bed, sweet bed.

My body said sleep, but my mind said think. Luckily, it wasn't a weeknight. I could stay awake all evening if I chose to.

What I chose to do was remember Justin. He was so excited about getting a real Mayo Clinic doctor, said it was a gift from St. Jude. He had me believing there was nothing to worry about. I guess that was just what he wanted me to think.

Did Justin know Dr. Friedman was related to Sabrina? Justin was a proud man. He wouldn't have accepted a favor that large. Of course he didn't know. And Sabrina was smart enough not to tell him.

God, how I wished things had turned out differently.

I tossed and turned for a bit, thinking about the evening's events. I smiled, remembering Kathy's heavy Irish accent. Some of the phrases she'd said were so funny to hear. The super-models were all right, as nice as they could be to an ordinary woman like me, I guessed.

I closed my eyes and began drifting off. And, in a far corner of my mind, I found myself thinking about Gordito, the cat.

Chapter 14

Sunday morning, I woke up to the smell of breakfast. Usually I helped with that, but my late night thinking threw me off schedule. If I were a normal person, I'd have a hangover.

I climbed out of bed and shuffled to the kitchen. "Hey, guys," I said.

"Hi, Mom. How was your friend's party?"

"Oh, it was okay. Lots of different kinds of people." I paused, then added, "You know what was really good? The food."

I sat down and pushed my chair in. I was starving. Mom and Tyler sat down too.

"So that's it then?" she asked. "No details?"

I shrugged and put a scoop of scrambled eggs on my fork. "Let's see," I said. "I met a bunch of people. A doctor. A lawyer. A computer consultant from Ireland. Oh, and I met two super-models who do ads for Sabrina."

"Neat," Tyler said. "And you thought it wouldn't be any fun."

"Not as fun as hanging out with you," I replied, elbowing him.

"And your dress, did that work out?" Mom asked. "Did you get any compliments?"

I thought of what Miguel had told me. "Yeah. Sabrina

said she loved it. That it was a perfect choice with my hair."

Mom and Tyler seemed satisfied. We continued eating and then moved on with our regular weekend plans. Mom had to run some errands, so I cleaned up and got up-to-date on Tyler's homework and art class project. In the evening, we did our workout routine.

*****

Monday morning, I got up early and dropped the borrowed dress at the dry cleaners. When I arrived at work, I discovered a relaxed, easy-going atmosphere.

"What's going on here?" I asked Barb.

She was sitting with her feet up on her desk and her arms crossed behind her back. She looked like she was sunbathing. Fatima sat in her chair, texting.

"Dave had a family emergency. He had to go out of town. He'll be back Wednesday."

"Who's in charge then?" I asked.

Barb looked smug and replied, "Nobody."

My co-workers were acting like crazy people. I decided to ignore their odd behavior and get started on my own work.

After a while, I heard Barb put her feet down, and papers start shuffling. The rapid clicking sounds ceased from Fatima's direction, too. I guess if I wasn't going to act mutinous, they wouldn't either.

They suggested we go out to lunch as a group. I didn't want to be a stick in the mud, so I went along. Thank God we were back in time, because Dave called in. I just managed to make it to the phone.

"We're holding down the fort," I told him.

"Everything's fine, same as usual."

The line cracked in and out on his end. "Things are not going well here," he said, "but I'm doing my best. Tell everyone to just continue with their tasks. You ladies know what to do. I'll call back tomorrow."

He hung up. He never elaborated on what was going on with his family.

Later that evening, I logged onto the computer to send an email to Sabrina.

I wrote: "Thanks for inviting me to your party and lending me the dress. I dropped it at the cleaners this morning. It will be ready on Friday. I hope everything continued to go well after I left.

"Oh, and an odd thing happened to me on my way out. I bumped into Dr. Friedman. He said he was stopping by to surprise his cousin, whom I found out is you.

"Sabrina… I know what you did for us. And I cannot find the words to express how grateful I am. You have no idea how much having Dr. Friedman there meant to Justin. He thought him showing up was a miracle straight from God.

"I realize me bumping into him was purely by chance, and that you had no intention of telling me about it. But things happen for a reason, I guess.

"I want you to know that I feel so lucky to have a friend like you."

I signed it Amy, and then hit send.

*****

Tuesday was a normal day at work. Dave had called in and spoken with Fatima, and she assured him everything was still okay. He still didn't share any details of his family emergency, but that didn't surprise any of us.

That night, my mom had her book club so Tyler and I went to the library so he could look for a yoga DVD.

"How come we're looking for a yoga video?" I asked him.

He scanned the titles, tilting his head to the side. "Sam's doing it twice a week. He says it loosens him up and makes his parkour moves better."

Understood. Tyler was going to do anything Sam did. I was thankful he was a nice kid and was into sports instead of trouble.

"Here's one," I said, holding it up.

Tyler checked the description. He decided it would work. All we needed to do was stop and get the yoga blocks at the store.

Doing yoga with my son that night was one of the most relaxing things I'd experienced in years. Tyler thought so, too, then went to finish up his homework.

I decided to check my email before bed. Lots of junk, and a response from Sabrina. It read: "I'm glad you enjoyed the party. And you didn't have to clean the dress. But since you did, do you want to come by with it this weekend? We could swim again or do something else. I just can't do the following weekend because there is a legal matter I have to take care of and I'll be out of town."

I was surprised she didn't say anything about Dr. Friedman. Was she embarrassed? Did she not want to take credit? With her there was no way to know for sure.

I wondered if Miguel would go with her to address the legal issue she mentioned. Why hadn't they gotten together? He seemed genuine, sincere. Maybe Justin actually was helping her, putting someone right under her nose, but she wasn't paying attention.

I responded to her email and said Sunday would work. I planned to bring up the subject of Dr. Friedman then. It was much too big to ignore.

When Dave returned to work Wednesday morning, he seemed to have aged in the few days he'd been gone. He never told us what happened, which was typical of his character. I wondered why he acted that way? After Justin died and I was devastated, Dave had been very comforting. He'd spent time listening to me sob at my desk, without complaining. And I'll never forget how he gave me two weeks off with pay—weeks I didn't have coming—to rest and recover.

I appreciated all he'd done for me. Maybe that's why I didn't revel in his absence. I respected my boss. And if not talking about his family emergency was what he preferred, then I wouldn't pry.

*****

Wednesday night, Mom offered to take Tyler to Josephine's.

"Are you sure?" I asked.

She smiled. "He's turning in his assignment, the one of my hand."

I could see it was important to her, and I didn't want to take away her chance in the spotlight. "Be my guest," I said.

I mused about how being a model for a child's art project could make a person feel so good. I could only imagine how the models who worked for Sabrina felt.

After they left, I sat on the sofa and closed my eyes. It

felt good to just do nothing. When I opened them a few minutes later, I saw the yoga blocks resting on the floor by the TV. We usually skipped working out on Wednesdays, but I felt compelled for some reason, so I walked over and picked up the DVD.

The instructor looked to be over fifty, yet she had the nicest figure. Health seemed to emanate from her. I want that, I thought.

After I finished the workout, I lay down on the floor. It was the second most relaxing night I'd had in years. We would have to buy our own copy of the DVD after returning this to the library.

I had more time to myself, so I curled up on the sofa and picked up a book to read. In a little while, I heard Mom and Tyler come back, so I got up to greet them.

"Hey, honey, how was your lesson?" I asked Tyler.

"Good," he said. He wore a smile that ran from ear to ear.

I looked at my mom for an explanation. She winked as she passed, code for "I'll tell you later."

Tyler left to use the bathroom, and Mom whispered in my ear, "He showed Josephine some of his jumps. You should've seen her. She was so impressed. All she kept saying was how cool he was."

This news filled my heart with joy.

"And how did he do with his assignment?" I asked. "Did she like your hand?"

Mom lifted her hand in the air, displaying it. "She specifically said she loved the model. Said the wrinkles added character to the work."

"Character, huh? Is that what they call it?" I said, ribbing her. "Oh, you know what, I told Sabrina I could stop by on Sunday and return her dresses. Could you watch Tyler for a little while?"

She shrugged. "Sure. *Vogue* magazine hasn't called yet."

I laughed. My mom was a good sport. I loved having her here with us.

Tyler walked into the kitchen, still wearing his massive grin. He'd also changed into sweatpants. Probably planning to go out in the yard and practice a few more moves, just to stay "cool."

*****

Sunday morning, I rose early and made breakfast for everyone. I felt guilty when I found out my mom was taking Tyler to the community pool and I was going to swim at Sabrina's.

On the way to her house, I thought about how I used to be uncomfortable having such a rich friend. Now it didn't seem to matter. It was funny how much had changed and in such a short time. Just a few months ago, I'd despised and not trusted this woman. My life was filled with sadness, constant memories of the past. Now, neither was true. And it surprised no one more than me.

When I got to Sabrina's, Henry answered the door. I hadn't seen a lot of him lately and assumed he was only working special events, like her party. Since I didn't have a jacket to hand him, he just welcomed me back.

Sabrina wasn't there, so I stood in the foyer, waiting. A minute later, the door opened and she walked in. She was outfitted from head to toe in stylish active wear. She must've been out running.

"Hey. Perfect timing," she said. "Now we can hit the pool."

I'd wondered how she stayed in shape. She had such a nice figure. Of course, she hadn't had any kids yet, so she was ahead of others our age.

"I'll go change into my suit," I said.

While in the guest bathroom, I noticed for the first time that my own figure had improved. I could finally see some benefits of the family workout routine.

When I got to the pool area, Sabrina had already gotten in, so I climbed in, too.

"It's funny," I said. "My son went swimming at the community pool with his grandma today."

Sabrina frowned. "You should've brought him here. He's welcome to come."

"Thanks," I said. "Maybe I'll bring him another time."

Sabrina began doing laps, taking her pool time a bit more seriously. I did the same. And as I listened to the sound of the water splash in my ears, I wondered why I hadn't thought of bringing Tyler here before. She'd mentioned wanting to have a kid to play with, and he would get a real kick out of this place. I guess I was just too protective. I never let anyone into our world until I was sure.

Sabrina veered off course and swam up to me. I saw her coming and stopped, and began treading water to stay afloat. "Do you remember my friend, Miguel? The lawyer you met at the party?"

"Oh, yeah, I think I do," I replied, trying to appear calm.

Sabrina wasn't buying it. She knew I was nervous, but because she was polite, pretended not to notice.

"Well, he's helping me solve a major problem next week. He stopped by earlier so we could discuss it. I feel confident we can get it fixed. Oh, and he dropped off a

CD and asked me to give it to you." She raised her eyebrow in a question.

I wanted to sink to the bottom of the pool.

"That was thoughtful of him. So what kind of problem do you have?" I asked, quickly changing the subject.

"Well, it's complicated, but if I were to sum it up, it would come down to knock-offs."

"Like copying your designs?"

"Yes," she said, then leaned forward and began swimming again, "except at a highly-reduced price."

I began swimming again too and hoped the conversation would stay focused on business.

"We can't allow people to copy us," she said from across the pool. "We lose money and it puts us in a bad position, especially if we want to do a lower-priced line of our own someday, with a store like Target, for example."

I couldn't believe she had taken my idea seriously. I felt proud.

"So I have question. Kind of on the same topic," I said. "Last week my mom was a hand model for Tyler's art project. And it got me wondering, how come a magazine like *Vogue* doesn't have a senior edition?"

Sabrina stopped swimming. This got her full attention. I wasn't sure if she was offended or intrigued.

"It's interesting that you'd ask because *Vogue* has many editions—international ones, a *Teen Vogue*, but they haven't ventured into the market for older individuals."

"Why not?" I asked. "Aren't they the group with the largest population growth? And with the most money to spend?"

Sabrina climbed out of the pool and grabbed her towel. I followed.

"You want to know the truth?" she asked.

"Sure," I said, while grabbing my own towel and drying off.

"In the fashion world, youth is valued above everything else, worshipped even. No one wants to embrace women aging gracefully, losing their beauty, so they ignore it. They continue to sell the same proven concept. And indeed, they may shun the older, wiser woman with money to spend."

"Well, I'm not too into fashion myself—no offense—but I think they should have a *Vogue Senior* or something like that, something older women can connect with, so they can feel good about themselves."

Sabrina nodded rapidly. "Yet they don't. It's because they don't place value on that type of beauty. They can't sell the dream of reality."

She must be right, otherwise they would've done it already. If they could've made money on it, it would exist.

"Getting hungry yet?" Sabrina asked.

"Yeah."

I finished drying off and changed in the bathroom. When I got to the kitchen, I saw Henry had put together some good-looking sandwiches.

Sabrina sat down and handed me a plate. "You have a head for business," she commented.

I rolled my eyes and grabbed a napkin. "I doubt that. All I do at my present job is data entry. I helped some with Justin's business, but mostly little things... like depositing the checks."

"You sell yourself short," she said, before taking a bite of food.

She meant it as a compliment. But I thought my ideas were as ordinary as the next person's. I was feeling a little embarrassed, so I decided it was time to steer the conversation toward Dr. Friedman.

"So how did the party go after I left? Anything exciting happen?"

"No. Not really," she said.

"Were you surprised to see your cousin?" I asked.

The room instantly tensed up, and Sabrina said, "I was very surprised… and happy. It had been a long time."

Sabrina got up and went to the refrigerator. She pulled out two healthy-looking fruit and yogurt desserts. "My cousin would approve of these," she grinned.

I took mine and set it next to my drink. "I was wondering," I said, "if Dr. Friedman has an office in the Illinois area?"

Sabrina shook her head no.

She obviously didn't seem to want to talk about him. I didn't care, though. I was going to continue.

"You know what was odd," I said. "I never received a bill from him, or any bills from the insurance company showing he'd submitted anything."

I reached for my dessert and sat staring at her.

She kept her eyes down and replied, "I know."

She was acting weird. Evasive.

"Sabrina," I said.

She finally looked up.

"Did you pay those bills for us? Or did your cousin do it as a favor?"

"Does it matter?" she asked.

I thought about it for a minute and said, "It does to me."

Sabrina sighed. She paused for a while before responding. "Okay, if you must know… it was a favor."

I couldn't tell if she was telling the truth, but what was done was done. What I did know was that I felt immense gratitude swelling in my heart. I didn't think I could find the words to express how thankful I was.

"Sabrina," I said.

She made eye contact with me again, reluctantly.

"I want you to know how truly grateful I am, that we both are. I mean, if Justin could speak he would've been so thankful had he known. I guess what I'm trying to say is I don't think I could have asked for a better friend. Not in my whole life."

Sabrina managed a half-smile. Had I made her uncomfortable?

"You've become a good friend, too," she said.

As usual, time moved fast while away from home.

"Well, I guess it's about time for me to get going soon. My mom could probably use a break by now."

Sabrina's expression seemed to brighten. "Don't forget to bring your son next time. He's always welcome here."

I decided I would do that. Then I stood up and excused myself for one last bathroom break before leaving. When I returned, I grabbed my car keys out of my purse and thanked Sabrina for lending me the dress.

"Good luck with your business problem," I said. "I hope you get it fixed."

Sabrina's eyes widened, and she darted from the room. She returned holding a CD. "I almost forgot," she said. "Your music."

She handed it to me.

I played it cool and said, "Thanks. And, more importantly, thanks again—for everything."

We walked to the foyer and she opened the front door. "See you next time," she said.

I smiled and waved goodbye.

I drove home listening to talk radio. Occasionally, I

glanced at the CD lying next to my purse. The news was a broken record. Hot weather with high humidity, falling stock prices, and another murder on the south side of Chicago. I listened to traffic and weather updates every eight minutes all the way home.

When I pulled into the driveway, I stared at the CD again. Then I stashed it in my purse and went inside.

Chapter 15

The house was unusually quiet when I got home. I went in search of Tyler and found him in his room. He had a weird expression on his face. "Hey, Mom," he said. "We just got home."

He had gotten five shades tanner. He'd only been out a few short hours.

"Where's Grandma?" I asked.

His expression worsened. "She's resting. I don't think she feels too good."

I set my purse down and decided to check on her. When I knocked on her bedroom door, there was no answer. I opened it a crack to peek inside. My mom heard the sound and moved. She was awake.

"Mom. Are you okay? You're as red as a lobster!"

She sighed. "I know. I forgot my 30 SPF and it was overcast—"

"Do you want me to run out and get you something?" I asked.

"No. I'll be fine. I put some aloe on. I just need rest."

"Do you want something to eat or drink? A glass of lemonade?"

She shook her head. "No. I'm just going to sleep."

I got up and gently closed the door. I felt terrible. Then I began making dinner while Tyler did his homework.

When the food was ready, I offered my mom some,

but she couldn't eat. She said she was too nauseous. Tyler and I ate dinner, then skipped our workout since we both swam all day. After the heavy meal and the heat, we were both tired and went to bed early.

The next morning, before work, I checked in on my mom. She still looked horrible, like she'd been roasted alive.

"I feel a bit better, really," she said, trying to reassure me.

Once again, she wouldn't let me take care of her. Since Tyler was out of school, he promised to keep an eye on her while I went to work.

It was a hectic day. There were computer problems, clients with issues, the phone rang off the hook. Yet I still managed to find time to worry about my mom in between.

When I punched out for lunch, I noticed the Spanish channel was playing in the office.

I sat in the cafeteria alone with my peanut butter and jelly sandwich. As I pulled out my bag of chips and milk, it reminded me of being a kid at school again. I chewed my food and began zoning out. My relaxing moment was interrupted when Dave came in, looking frantic while listening to a voicemail. Once he hung up, he noticed me sitting nearby.

"Everything okay?" I asked.

He looked to be on the verge of a nervous breakdown, but he smiled and said, "Yep. Just family stuff."

I felt bad for him. It made me think of my mom, so I gave her a call after I finished eating.

"Hello," she answered, her voice sounding raspy.

"Mom. It's me. Are you feeling any better?"

"Yeah," she said, clearing her throat. "I took a cool

bath and put on more aloe. I'm gonna be fine. I just hope it doesn't peel."

"Okay, well, take it easy. I'll make dinner when I get home. Just relax."

Around 3:00 p.m., I stretched and took a break. Fatima got up and walked over to the radio, and then turned it up.

"What are you doing that for?" I asked.

Fatima spun around and began dancing, some salsa-type moves. "Because I like this song."

I cracked up laughing. "You don't even know what they're saying."

"Don't have to," she said, while smiling and shaking her butt.

It was pretty funny until Barb spotted Dave coming down the hall. She flagged Fatima to turn it down, and she returned to her desk.

At 5:00 p.m., I punched out and began digging through my purse for my car keys. It was becoming an annoying habit, searching through this dark, endless cavern of a bag. I didn't know why I carried such a large purse. Finally, I found them, right next to the CD from Miguel.

I got in the car and, out of habit, turned on the radio. A small voice in my head suggested listening to the music I had in my purse, but I quickly dismissed it. I didn't have time for that. I needed to focus on helping my family.

Once I got home, I went to check on my mom. "Knock knock, permission to enter," I joked.

"Come in," she replied.

I opened the door and saw my poor mother. She sat on the bed in her pajamas. Her hair was a tangled mess, like a bird's nest. Her red skin had blistered. She would peel for sure. Just what she wanted to avoid.

"Oh, no," I said.

She frowned. "At least I'm feeling better. You know what? I could go for a cheeseburger and fries from McDonald's."

It wasn't what I'd planned for dinner, but I didn't mind the change in plans.

I smiled. "Whatever you want. Let me just see what Tyler wants and I'll be back."

When I returned, we sat together and ate. Mom seemed to be enjoying her fries.

"Hey, T.," I said, glancing in his direction.

"Yeah."

"I don't know if you'd be interested, but my friend invited you to come over and swim at her house next time I go."

Tyler's eyes lit up. I guess he was more interested than I'd imagined.

"Cool," he said. "Can we go next weekend?"

"No, honey. She's out of town next weekend. Her pool is indoor, though, so we can go anytime."

He took a drink of his soda and set it back down. "Nice," he said.

While I cleaned up the paper plates and wiped down the table, I thought about Sabrina travelling with Miguel. Maybe they'd hit it off. Maybe she'd open her eyes and see the catch Justin had deposited right in front of her. If Justin were here he'd point to him and say, "Look, woman. There."

I laughed to myself thinking about it. My husband... how I missed him.

Tuesday night, Mom insisted on going to her book club, even though her skin was peeling and she thought she looked silly. Tyler and I hung out together while he worked on his art project.

"You're getting really good, you know," I told him.

He continued concentrating on his piece. "Thanks."

"So how come you're painting this week instead of drawing?"

Keeping his eye on the canvas, he replied, "Josephine suggested moving on to another medium. She asked me to create a painting of whatever I wanted, so she could figure out what level I'm at, where I need help."

"Smart," I replied. "Looks like you're doing something tropical."

"Yeah. I'm painting the beach in Bora Bora, with Mt. Otemanu in the background."

So that was the name of the mountain. Justin and I had looked at it so many times.

The rest of the evening, I stayed at his side, opening paint containers, handing him brushes, providing critique.

He was my little Gauguin.

Wednesday night, I took Tyler to his art lesson. There was no way Mom was running him around again. She needed her rest. After I dropped him off and said hi to Josephine, I ran to the bank and managed to return early. I didn't want to disturb them, so I decided to hang out in the car and relax.

I turned on the radio and tried to find a good song, but every station was stuck on commercials. I closed my eyes to take a nap instead. As I relaxed and got comfy, that little voice in my head suggested once again that I should listen to the CD in my purse.

"All right already," I cursed out loud. "Give it a rest."

Was I yelling at myself? *Out loud?* Wasn't that how mental illness started?

I sighed heavily, hoping I wasn't losing it. Then I gave in and reached into that black hole of a purse and pulled out the CD. I took a closer look at it. The cover was a photograph of an acoustic guitar.

I opened the case. Inside was a picture of a fat black and white cat. "Gordito," I mused, still talking out loud to myself.

He was a cute cat, a black and white short hair with big green eyes. Everything about him seemed larger than life. That cat needs to go on a diet, I thought.

I slid the CD into the car stereo. The music started right away, a gentle picking and strumming of what sounded like a classical guitar. I was surprised by the clear sound quality. It had a studio feel, not home-made at all. Within a short time, the melody grew more intricate and decidedly romantic. I felt my muscles tighten as I listened. At the same time, I couldn't help but notice what an accomplished player he was.

Then the singing began.

Beautiful lady in a borrowed gown, I never thought I'd meet someone like you.

I laughed, but still felt tense.

There was a pause in the singing, and then the cat began meowing loudly, over and over, in sync with the guitar strums. My jaw dropped. I couldn't believe how hysterical it was.

It has been such a long time since I have felt this way.

The strumming accelerated, quickening its pace, and Miguel continued.

But if you would like to meet with me, even just for a coffee, it would make my heart skip a beat.

Gordito howled in the background while he sang. It sounded like a cat fight, and I lost it. I began laughing so hard I started crying.

Toward the end of the song, it slowed down again, and Miguel sang his phone number, requesting that I call him.

I sighed, then I wiped tears of laughter off my cheeks. I pressed the eject button and put the disc back in its protective case. Before closing it, I took one last look at Gordito, and I put the CD back inside my purse and out of my mind.

Tyler came out of the house, and I got out to meet him.

"What did she think of your painting?" I asked as he got closer.

He smiled a goofy smile. "She liked it," he replied. "She made suggestions on how I could improve it, and that's what I'm working on this week, and probably the next few weeks."

"Sounds good," I said, full of pride.

That evening Tyler and I did the yoga workout. Afterward, he worked on his parkour moves in the backyard. I checked in on my mom. She looked less crispy as she sat in her room reading.

Later on, as I lay in the dark, I thought about Miguel's song and started giggling all over again.

Then I felt a strange feeling. I was lying in my bed—mine and Justin's bed—thinking about another man.

It unsettled me.

I jumped up and turned on the light, then flew across the room and grabbed my purse. I rummaged through it and dug out the CD, and then opened my bottom dresser drawer and stashed it beneath a pile of chunky sweaters.

I wanted it to go away.

Chapter 16

The weekend Sabrina was out of town turned out to be a fun one. Tyler and his friend Sam invited my mom and I to watch a group of their friends perform parkour outdoors. They both participated, and we had a blast watching them. I knew without a doubt Justin would have loved this sport. It was funny how much Tyler was like his dad.

Sunday night, when I logged onto the computer, there was an email from Sabrina. "Amy, I'm in New York with Miguel. We're gaining some positive ground in the legal matter. Thought you might like to know since we discussed the topic. And, not sure if this is too repetitive, but if you'd like to swim next Sunday and bring your son this time, let me know. Or we could do something else and bring him along? I'll leave it up to you. Of course, all provided you are free that day. Sabrina."

I looked down the page and saw there was more. "P.S. Miguel asked if you had a chance to listen to his CD?"

I read through her email a second time before replying. I couldn't believe she mentioned the CD. Had he told her about the song? I hoped not. I wrote back. "Sabrina, Swimming this Sunday with Tyler sounds good. He can't wait to come and see your house. You said you'd like to have a kid to hang out with, right? Well, be warned, he's a talker! Oh, and the CD. I haven't gotten around to listening to it yet. Amy."

I hit send and logged out. I didn't want her to know I'd listened to Miguel's CD. I didn't want him to know, either.

During the week I sat with Tyler while he began his second island painting. Mom's skin condition improved. And I started doing more research on dog adoption. It was getting close to being time for us to afford it.

*****

When Sunday morning arrived, Tyler was amped up, psyched about his adventure to Sabrina's indoor pool.

On the drive there, he listened to songs on the radio and sang along, tapping his feet. He was unusually wired, almost as if he'd drank a bunch of coffee. I hoped he would behave. He usually did, of course, but I didn't want to go and ruin Sabrina's idyllic vision of having kids.

As we pulled into her driveway, Tyler looked around. "Holy cow! This is the place?" he asked.

"Yep."

I winked at him and put the car in park. Then we got out and gathered our things from the trunk.

"Oh, and just so you know, my friend may answer the door or an older gentleman may. If he does, just act normal. He's her employee."

The way Tyler looked at me, I could tell he didn't understand. He nodded, though, and we began walking toward the house.

Before I could even ring the buzzer, the door opened. It was Sabrina.

"Hello," I said. "This is my son, Tyler."

Tyler stepped forward and offered his hand. Sabrina leaned down and shook it.

"Pleased to meet you," Sabrina said.

The look on her face was unlike any I had seen her make before. It was an expression unfolding. First there was surprise. No doubt the resemblance to Justin shocked her. Then I saw joy. Maybe seeing him, a miniature version of someone she cared so much for, was like having a part of him come back. Then I saw something I couldn't quite place. Was it envy? It was hard to tell. Each nuance lasted only a fleeting moment.

"Pleased to meet you too," Tyler replied, sounding three times his age.

We stepped into the foyer, and as we did, Tyler studied the room with a careful eye. Sabrina noticed.

"Would you like to see the whole house before we go swimming?" she asked.

"Okay," he replied.

Sabrina spoke to him as if he were an adult. She hadn't adopted the little kid voice people so often use. I wondered if that was how her parents spoke to her while she was growing up.

"Excuse me," Tyler said, interrupting my thought. "While we're looking at your house, can you show me the stuff my dad did?"

My eyes met Sabrina's, and we smiled in understanding.

"Of course I can," she said. "How about we start right here."

A renewed sense of enthusiasm filled Sabrina's voice. It didn't bother me anymore, her being so thrilled to talk about Justin. I was more excited to see Tyler being proud of his dad's accomplishments.

As we stood in the foyer, Sabrina began. "Under our feet, you'll notice a beautiful Italian tile, something your dad suggested for its wow factor."

The three of us looked down. It looked expensive. And if anyone could talk someone into spending more than they planned to, it was Justin. He was quite the salesman. Tyler didn't say anything. He merely observed and nodded, and we moved on.

While we walked, Sabrina described the details of each room, and what Justin had done to improve it. I was only half-listening, though, as the projects themselves didn't really interest me. Instead, I was fascinated by the way Tyler and Sabrina interacted. Tyler seemed more behaved and grown-up than usual. Sabrina seemed softer, a bit animated.

When the house tour finished, Sabrina showed Tyler and me to the guest bathroom.

"See you at the pool," she said, before walking away.

Tyler opened his bag and pulled out his swimsuit. Before closing the bathroom door, he asked, "Is your friend a movie star?"

I smiled. A month ago that would've annoyed me. "No, honey, remember, she owns a fashion design company."

He shrugged his shoulders, a sign that he couldn't care less, then closed the door. In a few minutes, he came out and I went in and changed. When I finished, I noticed he'd made his way down the hall.

"Come back here," I hissed.

Tyler spun around and ran back.

"Don't wander off. It's not our house. And it's rude."

He looked down. "Sorry."

Tyler and I walked to the pool area, where Sabrina was waiting. I noticed a few kid-friendly toys floating in the water. I couldn't believe she went through all that trouble, but I was thankful.

Before we even got in, Tyler started with the questions.

"Sabrina?" he asked.

"Yes," she said, while laying her towel out on a chaise.

"Do you live here all by yourself?"

"Yes."

I glared at him, hoping he would stop, but he was looking the other way.

"Is it scary?"

Sabrina laughed. No doubt she realized this could go on indefinitely.

"No. It's not scary," she replied, and went to sit by the edge of the pool, putting her toes in the water.

Tyler jumped in but was careful not to splash. I sat near Sabrina, with my legs dangling further in than hers.

"Is the lady in all the paintings a relative of yours?" Tyler asked her.

"No." Sabrina said, "The woman in the paintings was a model from long ago, for an artist called John Waterhouse."

"I think I've heard of him," Tyler replied.

I jumped into the deep end and flashed her a "you asked for it" look, and began swimming laps.

Sabrina didn't seem to mind. She kept it going. "I hear you're an artist too."

Through the splashing water, I heard Tyler reply, "Yeah. I'm a beginner."

"Well, we all have to start somewhere, don't we?"

"Do you have a painting of yourself?" Tyler asked her.

Sabrina, who had now gotten into the pool, tilted her head and said, "No."

"How come?"

If Sabrina was losing patience, she didn't show it. "Umm, I don't know. I guess I like to collect other artists' work. I've never thought of having one of me done. Maybe someday you could paint my portrait. Once you're experienced enough to take on the task. What do you think?"

I stopped swimming and watched Tyler's face light up. "Like a real artist?" he asked.

Sabrina and I made eye contact.

"Exactly," she said to him.

Tyler, thrilled beyond words, swam over to an orange floating noodle and hung onto it.

"He just did a drawing of his grandma's hand the other day," I added. "He's working his way up."

I grabbed a floating beach ball, thinking Tyler might like to play catch, but he began chatting again.

"I'm doing a painting this week. My teacher had me create one (whatever I wanted) and she's showing me how to improve it."

"Wonderful," Sabrina replied. "What did you choose?"

Tyler leaned forward to answer, then slipped off his noodle and fell into the water. He reemerged laughing.

Unfazed by his accidental dunking, he answered, "It's a tropical scene. Of Bora Bora, with Mt. Otemanu in the background."

Sabrina must've decided she didn't want to go there. She changed the subject.

"So, Tyler," she said, herself now leaning on a purple noodle. "How do you like school? Do you have any other hobbies?"

They both seemed equally interested in talking to each other. And I was glad it didn't make Sabrina uncomfortable. I abandoned the ball and swam toward the last available green noodle.

"I'm off for summer now," Tyler said. "But there's a sport I'm learning called parkour."

Sabrina's face looked blank.

"What kind of sport is that?" she asked.

Tyler loved this. It wasn't often an adult he didn't know gave him this much undivided attention.

"It's kind of hard to describe. It's better to see it. I can show you later if you want?"

Sabrina smiled. "I'd love to see it."

While in Tyler's company, Sabrina seemed to glow. I wondered if it was because she wanted to have kids of her own or if it was just because he was Justin's child. Someone like her ought to have a child of her own. She certainly had the space and the means to afford it. And she had plenty of love to give.

Interrupting my mental banter, Sabrina said, "Anyone getting hungry yet?"

"I am," said Tyler, throwing his noodle aside.

"Honey, did you want to eat and then jump around like that? Or do you want to show her the moves first?"

Tyler thought about what I said. "Yeah, I should show you first, then eat."

Sabrina climbed out of the pool and wrapped a towel around herself. "Whichever order you prefer."

Tyler and I got out of the pool and dried off enough so we could walk back through the house and change. Afterward, Sabrina met us in the hallway. I was surprised when I saw her. She'd changed into capri jeans and a t-shirt. She looked normal.

"So where do we go to see the parkour?" Sabrina asked.

"I usually do it in the backyard at home. I need to be

able to run around and jump off things, like the side of the house."

Sabrina raised an eyebrow. She led us to her backyard. "You can use the side of the house and any unbreakable objects that are out there," she said.

Her back yard was more like a mini forest preserve, meticulously landscaped. I hoped Tyler would realize he couldn't just trample through her flowerbeds and plants.

Sabrina opened the large French doors that revealed a massive stone patio, the kind with bits of moss growing in-between. Luckily, I didn't have to tell Tyler. He glanced at me and caught on quick. We weren't at home, with weeds fighting to survive no matter how often we pulled them, and sod that faded in the summer sun.

"Whoa," he said. "Let me look around first. I need to see where I can do this without ruining anything."

Sabrina and I stood still while he walked around, surveying the area.

"Okay. This spot seems safe for a demonstration."

We walked closer to where he stood, and Tyler began shaking his limbs, loosening up.

Sabrina glanced at me and giggled.

"Be prepared," I said, teasing her.

Of course, she couldn't be. Unless you'd seen it, it always came as a big surprise.

In a moment, Tyler began running. He came up to a stone bench, did what looked like a cartwheel over it, landed and began speeding toward the side of the house. Then he did his signature move. He appeared to climb the side of the wall, flipped over in the air, and landed back on his feet.

"Oh, my God!" Sabrina gasped, holding her hand over her mouth.

"Pretty cool, huh?" I said to her.

Sabrina's eyes were wide. Tyler came sauntering over to get her reaction.

"That was amazing! I've never seen anything like it," she said.

Tyler blushed. "Thanks. I'm still learning this stuff. You should see the older kids."

I rubbed my son's head, messing up his hair. He looked up at me and smiled.

Sabrina watched us, then said, "Now you've got to be starved."

We followed her to the kitchen, where we took a seat at the table.

"Your mom tells me you like vegetarian food," Sabrina said to Tyler. He looked at her and nodded. "Well, I've got something prepared you'll probably like."

I watched as she turned the oven on and pulled out a few slices of flatbread. She sprinkled a little water on each piece and popped them in the stove.

"Have you ever had Mediterranean food?"

My son looked confused, which meant no.

"Well, I've got some pre-made falafels from Trader Joe's, and I'm going to heat them up and serve them with lettuce, tomato, and tahini sauce. It makes a hearty sandwich."

"Cool," my son replied.

I was open to anything. I'd often discovered some of my favorite meals this way in the last year.

Once the sandwiches were ready, Sabrina sat down with us and we began eating. They were delicious. Tyler must have agreed because he wolfed down his whole meal like he'd never eaten before.

"I can help clean up," I offered after we'd finished.

Sabrina shook her head no, then she set the dishes in the sink and came back to sit down with us.

"So are you excited to go back to school? It's coming up soon, isn't it?"

"Sure," Tyler replied. "But being off for the summer is fun, too."

A wide smile crossed Sabrina's face. "I remember those days like they were yesterday," she said.

I smirked. "How did you spend your summer vacations?" I asked her.

Sabrina sat up straighter. "Oh, my parents took me and my sister to Europe for about a month. One year it was the French Riviera. I'll never forget how my sister embarrassed me, pointing out the topless women on the beach. My mom had to apologize and drag both of us away."

We all laughed.

"Where else did you go?" Tyler asked. He was having so much fun I didn't think he'd want to go home.

"Ah, let's see," Sabrina said, trying to remember. "We went to the Greek islands one year. Italy the next. My parents were a lot of fun."

"Do you still see them often?" Tyler asked.

Sabrina glanced at me, not sure what to say. I nodded to her.

"No... I don't," she said, her voice sounding softer now. "They both passed away in a plane crash."

Tyler didn't respond right away. He just stared at Sabrina. He seemed shaken by what she'd said. Then, he reached out and held her hand, acknowledging her loss in his own little way.

"I lost my dad, too," he replied, looking sad.

"I know," Sabrina responded. "I'm sorry that

happened to you."

Tyler's eyes met Sabrina's. They had something in common.

The mood had changed from playful to somber. I figured it was a good time to wrap things up and head home. "Well," I said, while getting up. "I guess we should be going back soon."

Sabrina stood up and smoothed the front of her capris. "Of course," she said. "Thank you both for stopping by."

I put my hand on her shoulder and said, "Thanks for having us. We had a great time."

Sabrina walked Tyler and me to the front door and handed us our bags. To my surprise, Tyler turned around and hugged Sabrina goodbye. He never does stuff like that to people he's just met. Sabrina wasn't expecting it either.

As I walked down the drive and waved at her, I could see her eyes had filled with tears.

*****

The drive home was much quieter than the one there. I put on an easy-listening channel, and Tyler rested his head on the passenger window, staring out. I knew not to bother him. I would leave him alone with his thoughts.

When we got home, Tyler decided to take a nap. He said he was tired, and I guess he could've been from all the swimming. I suspected he also wanted to be by himself so he could talk to Justin.

The following day, after I'd clocked out from work, I noticed I had a voicemail. It was Sabrina. She hoped Tyler didn't leave her house upset? She was worried he may have had a bad time. She was over-thinking the whole thing.

I decided to call her. She picked up after a few rings.

"Hello?"

"Sabrina?" I asked.

"Amy. Hi. I'm glad you called. I've been worried about what I said to your son. I hope I didn't ruin his day?"

"He's fine," I assured her. "Honestly, you don't have to stress out. He had a blast. He's dealing with loss just like you did, day by day."

"I guess," she said. I could tell I wasn't convincing her.

"We had a great time. Real life comes up, that's all. Don't worry about it. He's fine."

"If you say so," she replied.

There was a long pause, and she said, "Hey, my grandmother sent me some bottles of wine from France. I have to go over new designs this week, for the next collection. How about you come over for a wine tasting and give me your opinion on the clothing?"

I didn't have any plans, so I accepted. "I could taste some wine with you, but I'm not sure if I can be helpful on spotting the best fashions."

Sabrina laughed. "Is it possible for you to come over one day this week?"

Weeknights were tough, especially with her living so far away. "I guess I could come on Friday," I replied. That way, if I had a headache, I could sleep in on Saturday.

"Sounds good," she said. "See you then."

The rest of the week flew by. Thankfully, Mom offered to babysit Tyler while I went to Sabrina's Friday night.

"What are you guys gonna do? Can I come?" Tyler asked.

I frowned. "No, honey," I said. "This time is for grown-ups. She's going to have me look over some project she brought from work. It's something you wouldn't be interested in."

"Oh," Tyler said. "Grandma and I are going to watch a movie anyway." Once he realized we wouldn't be swimming or doing something fun, he didn't seem to feel left out.

I leaned down and kissed the top of his head. "You two have fun then. I won't be gone long."

Mom waved me off, reassuring me babysitting wasn't a problem. They would do what we always did that night, except without me.

Driving to Sabrina's house usually felt relaxing. This time, after working a full day, it drained me. I arrived yawning and continued to do so as I walked toward her front door. I hoped I could stay awake for the short time I'd be there.

Sabrina answered and looked tired too. While I followed her to the living room, I noticed an open bottle of white wine sitting on a table, half empty.

"I've opened a bottle of Chenin Blanc, from the Loire Valley. Would you like a glass?"

"Sure," I said, peeking at the nearby appetizers she'd set out: cheeses, crackers, and fruit.

I took a small plate and filled it with a variety of everything before she handed me a drink.

I held it up and toasted. "To Grandma."

Sabrina smiled, her eyes already a little glassy. "Merci, Grand-Mère," she replied.

I took a sip. It was fruity and smooth. I didn't have

much experience in the wine department, but my taste buds told me this one was a winner. "It's so good," I said, and bit into a cracker with cheese.

"I know," she replied. "I'm afraid I started without you, about an hour ago." She winked at me and flashed a smile.

"Nothing wrong with that. It's not like you have to drive anywhere, and I'm sure you don't do it all the time."

A look of melancholy came over her, and she whispered under her breath, "I never do it."

Who was I to judge? Maybe she decided to let her hair down, to have some fun.

Sabrina munched on a few snacks, finished her drink, and poured herself another. Then she headed across the room and grabbed a big book. She walked back toward me and set the album on a nearby table. She pulled a chair up so I could take a seat. "Go ahead and look through the photos," she said. "Tell me what you like and what you don't like."

I glanced up at her, unsure. What if I said something was ugly and it hurt her feelings? What if I just had bad taste?

Sabrina noticed my hesitation. "Don't worry. You don't have to give details," she assured me. "Just see it and respond."

She made it seem so simple.

I sat down and took another sip of wine, and then I opened the book. The first photo was of a casual dress with a bold, geometric print. "I like this," I said.

Sabrina took another long swig of her drink. After I'd gone through a few more pages, she stopped me. "Hold on," she said. "This is good. We are getting somewhere. But first I need to open another bottle of wine."

I nodded as she walked out of the room. I helped myself to another serving of food and continued sipping my drink. I wondered why Sabrina was drinking so much. She had said it was out of character for her.

She returned with another opened bottle of wine. After pouring herself a glass, she was getting ready to add some to mine.

"No, thanks," I said, stopping her. "I've got to drive back later."

Sabrina set the bottle down. "Of course, I almost forgot."

She was halfway to drunk by now. I found it amusing.

Sabrina waved a hand, motioning for me to look at more of the collection photos. I felt bad when I came upon an outfit I didn't care for. "Don't like," I announced.

She grabbed a red sticky note and stuck it to the top of the page, and said, "Please go on."

I continued making my way through the photos, commenting as I went along. In the background, I heard her pour another glass. Then another.

A little while later, as I approached the end of the book, I heard sniffles. I looked up at Sabrina, and she was crying.

"Is everything all right?" I asked.

Sabrina wiped tears from her cheeks with the back of her hand, and said, "Sure… Everything is as it should be."

I had no idea what she meant by that. I stood there and watched as she continued crying, ruining her makeup. I handed her my cocktail napkin, and she used it to wipe away some of the smudged mess.

"Is there something wrong?" I asked. "I mean, if you

want to talk, I'm here for you."

Sabrina began sobbing harder now. "I know you are," she said.

I'd never seen her act like this, so I just stood there, staring, while she cried like a baby.

Finally, she calmed down a little and began to speak. With a raspy voice she mumbled, "I've been reading that email you sent me over and over. The one where you told me I was the best friend you ever had and thanked me for all my help."

Her reaction didn't make sense. "It was a compliment. Nothing to get upset over," I assured her.

Sabrina shot me an odd look, one that didn't seem to match the conversation we were having.

"It's just," she went on, between sniffles, "I want more than anything for that to be true. I want to be that person."

Of course she was that person. This was probably just the alcohol speaking. "Come on now," I told her. "You know it's true. Please just accept my gratitude and be happy about it. Don't cry."

She paused, wiped her face again, and looked up at me. "No. It's not true," she said. "I'm not the person you think I am."

As my eyes locked with hers, an old, familiar ping gripped my gut.

Sabrina must have sensed that I understood. She surely noticed the slight flicker of panic on my face, because once again she began to cry. I wanted more than anything to sit down, but I couldn't; I was rooted in place by fear.

Sabrina set her wine glass on the table. She managed to clear her throat and calm down enough to continue.

"You see… we are good friends… now."

She paused, and it felt like an eternity before she continued, "But it wasn't always this way," she said.

I stood still, listening.

"When Justin worked here, you didn't exist to me."

I didn't like where she was going with this.

"I'm a woman with money and power. Most anything I want, I can usually have. And I know how to get what I want."

My body heat rose as Sabrina spoke. My insides began to quiver. Still, I said nothing.

"But," she said, and this was followed by a long pause, "the one thing I wanted most—"

"Justin," I said.

"Yes," she agreed, and lowered her eyes.

A wave of disappointment hit me like a tsunami. I was heartbroken in a way I'd never quite experienced before. Then I cursed myself for being so naïve, for trusting her so quickly.

"Why are you telling me this? Why now?" I asked.

Sabrina looked up at me, and with a soft, sincere voice said, "Because you *are* real to me now. You're not someone who is in the way of what I want." She paused, looked me right in the eyes. "You're my friend."

The emotion that coursed through me caused tears to spill down my face. I was shaken on so many levels, I wasn't sure how to react. Then, the heat that had begun rising earlier turned into rage. It filled every cell of my being.

Sabrina took a step toward me.

"Don't touch me," I said, throwing my hands in the air and stepping back.

Sabrina looked confused. In her drunken stupor this

must've seemed like a good idea. "I'm only telling you this because I am so sorry. I want to ask for your forgiveness. I want to be the friend you think I am."

I stood there, shaking, with tears streaming down my face. What could I say to her now except the truth?

I exhaled deeply, and as I did, a hardened look came over my features. "There is no way in hell you could ever be that person to me. Not now. You were trying to steal my husband from me. I can't forgive that."

Sabrina let out a gasp.

She had gone and screwed it all up, beyond repair. How could she have been so stupid?

"I was hoping if I was honest with you, if I confessed, that maybe things would be better," she said in a hysterical tone.

I shook my head and laughed like a cynic. "You know what? It's obvious that you're still having a difficult time dealing with your past actions. Still, I see no reason why you should throw all this on me." Pointing at her, I added, "This was yours to deal with, on your own. You could've suffered in silence and let it eat at you like a normal person, or you could've told it to a priest, or whatever people of your faith do. But laying this on me now, after I thought we were friends, after I even brought my son here… it's too much."

I could see she realized this wasn't going how she thought it would. Yes, she was drunk. People said stupid things when they were drunk.

I, on the other hand, wasn't wasted. I wasn't even buzzed. I was sober and unbelievably pissed.

"I'm going to ask you one final time," I said with unusual calm. "Did anything happen between you and Justin?"

"No," she responded quietly.

Sabrina was broken, but I didn't pity her. Instead, I gave her a look that was filled with disgust.

"Please," she said. "Please say something. You're just standing there looking at me like you despise me."

I shook my head no. "I don't despise you," I said. "It's not worth the effort." I wanted nothing more to do with her, but this was my opportunity to find out the truth. The whole truth. "How about your cousin?" I asked. "Doctor Friedman?"

Sabrina looked down again. No doubt she realized she'd made a major mistake. Finally, she cleared her throat and said, "I asked my cousin to help. He said he'd come down and assist me, as a favor, since he knew how important Justin was to me."

Sabrina shifted from one foot to the other before continuing. "But I wouldn't let him. I paid him—even though I told you I didn't because I knew it would make you uncomfortable—I paid him his going rate. And I paid for his hotel stays, and all his meals." Sabrina looked back into my eyes now as she spoke. "I would've given him every last cent I had if it could've helped."

I would've given anything in the world if it could've saved him, too. But that was my line! My truth! She had no right talking that way. Knowing the dark truth behind the doctor's help made me sick.

"I guess money can't buy you everything," I said. "Not even more time to try and steal another woman's husband."

Sabrina's face crumpled, and she began sobbing heavily. "I'm so sorry Amy," she cried. "I was selfish. I never thought of you. You were never real to me."

I'd had enough of this insanity. Truly enough.

"You want to know what's real?" I asked.

Sabrina looked back at me, eager and afraid.

"You *were* my friend. But now, after finding out all this, I hope to never lay eyes on you again!"

With that said, I pushed the book aside and grabbed my purse. I spun on my heel and stomped out of the room. Sabrina didn't say another word. I heard her collapse into a stuffed leather chair and start sobbing again.

As I left the house, I slammed the front door, rattling the windows before driving off into the night.

Chapter 17

When I got home and walked in the door, I felt safety and comfort return. This is my family. People I know and can trust. I'd never been happier to see them. At the same time, I didn't know what to say about what just happened.

Maybe it was nearing time for me to tell the whole truth, too.

"Honey, are you okay? You seem upset?" my mom asked.

"That's an understatement," I said, then stormed past her and into the kitchen.

I was starving, and as I rummaged through the leftovers, Tyler approached me. "How was your night with your friend?" he asked, looking innocent and adorable.

His face was like that of an angel. I didn't know how to respond.

"We had a fight," I said, simplifying the truth. "And we're not friends anymore."

Tyler stared back at me, surprised. In his short life, he'd never experienced his mom in a fight with anyone. I doubted he'd ever seen me this angry before, either.

"I'm sorry," he said, trying to comfort me. "Do you want to come with us? Grandma and I were going to watch the rest of the movie?"

Watching television was the last thing I wanted to do. What I wanted was to punch something—anything—repeatedly. But how could I say no?

"Sure, honey," I replied. "Let me heat up some food and I'll be right in."

He walked out of the room and sat on the sofa. Maybe to a kid it's that easy. If you're not having fun, go do something else. If only adult life were that simple.

I found my mom's famous spaghetti and meatballs in a plastic container. I nuked some and began attacking the noodles with my fork like a savage. The more I ate, the more relaxed I became.

Mom and Tyler were kind enough to pause whatever they were watching until I had finished. When I came in the family room, they filled me in on the story before pressing play. For Tyler's sake, I feigned interest. But I couldn't pay attention to the film. All I kept thinking about was Sabrina, and how angry and disappointed she had made me.

When the movie ended, I kissed Tyler goodnight. Mom looked my way to see if I wanted to talk.

I put my arms up and stretched. "Goodnight, Mom. I'm exhausted."

She had a concerned look on her face. "Goodnight," was all she said back.

Once I got into my room and changed into pajamas, I realized I couldn't sleep. I decided to go wash my face and brush my teeth. When I finished with that, I found I was still wide awake, so I got back up and flossed, then did an exfoliating facial treatment followed by a deep moisturizer.

I still wasn't tired. I hated to run the water so late, but I figured a hot bath with aromatherapy salts might help.

Once the tub was filled, I lowered the lights and sank in. Then I reached for the pumice stone and proceeded to scrub the heels of my feet, removing all the dry, flaked skin, and some healthy layers while I was at it. I shaved my legs. Then, after I finished all those tasks, I moisturized and dressed again in my pajamas.

And still I couldn't sleep.

With nothing left to wash, I decided to head into the family room and read my novel. That lasted for about five minutes. I gave up when I found myself reading the same paragraph over and over. I cast the book aside and exhaled loudly. Across the room I noticed the yoga blocks lying near the DVD. I went over and picked up the case and read the cover for the first time. *PM Yoga*, it said. The older woman shown was named Patricia Walden. She was older than me. She had a kind face. I liked her. And I liked exercising with her.

She could be my friend, I thought.

I turned on the TV and muted the volume. I'd done this routine so many times I didn't need to hear her voice. After twenty-five minutes I began to feel relaxed. I could always count on virtual pal, Patricia.

The next morning, I slept in late again. This was becoming a familiar trend. Tyler woke me up with the news that breakfast was ready. After eating, he asked me a favor. "Hey, Mom. Can I go with Sam and his older brother to watch a parkour event?"

"Sure," I replied. "I can take you. No problem."

Mom asked to join us, and after we dropped him off, she offered to take me out to lunch.

The hostess put us in a booth, far away from a group of screaming kids who were having a birthday party.

Mom and I sat down. After ordering our food, and

without her prompting, I decided to tell her everything about Sabrina. The whole story.

I told her about the daffodils and the multiple visits to the cemetery to try and find her. I laughed a nervous laugh when I talked about how I'd played private detective that day, and how it had paid off since I was able to finally confront her. I told her about our unusual friendship, and what had occurred on our visits. I told her about meeting Dr. Friedman at the party, and even fessed up about being introduced to Sabrina's friend, Miguel. Then I told her about the fight, and how everything had ended.

"That brings us to now," I said, taking a sip of my Coke.

A moment later, the server arrived with our food. Mom was sitting across from me with visible shock on her face. It was a lot to take in all at once.

I let her absorb what I'd said while I took a bite of my salad.

"I'm not sure what to say," she finally said. "That's an incredible story. I'm surprised you were able to keep it from me for so long. And maybe a little sad, too."

"You know Mom, I didn't want to keep it from you. But it was complicated, and I didn't know how it would turn out. Also, I didn't want your opinion of Justin to change."

We made eye contact and she nodded. She understood what I meant, but we weren't going to go there. In all our years together, we never did.

"Later on, I figured it didn't matter how Sabrina and I had met. We had become friends. Life had brought me something nice. But now, now that I've discovered the truth, I had to share it with you."

Mom took a bite of her sandwich. She was my real best friend. Always had been.

"You know," she began, once she'd finished chewing, "Justin was a wonderful man. He truly was. But for a person to become so obsessed like that… it's just not healthy, you know."

I nodded and took another bite of my salad.

"I'm really sorry this happened to you," she continued. "But I'm glad you told me. I could tell how upset you were last night. But boy, never in a million years would I have guessed the reason."

I cracked a smile. I was glad she wasn't angry with me.

Mom grabbed a menu. "I'm stuffed," she said. "But I think there may be room to split dessert. They have key lime pie. Do you want some?"

"Sure."

The waitress came and took our order. Soon we both dug our forks into the delicious green concoction, and the conversation led to other things like my mom's book club and what was going on with her lady friend. It was a nice change of pace.

Before we knew it, it was time to pick up Tyler. Mom paid the bill. I thanked her for treating me, and we left for Sam's house.

On the way there, Mom said, "It's too bad about that Miguel fellow. He didn't do anything wrong."

I was wondering when she'd get around to mentioning him.

"I know he didn't," I said. "It doesn't matter, though. I had no plans to call him anyway."

She didn't press the issue further. It was just like her to bring it up, though. She couldn't help herself. I reached over and turned on the radio, and we drove the rest of the way listening to the oldies channel.

When we got to Sam's, I didn't see the minivan. Tyler and the others weren't back yet. Mom and I reclined in our seats and closed our eyes. I was in a food coma. Mom must've been too, because she quickly fell asleep.

I didn't hear the Caravan pull in, but I woke up when Tyler knocked on the driver's side window. Right away, I noticed scrapes grazed his left elbow.

I opened the car door. "What happened?"

"Ah, not much. Just some road rash from a move that went wrong."

That's exactly how Justin spoke when he'd fall off his skateboard back in the day.

Tyler climbed into the back seat. "Well, when we get home I'll clean it and put a bandage on it," I said.

He shrugged. He didn't care either way. He was having a good time. No doubt the minor injuries only added to his "cool" status.

*****

Saturday night, I sat down with the budget. The gym membership was expiring, and after crunching a list of numbers, I discovered we could indeed afford a dog. It was time.

I got up and walked down the hall to Tyler's room, then knocked.

"Come in," he said.

He was on the floor, organizing his art supplies.

"It's time," I stated.

"Time for what?" he asked, looking confused.

"Time to get a dog."

Tyler shot to his feet. "Awesome! Can we go tomorrow?"

"I don't see why not."

"I'm going to tell Grandma," he said, then pushed past me.

The rest of the evening the three of us searched the Petfinder website. We were so excited sitting there, browsing for pooches. I let Tyler take the lead, picking his favorites, while I took notes. Mom sat on his other side, adding her opinion.

Tyler was all over the board with breed choice. It wasn't like he was fond of one over the other. He liked them all. The list I was creating, with the dog's name and locations, was growing way too long.

I stopped him. "Honey, here's what we've got so far." I showed him the notepad. "Maybe we should take another look and scratch a few off? Narrow the list a bit?"

Tyler reviewed the choices. He was having a hard time eliminating any of them.

Sensing we were getting nowhere, Mom said, "Maybe we should go there in person. Have a look at them and see what happens. Find out which one you like best. Or maybe which one likes you best!"

"Good idea," Tyler agreed.

It was decided. Afterward, we each went our separate ways. I lay in my bed, thinking about our family, and how we were finally getting a pet. We would have had one years ago, but for Justin's allergies. Then I thought of Sabrina. And I wondered how she'd fill her Sunday.

She could go to hell. I punched my pillow to fluff it and reached over and turned off the light.

*****

Sunday morning, the house buzzed with energy. It felt like Christmas. We ate our breakfasts, then scurried around, washing dishes and showering. We climbed into the car, and after arriving at our destination, sprung from our seats like Jack in the Box toys.

The shelter had big dogs, small dogs, even puppies. I walked the rows, staring at each prisoner. I soon realized if I looked too long at any one of them, it would feel like tiny arrows were piercing my heart. I loved them all, but I wanted Tyler to choose. This was for him.

Tyler walked slowly, up and down the aisles several times, stopping once and a while to make baby talk with a few of the dogs. I was surprised he didn't want one of the puppies, but I kept my mouth shut.

"I like him," Tyler said, pointing to a scruffy, caramel-colored terrier mix. "Can I see him out of the cage?"

"Let me go and get someone to let him out," I said.

Mom had already found someone and they were on their way over. "Okay," the man said. "This is Moose. Let me tell you a little about him."

The three of us stopped and gave him our undivided attention.

"Moose was found in his family's backyard after their house had gone into foreclosure."

Mom and I looked at each other. We both knew where this story was going.

The man continued, "The neighbors heard him barking and didn't know who he belonged to since the people had already moved away. They found him with empty food dishes, his hair matted and dirty, lying next to one of his toys." The shelter attendant pointed at the dog toy. A well-worn braided green and white rope.

"So we picked him up and had him checked out. He's in good health. He was just hungry and in need of a bath. Now he's ready for his forever home."

I looked at Moose. His eyes were a warm, chocolate brown. His hair was caramel in some spots, beige in others. Despite all he'd been through, he seemed upbeat, panting and wagging his tail.

"I'd like to play with him," Tyler told the man.

The attendant leaned over and opened the cage. Moose bounded out, full of energy. He jumped up and began licking Tyler's face.

Tyler laughed, then reached in and grabbed his rope toy and threw it. The dog ran down the slippery tile floor to catch it. When he returned, he wanted to play tug of war.

Tyler petted the top of his scruffy head. "I think he likes me."

"He definitely does," Mom agreed.

"Is he the one you want?" I asked.

Tyler and the terrier with a sorrowful past stared at each other, like they were Zen masters. Then, the funniest thing happened. Moose seemed to smile.

"Yes," Tyler replied.

With that decided, Mom and I got up to sign the paperwork. Tyler continued to throw the rope for Moose, and the dog chased after it each time. Of course, we weren't prepared with pet supplies, so we loaded Moose into the car with us and went back home, and then I left to run to the store and get the items the shelter attendant said we'd need.

When I got back, Tyler and my mom were in the yard playing with the dog. It was one of those moments I wanted to remember, so I stopped to watch before joining them. The sun shone partially through the trees, illuminating them as they ran in and out of bright patches of light. Moose's bark combined with their laughter, and I stood there absorbing it all. I wished Justin could've seen it.

I opened the door to join them and noticed the air had grown a little colder. Autumn was coming, and I was grateful. It was my favorite season.

I stepped into the commotion. Moose ran from Tyler to my mom to me, and back to Tyler again. His energy was endless. It was hard to believe someone had left him behind. I decided to stop thinking of it though and enjoy the fact that he was with us now, forever.

The rest of the evening we did everything we could to make our new family member comfortable. We set up his food and water area. We attached his nametag to his collar, and left his leash lying by the front door. His bed was placed on the floor next to Tyler's. The air was filled with the word *Moose,* over and over again.

The three of us came up with a plan for his bathroom needs. Mom would let him out in the morning and during the day. She'd be in charge of picking up and cleaning out back. Tyler would walk Moose after school, giving him exercise and fresh air. It would be their special time. Then I'd walk him once more after dinner, for his evening bathroom break.

With the fine details figured out, everyone kicked back on the sofa. We stared at Moose. He lay resting on the floor in the center of the room, sleeping. He was worn out.

"I love him," Tyler said, wearing a smile that lit up his whole face.

"Me, too, honey." I looked over at Mom to see what she had to add, but she'd fallen asleep.

"Do you think he misses the other people? The family that left him behind?" he asked.

"I'm sure he does. But... they're gone now, and he has us. We're going to take good care of him."

"Yeah," Tyler agreed.

The night lingered and we sat and watched Moose sleep. It was like we were hooked on some new reality show. Everything he did fascinated us. We couldn't get enough. It was hard to believe we'd finally done it.

Monday morning, my mind wandered to Sabrina and how pissed off she'd made me, but then Moose came into my room and poked his head under the blankets.

"Hey, boy," I said. "Come here."

I rubbed the top of his head, and he jumped up onto the bed. He rolled over on his back and exposed his tummy for rubs.

"You're so sweet," I said in a cooing tone. "Yes, you are."

Moose lay there peacefully, enjoying the attention. I could play with him all day long and not get bored. I had no desire to leave for work. But I had to make money to support the family, and he was now a part of ours, so I forced myself to get up, shower and leave. Mom and Tyler assured me they'd keep him plenty busy.

I told Barb and Fatima right away. They were excited for us about the new addition. Then I explained how he came to be at the shelter.

"That's criminal!" Barb said.

"It should be," I replied.

"Do you have a picture of him?" Fatima asked.

I didn't. But his picture was still up at the Petfinder

site. I clicked to it.

"There he is," I said, with the pride of a parent whose child has just won an award.

"He's handsome," Barb commented.

Fatima agreed.

*****

Monday night couldn't come quickly enough. When I got home, I found Tyler in his room, creating a pencil sketch of Moose.

"Hey, honey. How's our boy?"

Tyler sat up. "Oh, he's good. I walked him right after school, and I picked up his poop with the bag—gross!" he exclaimed, while making a sickened face.

"Well, you know that's part of it." The second I said the words, I realized I'd have my chance to experience the same thing after dinner.

Throughout our meal, I noticed something different in our house. There was a feeling of fullness. It was like we had found something we didn't know we'd been missing. And now that we had it, things were just right. There was balance.

Tyler offered to do the dishes with Mom so I could walk Moose. I changed into gym shoes and attached the leash to Moose's collar.

"Don't forget this," Tyler said, while handing me a plastic bag.

I took it from him and smirked. This wouldn't bother me. I had changed diapers and raised him, after all.

It was chillier outside than it looked. I grabbed a light jacket and headed down the street, Moose gently pulling me. He didn't pull on the leash like I'd expected. He was very well-behaved. Once he got my pace, we moved forward together, in sync.

I made it to the end of the block and wondered how he would do with jogging. I looked down at Moose. He looked back at me, his expression almost saying "just do it!" So I stepped things up, and he kept even stride. As I jogged, I periodically checked on him to see if he was okay. He was trotting with plenty of energy. What the heck, I thought. I'm going to run. I glanced at Moose and imagined him giving me the paws up to go for it.

I started running at full speed. I hadn't done that in years. If I hadn't been swimming and working out with my family, I wouldn't be able to run at all. It felt good, though, almost like I was moving in slow motion. I peeked at Moose. He ran with the style and grace of a winning horse.

Within ten minutes, my heart was pounding hard in my chest. I'd pushed it too far. I slowed down and began walking, and as we turned the corner, Moose paused and found a place to do his business.

When we got back home and I took off Moose's leash, he ran straight to Tyler's room. I went to the garbage and threw away the bag of poop, washed my hands, and collapsed on the sofa. I was tired, and I was elated. I couldn't wait to do it again tomorrow.

After I cleaned up in the bathroom, I noticed I'd gotten a voicemail. I was hesitant to check it. I didn't want Sabrina to ruin my evening. I finally gave in. It was Josephine. She had to cancel this week's lesson because she had the flu.

The rest of the week, I was in great spirits. Moose had that effect on people. He even seemed curious about Tyler's parkour routine. So curious, in fact, that we had to lock Moose indoors otherwise Tyler couldn't practice. Moose kept finding his way under Tyler's feet.

I sat on the sofa drinking a cup of green tea. I rubbed Moose's head and hoped he was just as happy to be here as we were to have him. Did he miss his old family?

It didn't matter now, I thought. He was one of us.

Chapter 18

I read somewhere that petting a cat can lower your blood pressure. I wasn't sure what dogs could do. All I knew was what Moose had accomplished and in such a short time.

Over the course of a few weeks, my life had gone through a major transformation. No area was left untouched. My workdays went smooth. Everything just flowed. My physical health improved. I was relaxed, yet my muscles felt toned. The poor-postured, flabby woman I was before was no longer. Maybe Moose didn't do all that. Maybe it was a cumulative process, and I just hadn't paid close enough attention. But I was happy to give him credit.

Each night, we ran together amidst the autumn landscape. As my feet hit the pavement and I heard his paws shuffle through the golden, crunchy leaves, I felt my heart grow lighter.

I was set free.

I didn't even know I was a prisoner until I'd escaped. I was full of layer upon layer of anger for Sabrina. Because of what she did, and because of what she would've done if she had had the chance. I hated her for all those reasons. But what hurt most was the deception of our friendship. If she felt something for Justin years ago, so be it, but she shouldn't have tried to befriend me.

Each night, as Moose and I ran, I realized I didn't

need to understand the "why" of her choices. It no longer mattered. All the Irish anger I'd built up on the subject simply vanished.

A few more weeks passed peacefully. Sabrina didn't call or email me. She respected my request and stayed away. Josephine got over her cold, and Tyler and I brought her pictures of Moose. There was a lot of play time around the house. Mom got an Elvis cookbook from the library, and we made fried peanut butter banana sandwiches. We rented a slew of great movies. Even my boss, Dave, seemed happier. No doubt he'd solved his family problems, whatever they were.

On Halloween, Mom surprised us by buying Moose a pumpkin costume. Tyler dressed up as Charlie Brown, and I stayed in jeans and a sweater. The weather was cool but not rainy, which was great for trick-or-treating.

As we walked the neighborhood together, Tyler asked me a question. "Hey, Mom. Do you think you're ever going to make up with your friend?"

I couldn't see my son's face because it was covered by his mask. I was surprised because this was the first time he'd mentioned her in weeks. The answer was easy. I would never see Sabrina again. We weren't kids who'd had a minor disagreement that could be smoothed over.

"I don't think so, T.," I said.

"Whenever I've gotten into fights with someone, you've always told me to say I'm sorry," Tyler blurted out.

I hated when children were wise enough to use your own words against you. But surely this wasn't that kind of situation.

"You know, honey, it's not that kind of fight. It's a complicated grown-up thing. And in this case, it's not me who needs to say sorry."

Tyler paused, then reached for a piece of candy and pulled his mask off to eat it. "Want one?" he asked.

"Sure."

Tyler handed me a mini Snickers. "Well," he sighed, while chewing his chocolate bar, "Maybe she should apologize."

Tyler threw the candy wrapper into his bucket and put his Charlie Brown mask back on. How could I tell him that she already had? He might be an old soul, but he could never understand the complexities of the situation. He was too young.

"You know what?" I said. "It doesn't really matter to me anymore. Maybe sometimes you're only meant to know someone for a short time."

"I guess," he agreed.

We noticed a large group of kids congregating in front of a particular house. "They must have the good candy," Tyler exclaimed. "Sour Patch Kids, WarHeads… let's go there next."

We crossed over and rang the doorbell. The woman filled his pail with Lemonheads and Sour Patch Kids. She had the mother lode of kid candy. I didn't even ask how he knew that. I just snagged a box of his Lemonheads and began to eat them.

In a short time, it was getting dark. We'd amassed an array of treats to last us a whole week. Moose had even scored himself a biscuit. The rest of the night, Mom, Tyler, and I overindulged in one piece of candy after another. We knew we'd get sick to our stomachs later, but it was tradition.

The next morning, I woke up to cold, rainy, gray. The beautiful Indian summer was over. We'd been lucky on Halloween. It was cool and crisp, but the kids didn't have to layer heavy coats over their costumes.

I didn't mind the dreariness because it was Saturday. And it was good sleeping weather. All I had planned was to run errands, do some grocery shopping, and go with Tyler to see an indoor parkour event.

I got to sleep in, but this time no one came pounding on my door saying breakfast was ready. Moose didn't even bother me. He must've been zonked out somewhere cozy.

Justin liked to sleep in late. During the work week, he always had to get up incredibly early. So he savored sleep on his days off. I thought about how we used to snuggle those lazy mornings. We'd eat some toast and juice, and then collapse right back in bed. I still missed him all the time, but strangely, it didn't hurt as badly. I worried, wondering if I was forgetting him.

I could never do that. I wasn't sure what was happening, but my gut feeling was that I would be okay.

Everyone eventually rose and found their way to the kitchen. After eating, Tyler and Mom stayed behind while I ran to the grocery store and bank. While waiting in line to speak to a teller, I felt my phone vibrate.

When I hopped in the car I checked to see if it was a message from home. Caller ID showed a local number I didn't recognize, so I didn't bother to check voicemail. I drove back home, put the groceries away, and played tug of war for a while with Moose.

I couldn't believe how sleepy I felt. I thought it best to take a nap before getting cleaned up to leave with Tyler for the parkour event, so I kicked off my shoes and lay down. The bed felt so comfy and inviting; I could've slept in it all day. But then I remembered the voicemail. I couldn't rest until I got up and checked it.

I keyed in the password and listened. "Hello, Ms. White. This is Henry, Sabrina Bergman's assistant. I'm calling you from Lake Forest Hospital. Ms. Bergman has been in an automobile accident. She's in critical condition and is asking to see you."

I hit save and replayed the message again. I wasn't sure what to think or feel. I was too shocked. I hung up the phone and flew through the kitchen to the family room.

I passed my mom, who was looking for a snack in the refrigerator. "Hey. What's the hurry?" she asked, as she followed me into the family room.

I didn't answer her. I was too busy logging onto the Internet. I cut and pasted the address of the hospital into the destination box and hit "Get Directions." Then I paused to look up at my mom. "Sabrina has been in an accident. She's in the hospital in critical condition."

"Oh, my God!" she said, covering her mouth with her hand.

After the directions popped up, I hit print. Then I remembered Tyler's parkour event. "Tyler is going to be so disappointed. I can't go with him tonight."

"Don't worry," Mom said. "I can take him. You just go. I'll handle things here."

I hugged my mom, and rushed to the closet to grab a jacket. I was out the door so fast I'd forgotten to grab an umbrella so I pulled my jacket over my head as I ran to the car. Once I started it and the defroster began working, I realized I'd better take a few deep breaths and calm down. I looked at the directions and noticed they'd gotten hit with a few raindrops but were still legible. The hospital wasn't too far from Sabrina's house.

On the way there, I kept the radio off and my hands firmly on the wheel, paying extra attention to the road. I played with the windshield wiper levels until I decided to just leave them on high speed. I stayed focused. My mind didn't wander.

But the closer I got to my destination, the more a sense of dread grew. It spread from a place deep within my abdomen and eventually enveloped me, like an old, heavy blanket. I didn't like hospitals. Never had. And the last time I was at one was when Justin died. I shook my head. I couldn't believe this was happening.

I saw the Lake Forest Hospital sign and turned into the parking lot, then found the visitor section and picked a space. I spotted my umbrella on the floor in the passenger side and leaned over to grab it. On my way back up, I caught a glimpse of myself in the rearview mirror. I looked like hell. For once I didn't care. There wasn't time for such nonsense.

The rain had started to come down harder, in big, fat drops that pelted me in the face even though I held protection over my head. I hurried through the onslaught and into the main entrance.

Even though I was in a hurry, I couldn't help but notice how lavish the place looked. The walls had beautiful wood paneling and wing back chairs near a crackling fireplace. Apparently the wealthy felt more comfortable surrounded by style and class even when they were ill.

The nurse at the front desk told me Sabrina's location, and as I headed there, the all too familiar smell hit my nostrils. The scent of sickness and surgery and medication. No amount of money could take that away.

My muscles tensed.

My pace slowed. I didn't want to go. I stopped in the middle of the hallway and recalled the last words I'd said to her. I had meant what I told her. My feelings on that hadn't changed... but the situation had.

Still, I couldn't just turn around and go back home. I needed to do this. So I began walking forward, down the outstretched corridor, to visit Sabrina.

I made it to her room and peeked in. She was asleep. I tip-toed in slowly, and as I got closer, I began to see how drastic the situation really was.

My once beautiful friend was covered in horrific purplish bruises. Her head was heavily bandaged. The elegant woman I once knew was reduced to a beaten, crumpled heap.

I broke down and cried. The sound disturbed her.

"You came," Sabrina whispered.

Her eyes were half open and looked glassy. No doubt she was on some serious pain medication. I wiped my tears away and smiled, trying to lighten the mood.

"I don't like this look on you," I joked.

Sabrina tried to form a smile, but it caused her pain and she closed her eyes instead. I stood beside her saying nothing. I didn't know what else to do.

"I went to the store for chocolate," she finally said, struggling to get the words out.

I didn't think she should be talking, but she continued. "I didn't want to bother Henry. I wanted to get it myself. I never saw it hit me. I just felt it."

I couldn't hold back the tears so I let them flow freely. I wiped them from my face with my left hand, and took my dry, right hand and reached out to hold hers.

Sabrina closed her eyes and kept them shut a few more minutes. I stood where I was, hoping I could provide some small level of comfort. I'd changed so much since our argument six weeks ago. Most of my anger was gone, but I still had no intention of making up, as my son had suggested. She had hurt me deeply. But none of that mattered now. Seeing her this way, in such a terrible position broke my heart. It changed everything.

Sabrina struggled to re-open her eyes. "You're tired," I said. "Do you want me to go?"

"No," she managed to whisper, and then cleared her throat to speak. "The first time you came to my house…" she said, and began coughing.

I looked around the room and found a jug of water. I poured some into a glass and helped her take a sip.

Sabrina settled down and cleared her throat. "I wanted you to come back again, to get to know you for myself. I was curious."

Sabrina looked up at me now. "You had everything I had ever wanted," she said, her voice cracking. "I wanted to know what you had that I didn't have."

I didn't have anything she didn't have. In fact, I had less than half of what she had. Sabrina was glamorous, wealthy, successful. She had travelled the world and had seen and done things most people only hope to see and do. And her house… it was every woman's dream home. How could she think that? How could she think I had anything she didn't?

"I don't know what you mean," I responded. "You have everything."

Sabrina closed her eyes and shook her head. "Everything I have is nothing without someone to share it with."

I wanted to tell her that there were plenty of someones out there, and that she would've found that person if only she had stopped obsessing over a man who wasn't available. I wanted to tell her the truth, but now was not the time or the place. Now was the time to listen.

"Through the years," Sabrina said, re-opening her eyes. I was so jealous. I would've given anything to switch places with you. And I did everything in my power to tempt him."

I stared down at my bruised friend and was sad. There was no reason for her to be jealous of *me*. There was no reason for her to have wasted so many years. She had everything to offer, the whole package. I didn't have a response.

"I'm not proud of that," she said, her eyes filling with tears. "Like I told you, you were never real to me. I just wanted him for myself."

I thanked God Justin had never betrayed me. Then I prayed to God to help Sabrina, make her well and send her a mate to share her life with.

"I'm sorry I hurt you," Sabrina said, interrupting my thought. "Amy, you are *very* real to me. The best friend I could ever have."

She began coughing again, and I rushed to refill her glass of water. I didn't speak the words "I accept your apology." But I did feel them.

In the end, maybe because of my walks with Moose, I realized none if it really mattered. I had had a good life with Justin. And that was in the past. Sabrina had wasted precious time wanting him, but that was her life, her choice. I had decided to forgive her.

Visiting hours were coming to an end. I wondered if we'd really see each other again after she recovered. Would we have a friendship like before? I hoped we would, but on some inner level I suspected we wouldn't. Something had changed. It was like we didn't need each other anymore.

I had enjoyed spending time talking with her, hearing new stories about Justin, learning things I'd never known. And she had satisfied her curiosity by meeting me. We'd gotten to know each other. She had even met my son.

It seemed there was nothing left for us to do but move on.

This truth depressed me. Yet there it was. I couldn't deny it. "One more thing before you go," Sabrina said.

I stared down at her, wondering what she could possibly add. She'd already said so much.

"Remember how I said nothing ever happened between me and Justin?"

"Yes," I replied.

"Well, I wasn't being entirely truthful." She didn't pause, didn't give me time to think about what that meant. "One time," she continued, while her voice cracked, "when he was in the hospital, right near the end of his life, I kissed him on the lips."

I wondered how she could've visited Justin in the hospital. I was there every moment I possibly could, and I had never seen her. Then I remembered her cousin, Dr. Friedman, and it all made sense. Of course, she could come anytime she pleased. A bonus of the arrangement.

"I was sitting next to his bed, filled with despair. I knew he wouldn't make it," Sabrina continued. "I leaned over, pressed my lips against his, and told him that I loved him."

I listened to this confession with surprising calm. There was no anger, no worry, just presence. Sabrina looked up into my eyes, waiting for a response.

"And what did he say?" I asked.

Sabrina managed a smile, perhaps grateful I could just be there for her, so she could get it out.

"He didn't say anything," she replied. "He was asleep."

I could see the scene just as Sabrina described it. It was so clear, like I was there myself. It brought me back to the time when they called me, telling me Justin had died, in the middle of the night, alone.

I knew it was coming. I did. Yet the pain was so vast it literally knocked me to my knees, like someone had swatted the back of my legs with two by fours. I tried never to relive that memory. I couldn't allow it. My mind tossed it around like a hot potato, not knowing what to do with it, before stuffing it into a far off place in my brain, never to be thought of again.

Sabrina's confession triggered the memory. And now I saw her leaning over and kissing Justin, telling him that she loved him, knowing he was going to die. It was easy to imagine the depth of her pain. Could it have been anything like mine? I didn't pretend to understand where she was coming from or how she felt. I knew one thing, though. She was a human being. She was my friend. And right now I felt overflowing levels of compassion for her. I would do anything I could to make her feel better.

Sabrina looked up at me, waiting for my response.

"He was sleeping, huh?" I asked.

She shook her head yes.

"Well, you know what I think?" I said. "I think if Justin were awake... he would've said I love you too."

The impact of the words was enormous. Her face lit up, a combination of surprise and joy, and then the tears began to flow. A smile that came from deep within her soul spread across her face, and all at once, she was beautiful again.

I reached down and held her hand, giving it a little squeeze. "Get better, okay? I'll see you next time."

I let go and waved goodbye. Sabrina didn't wave back. Instead, she continued to beam at me. Her happiness was a light that filled the lonely room.

I walked down the corridor, keeping that memory firmly held in my mind. Did Justin love her? I didn't know. But I knew Justin. He would have smiled and said it back to her. But his love for her would have been pure, platonic, something forged in friendship and nothing more. And he would have known how much it would mean to her to hear it.

As I turned the corner and left the Intensive Care Unit, I felt completely at peace. I couldn't ever remember feeling this way, and I wanted it to last forever. When I opened the door to leave the hospital, the rain was on a short break, and I was able to make it back to my car without the umbrella.

I sat in the bucket seat of my car, wondering if I'd see Sabrina again. Would there be a next time? I smirked. She was unpredictable. There was no point in trying to figure it out. I was just glad I came.

The drive home was easy, barely any traffic. Rain had that effect on people.

When I pulled into the drive, I saw Mom's car. She must've not taken Tyler to his event.

Moose greeted me at the door, followed by Mom and Tyler. They both looked very concerned.

"Is everything okay?" she asked.

I took my coat off, shook it, and hung it in the closet. "I hope so, but she looked terrible."

Tyler looked up at me. "Did you make up with your friend?"

"Yes, I did," I said. "That was your suggestion, if I'm not mistaken."

He smiled at me. Tyler might be the youngest in the house, but sometimes he was the wisest. He had a knack for simplifying everything.

"Good," he said, grabbing hold of my hand.

There were leftovers, and they'd picked up some DVDs from the library. It seemed they'd planned a nice, relaxing evening at home. I was exhausted and thankful.

*****

The next morning, I woke up feeling great. I had enjoyed a deep, restorative sleep. It was chilly, though, so I put a sweater on over my pajamas and headed to the kitchen. I started breakfast while Mom set the table and Tyler petted Moose. Then I heard my cell phone ring.

I lay the spatula down and rushed to catch it before it went into voicemail. "Hello," I answered.

"Hello," a familiar man's voice replied. "This is Henry," he said. "I'm afraid I have some terrible news. Ms. Bergman passed away last night."

"I see," I replied, choking up. "Thank you for contacting me."

"I thought you should be among the first to know," Henry said. "I will be in touch with the funeral arrangements."

The call ended. And just like that, Sabrina was gone.

I set the phone down and turned to face my family. Both of them stared at me in anticipation.

"She's gone," I said, then sat down in the kitchen chair and began sobbing. Moose came up and pushed his head under my arm, nuzzling closer to me.

Mom approached and gave me a hug. "I'm so sorry, honey," she said.

I glanced up at Tyler through glassy eyes. "Your friend is dead?" he asked.

I shook my head yes and cried harder. Tyler's face grew strained, and he ran into his room and slammed the door. Moose stayed by my side.

"Please, Mom. Go check on Tyler."

She went after him. And even though my heart was breaking, it now ached on a deeper dimension, knowing my son was hurting, too.

If only I hadn't introduced them, I thought, wishing I could re-write history. If only they hadn't met. Then he wouldn't be experiencing this pain.

Sorrow consumed me, but at the same time I realized there was no way I could protect Tyler from things like this, no more than my mom could protect me.

I reached for a tissue and blew my nose. Moose continued to try and comfort me by burrowing as close as he could to my body. I took solace in his love. I leaned down and hugged him and kissed the top of his head. Then Moose looked up at me, his chocolate brown eyes truly knowing. He began pawing at me and whining. He understood.

Within a short time, Tyler and my mom came back in the kitchen. My son's face was pink and his eyes were bloodshot. "I'm sorry about your friend," he said. I nodded and replied by giving him a bone-crushing hug.

Mom kept quiet and scurried around the kitchen. She began warming up our cold breakfast and filling our glasses with juice. We ate in silence. Afterward, she offered to clean up, so Tyler and I stumbled into the family room and found a comfortable spot on the sofa. I reached for a quilt and wrapped myself in it, and we both stared into space before falling asleep.

Chapter 19

When the alarm went off Monday morning, I cursed its existence. I didn't want to get out of bed, but I forced myself to do it anyway. Once at work, I headed to Dave's office.

"Can I come in?"

He looked up. "Sure."

Dave could tell something was wrong. I didn't want to share the whole story and decided it was better to keep things brief. "My friend passed away this weekend. The funeral will be one day this week. I'm still waiting to hear."

"Oh. I'm sorry to hear that," he said. "Just let me know which day and I'll apply one of your personal days."

"Thanks," I said, then returned to my desk.

I heard Fatima and Barb whispering behind me. I thought I'd spoken quietly, but they heard everything. Luckily, they left me alone so I could get my work done.

Before lunch Fatima came up to me. "I overheard your conversation with Dave," she admitted. "I'm sorry about your friend."

"Thanks," I replied.

I didn't want to talk about it. Sharing with my mom was one thing, but my colleagues and I weren't on the same level. Still, I appreciated their condolences.

Later in the day, Barb reached out and rubbed my shoulder. "You gonna be okay?" she asked.

I sighed, letting go just a little. "Yeah. It's just hard… losing people."

"I know," she replied, with her sweet, gnome-like smile.

The office remained quiet for the rest of the day. Not even the radio was turned on.

At five, I punched out and got into my car to head home. I noticed a voicemail, so I checked it. It was Henry. He said Sabrina's funeral would be tomorrow. So soon? I thought. Then I remembered something I'd read once about Jewish custom, where one had to be buried right away.

It was all happening so fast. I couldn't accept it.

When I came home, I smelled pizza. My mom and Tyler had it delivered, probably in an effort to cheer me up. I smiled and thanked them, then sat down to dinner. We ate in silence again. No one really knew what to say. Afterward, I put on a heavy sweater to walk Moose.

"I can take him," Mom offered.

"Thanks," I replied. "But I want to go."

She gave me a look of understanding and stepped back. I grabbed Moose's leash and attached it to his collar and we walked out the front door.

The air was cool but crisp. I saw a neighbor I didn't recognize wave at me, and I waved back. Then I looked down at Moose. We wouldn't run today. Instead we walked down our block at a steady pace. He was right there beside me, in the middle of it all, helping me make it through.

I felt so lucky we found him when we did.

Monday night, I called Dave and left a voicemail about the funeral. I tried to sleep that night, but couldn't. I tossed and turned and eventually went to the family room to surf the web. I Googled Sabrina Bergman. A few links popped up. The ones I'd seen before. Then I noticed a link to the Chicago Tribune. It read, "Fashion World Loses Another Friend."

I continued reading.

On Sunday, November 2nd, 2012, Ms. Sabrina Bergman, head of the Bergman Collection, passed away. She was 32 years old. Sabrina was the daughter of Don and Monique Bergman, founders of the line, both of whom were sadly lost in an airplane crash in Indonesia.

Sabrina was known for her intuitive direction and keen marketing savvy, often taking the collection into bold, new areas. Most recently, Ms. Bergman was in negotiations with Target, to create a limited-edition line of clothing for them, following in the footsteps of other successful designers.

I couldn't believe it. She hadn't told me anything about that. I kept reading.

Ms. Bergman suffered critical injuries from an automobile accident and died later at Lake Forest Hospital. She will be missed.

I wiped the tears away after I finished reading. Even though I didn't know the details, I visualized the accident and then immediately blocked it from my mind. I couldn't think of her that way.

Tuesday morning, as I lay in bed, a strong feeling came over me. I didn't want to go to the funeral. The service was to start at noon. It probably wouldn't last more than a couple hours, but I didn't want to go. I rolled over and turned on the clock radio. The announcer gave the weather forecast. Cold, rainy, gray. Again.

I hid my head under the pillow. I stayed that way, under the blankets, for as long as I could, until it was time to shower and dress for the funeral. I stood in front of my closet, dumbfounded. I considered wearing something fashionable. Then I decided against it. I was just too depressed. I changed into jeans, gym shoes and a sweater. I applied minimal make up and didn't style my hair, just blew it dry.

I stepped outside and climbed into the car. Then I checked the printed driving directions. It was a clear, direct route. I turned on the radio as I drove, then turned it back off. I couldn't handle any sound.

I made a wrong turn along the way, and found myself heading away from my destination. Instead, I was heading almost directly toward the Chicago Botanic Garden. I kept driving.

When I pulled into the lot, the attendant asked for twenty dollars. In my daze, I'd forgotten it cost money to get in. Luckily I had some cash on hand. I handed it to the man who took it and smiled.

The garden was not a popular choice on a dreary weekday in November, and that was fine by me. I welcomed the solitude. I grabbed my umbrella, put on my coat and locked the car.

Once I began walking, I realized Sabrina was right. Everything looked different from the last time I was here. It even *felt* different. I followed the same path she'd taken me on before, noticing the plants and their different colors, some of them heavy with raindrops.

I saw a puddle and jumped into it, creating a splash. Self-conscious, I did a quick scan for other people, hoping I didn't upset anyone. But there was no one around. My gym shoes were soggy and muddy, and I didn't care. I just continued on the path.

When I turned the corner, I came upon the area where

Sabrina had gotten married. It didn't look very pretty today and that made me sad. I wished my friend could've lived, that she would've fallen in love again, and had children. I wondered if her ex-husband would be at the funeral. I wondered if he'd be sorry.

I meandered over to the English Garden. I visualized Sabrina and her sister as children, running and playing hide and seek together, and I managed to crack a tiny smile.

The wind picked up, as it is so famous for doing in Chicago, suggesting I finish sooner than I would've liked. I looked to the sky and saw the makings of a storm. By the looks of it, a big one. I hurried over to the Japanese Garden, Sabrina's favorite place.

I had the area all to myself. As I crossed the main bridge, I stopped to notice the dramatic change that had taken place since I was here last. No plants had been moved, and the landscape remained the same, but something was very different. I blinked, and opened my eyes wider. I took a deep breath of cold, moist air and exhaled slowly, then I realized what it was. The cool formality of the place had vanished. It felt alive and dynamic now. And as I finished crossing the bridge and entered the garden, fog hung low, creating a mystical feel.

I knew this was where I was supposed to be.

The wind blew a little harder, so I reached into my bag for a scarf. I wrapped it around my neck. Even so, I wasn't going to let nature rush me today. I wanted to take my time here, in this special place.

I found my way to the Island of Everlasting Happiness. It was difficult to see in the mist. And it seemed further away than usual, at least to a mere mortal like me. I could still make out its graceful curves and tiny green hills, concealing secrets on the other side. The Japanese called this paradise Horaijima. Could Sabrina live there now?

My intuition told me she could. She could travel anywhere she liked whenever she pleased now.

She could even be… with Justin.

The idea didn't bother me. He could use a friend.

The wind picked up again, as if trying to tell me, "Go home. You're all done here." So I moved on, taking its suggestion this time. On my way out of the garden, I saw something I hadn't noticed last time, a giant weeping willow slightly tilting toward the water. I walked over to it. A sign read: Weeping Willow Point. A large boulder sat next to the side of the tree, so I decided to rest there for just a moment.

I climbed up onto the damp rock and took a seat. It began to drizzle, so I took out my umbrella and held it over my head. I closed my eyes and listened to the rain tap the fabric, and felt it splash all around me.

This was my funeral with Sabrina.

Now, more than ever, it would be appropriate to cry… but I couldn't. No tears would fall. Then a strong gust blew, nudging me from the spot. I got up and took one last look at the island.

"Take care," I said, then hurried away.

I made it back to the main building and used the restroom. The warm dryer on my hands felt so good. Before leaving, I noticed a gift shop. I was too soggy to go in, so I just scanned the contents from outside. That's when I saw the small bonsai tree. Instinctively, I walked in, forgetting about my shoes and their messy condition. I took the plant to the register and the sales associate rung me up.

On my way out, I wondered if I should take the tree to Sabrina's grave.

I got in my car, set my purchase on the passenger seat and made a monumental decision. I wouldn't do that. I wouldn't go to Sabrina's grave, and I wouldn't go to Justin's grave anymore. That was part of the past.

I drove home and found the house still empty except for Moose. After a long, hot bath, I rearranged the top of my dresser to find space for my new bonsai tree. It looked perfect right in the center, like it was always meant to be there.

I collapsed into bed and hoped Sabrina wouldn't be upset I'd missed her funeral. As I lay there with eyes closed, I reviewed my memories of the day and decided it felt right.

I must've fallen asleep because a knock on the door woke me up. "Hey, Mom. Are you okay?"

I rubbed my eyes. "Yeah. I guess I'm alright. How about you?"

I wondered how Tyler felt about all this. Mom had talked to him when it happened, but he hadn't spoken to me about it. I worried about him.

"I'm better now," he said. "Sad still. It took me by surprise."

"Me too," I said. He came over and gave me a hug.

"Dad's the only person I know that has died. And I just met her."

"I know," I said. "Part of me is sorry I had you two meet. I don't want you to be hurt."

Tyler gave me an odd look. "There's nothing you could've done to stop what happened. Why would you want to go back and change anything?"

He was right.

"Where'd you get the tree?" he asked, looking over at the dresser.

I smiled. "I bought it. Something to remind me of my friend."

Tyler responded by giving me another hug. Then he got up and left the room. Usually I'd have suggested we talk or play a game or watch a movie. Today I just let him leave, so I could be alone and rest.

Mom woke me late in the evening. "You hungry?" she asked. "It's after eight."

"Yeah. Come to think of it. I am hungry."

I followed her to the kitchen and re-heated leftovers.

"How was the funeral?" she asked. "Was there a big turn out?"

"I didn't go, Ma."

"You didn't go to the funeral?"

"No," I said calmly. "I did something else."

Mom knew I didn't do well at funerals, so she just smiled and looked uncomfortable, probably hoping not to say something that could further upset me.

"I went to the Botanic Garden," I said. "A place Sabrina and I visited once." I paused, and added, "Thanks for asking, though. A normal person would've gone."

Then I went over and gave her a hug.

Chapter 20

Weeks passed and life went on. I worked every day and ran with Moose each night. Tyler went to school and continued his art lessons. And Mom started a new book at her club. We were settling in for a long, boring winter.

A week after Thanksgiving, we got clobbered with our first real snowstorm. The kind that keeps you shoveling the driveway in shifts. I'd just finished my turn and came into the kitchen, collapsing in a chair. My fingers were cold even with gloves on. My face was beet red and pulsed with numbing pain. When I took my hat off, my hair sprung into the air from static.

Tyler laughed. "Mom. You look so funny right now!"

I smiled back at him, happy that my pitiful state could amuse him, then got up and headed to the bathroom so I could comb my hair and put it into a ponytail. I heard the doorbell ring, which I thought was odd because we weren't expecting anyone. I couldn't imagine it was Jehovah's Witnesses in this weather. I blew my nose and wiped it dry. I'd have to rest a while before my next round of shoveling. I decided to go lie on the sofa with Moose.

As I left the bathroom and headed down the hall, I heard my mom talking to someone.

"Why don't you come in out of the cold," she said.

I wondered who the heck she was talking to, so I

rounded the corner to find out. As I did, I made eye contact with the unexpected visitor.

It was Miguel.

Oh, my God! This can't be happening. He can't be here, at my house. I looked like a hobo who just lost her whiskey bottle—Unbelievable!

He'd already seen me and noticed that I'd seen him. There was nothing left to do but face him.

Mom had seen me too. "Amy," she called out. "A gentleman named Miguel is here to see you."

As Miguel wiped his boots, my mom eyed me, and a satisfied smirk crossed her face. I wanted to crawl into a hole and die. Instead, I walked forward to deal with the issue head on.

The electricity in the room, fueled mostly by my mother's excitement, scared me; I thought it might cause my hair to stand up in the air again. Miguel looked up at me with a confident smile, and then reached out to shake my hand. Moose came running in to see what was going on. He proceeded to run up and jump on our guest, pawing at him, wanting to play.

"Moose. Down!" I demanded.

"It's okay," Miguel replied. "He can probably sense I'm an animal lover. He smells my cat."

Gordito.

"I'm so sorry," I continued, shooing the dog away. "He's still kind of new to the family. We haven't trained him as much as we would've liked to yet."

"It's not a problem," he said.

Mom stood there, watching the awkward scene and decided to save me. "Why don't you leave your boots to dry and come into the kitchen? I can make coffee or tea. Which would you prefer?"

"Tea. Thank you," Miguel said, and followed her out of the room.

I walked behind them, embarrassed to think of him in my messy house, so completely different from Sabrina's beautiful place. And to top things off, I looked about as attractive as a troll. This thought made me pause. Why was I so concerned about how I looked? I knew the answer, but I wasn't ready to admit it. Not yet.

Miguel took the offered seat while my mom put some water in the teapot and began heating it up. I wasn't sure what I was supposed to be doing, so I shifted nervously from one foot to the other, wondering where Tyler was. I wished he'd show up so I'd have something to do. But he was nowhere in sight.

"Amy," Mom said. "You know where the tea is. I'll give you two space to chat." She proceeded to walk out of the room, leaving me alone with him.

Normally, in this house, Tyler, my mom, and Moose were everywhere. There was hardly a moment's privacy. Now that I wanted them around, they had scattered like rats.

"Amy… it is very nice to see you again," Miguel said.

"Likewise," I nodded.

He sat back in his chair and crossed his hands. I hadn't noticed it until now, but he was carrying a briefcase. He set it on the ground, next to his chair.

"I see that I have startled you, showing up this way. I should have called first," he said.

Miguel looked sideways at me, waiting for a response. I couldn't figure out how he knew where I lived, let alone what my phone number was. But I decided not to bring that up.

I heard the teapot whistle, so I turned my attention

back to that. "Is herbal tea okay?" I asked.

"Sure."

"Any sugar?"

"No. Thank you."

The politeness and the awkwardness was not a good combination. As I poured the tea into the mug, my hand shook.

"I thought I might see you at the funeral," Miguel said, as I placed his cup in front of him.

"Um, yeah… that would make sense." I pulled out a chair and sat opposite him. "I'm not too good at those things."

Miguel offered a sincere look of understanding. And I didn't feel judged. Instead, I felt compassion.

He took a sip of his tea. And as he did, I noticed his hands. He had neatly trimmed nails. The hands of a man who takes care of himself. One of the benefits of being in the white-collar profession.

He set his cup down and glanced at me. His face was still kind, like I'd remembered from when we met at the party. "I'll bet you're wondering why I'm here. Let me explain," he said, while reaching down and opening his briefcase.

Miguel pulled out a manila folder and set it on the table. "You may or may not remember that I am a lawyer," he said.

"I remember."

He smiled, and I noticed his perfect white teeth again. The feeling of wanting to escape came over me, like the last time. But I couldn't run this time. I was in my own house.

"Well, Ms. Bergman had me in charge of all her legal affairs, both business and personal. And I wanted to come and handle this in person."

Miguel's expression turned business-like. "Okay," he said, as he opened the folder and pulled out some papers. "I am here to inform you that Ms. Bergman left you something in her will."

My jaw dropped. Sabrina? Leave something to me? Why?

Miguel noticed the shocked expression on my face and then continued in a professional manner. "I will read to you exactly as it is written," he said. "To my good friend, Amy White, the person who has taught me the most about true friendship, I bequeath twenty thousand dollars—"

"What?" I shrieked. "Are you kidding?"

In my unbelieving state, I'd rudely interrupted. Miguel was kind enough to pause. I tried to compose myself and said, "I'm sorry. I'm in… just a surreal place right now. Please continue."

Miguel smiled and nodded. Then he backed up and continued. "I bequeath twenty thousand dollars to be used to travel to that special place where she has always wanted to go."

He stopped and looked up at me. I was experiencing a mixture of emotions. Disbelief, shock, gratitude, hysteria. I couldn't mentally process what was happening to me. With all my loud antics, I was surprised my mom or Tyler hadn't come into the room.

I stared at Miguel, overwhelmed with emotion.

"I guess I can see why you'd like to do these things in person," I said.

He leaned back in his chair. "It is one of the better parts of my job but not the only reason I wanted to come."

"Bet you changed your mind about that when you came in," I said, while pointing to my outfit. "There's no glamour in shoveling," I joked, a weak attempt to flirt.

"I suspect you could make moving snow seem elegant," he replied.

I couldn't hold back a smile. "Thanks," I replied. "Oh, and by the way, I listened to your CD."

This got his attention. He set the papers he was holding down. "And what did you think?" he asked.

"I liked it. It was completely unexpected and unique."

Pride swelled in Miguel, and he seemed to expand a little. He looked a bit like Tyler gets when I give him a compliment.

"And what did you think of the ending?" he asked.

Yes. I remembered the ending, the part where he gave me his phone number and asked me to call. I shifted nervously from one foot to the other, unsure what to say. "Well, as you know, I haven't called. I'm sorry if that hurt your feelings. But the truth is, I wasn't ready for that. I'm not sure I'm ready for it now, either," I answered.

Miguel seemed unfazed. He nodded his head and said, "I think I understand."

With that over, he reached back into his pile of papers and pulled out a legal-sized envelope and handed it to me. "Well," he said, "I guess all that is left is for me to give you this."

I took the envelope.

"Your check, for the trip," Miguel clarified.

I held the envelope in my hand, unable to comprehend it was actually mine, that she had given it to me.

Sabrina, even in death, was full of surprises. Her mysteries never ceased.

"Thank you," I told Miguel. "I really appreciate you

stopping by. This gift from Sabrina… I'm overjoyed beyond words."

Miguel winked at me. "Enjoy," he said, and as an afterthought added, "And now that you are a rich woman and my workload has slowed down significantly, perhaps you'll take pity on me and treat me to dinner sometime."

Not only was he kind, he was funny too. And apparently, he didn't give up easy. I responded with a nervous giggle.

"If anything comes up," he said, "I will contact you by phone or email. I got all your contact info from Sabrina's assistant, Henry."

Miguel got up, gathered his papers and shut his briefcase. "Well," he said, then handed me a card. "Here's my business card in case you need to reach me. Or if you want to send me any new clients. It would be much appreciated."

It killed me how he could make such a smooth transition from asking for a date to soliciting new business. I guess it came with the territory. Part of his job was communicating well.

"Will do," I replied.

I walked him to the front door and handed him his coat. He put his boots back on, buttoned his jacket, and put his hand out. I extended mine to shake his. Instead, Miguel bent down and kissed the top of it.

"*Nos Vemos*," he said.

I had no idea what it meant. I smiled and said, "Goodbye."

After I shut the door, I stood behind the drapes, watching him. Once he climbed into his car and pulled away, I allowed myself to breathe. I closed my eyes and inhaled deeply. I mentally replayed the memory of him kissing my hand, and as I exhaled, I let myself physically react to how it made me feel.

No. I'm not ready.

I snapped my eyes open and shrugged off the feeling. I looked down at the envelope containing the check in my left hand. I wondered when she had added this to her will. Before the fight? After? I guess I'd never know. And it didn't really matter. What was important were the words she'd written: To the person who taught me the most about true friendship.

A wave of sadness came over me. Even in the middle of this joy, it couldn't be stopped. I would never see Sabrina again. A tear escaped my eye, but I wiped it away and forced a smile. Then I turned and headed back into the kitchen.

Tyler and Mom had managed to show up without me noticing them.

"Who was that?" Tyler asked.

I glanced at Mom first. She still wore her smirk, then back at Tyler. "He's a lawyer, for my friend Sabrina."

Tyler usually had a response to everything, at least a question. But he just stood blank-faced, waiting.

I saw Mom eye the envelope in my hand.

"Mom. Tyler. The man who was just here came to inform me that my friend Sabrina left me something in her will."

Mom got it now, but Tyler was still confused.

I looked at my son. "When people want to leave someone a present, they have a lawyer put it in their will. It's like a gift they want to give you if they pass away."

Recognition showed on Tyler's face. I was surprised he didn't ask more questions. He stood there waiting for more, just like my mom.

"Sabrina left me twenty thousand dollars to go on a family vacation to Bora Bora," I blurted.

"Oh, my God!" Mom shrieked. She began jumping up and down, and Moose began barking and running in circles. Tyler just stood there, stunned.

"You mean your friend is sending us to Bora Bora? We're really going?" he asked, finally catching on.

"Yes!"

"Woo-hoo!" he cheered, and began jumping up and down with Mom, who was now teary-eyed with happiness.

I let loose and ran forward, joining them in celebration. We hugged and kissed each other, like we'd won the lottery. And, in a way, we did. I glanced down at Tyler. He had a permanent smile plastered to his face.

It was really happening.

"Ma. When are we gonna go?" Tyler asked.

"Maybe we could go on Christmas break? I'd have to check with my boss first."

Tyler's face lit up like a roman candle. I'd never seen him so excited about anything in his short life.

"Let's go online and look at hotels," Mom suggested.

We spent the rest of the afternoon snacking on Kettle chips and browsing travel sites, getting prices and reading reviews. We'd all but forgotten about the driveway. Airfares were steep and hotels were charging out of this world rates. It was how I remembered it when Justin and I had looked into it—completely out of reach... until today.

Twenty thousand seemed too much at first, but once I added everything up, it wasn't too off the mark.

"Why don't I stay home with Moose," Mom suggested.

"No." I told her. "No way."

"Well, who's going to watch the dog?" she asked.

"I don't know. We'll pay someone to do it."

Mom frowned. "You know, I really think it would be best if Tyler and you went together, a mother/son trip."

I looked at her with questioning eyes, wondering why she was doing this.

"It was always your dream to go there, not mine," she said in a soft voice. "I think you should have this time together."

I could tell it was what she really wanted, so I backed down and agreed. I secretly made plans to save some of the money to spend on a big spa day for her. Maybe at that Red Door place Sabrina went to.

Tyler had left the room and came back dressed in his winter gear. "My turn to shovel," he said. "I'll be right back."

"I'll help you," I told him, rising to get my coat.

"I'll start dinner," Mom added.

We all went about our business. Tyler and I cleared the fresh layer of snow away with renewed enthusiasm. We worked well together, like a machine. The only noise that could be heard was the rhythmic sound of metal scraping against concrete. It was a cold, but beautiful, symphony.

The next day, I went to work hoping I could get time off for the trip. Even if I hadn't accrued enough vacation time, I could afford to take some days without pay if they'd let me. I had my fingers crossed.

After I punched in, I saw Dave in his office. He didn't look to be in a bad mood, so I decided it would be best to hit him up before that possibly changed.

I knocked on the door. "Can I come in?"

"Sure, what's up?"

I smiled. "Well, I've got amazing news, but it requires me asking you a favor."

Dave looked intrigued. Probably because I never had amazing news. "Shoot," he said.

"Well," I began, trying to shorten my story, "A lawyer showed up at my door the other day. He told me my friend who passed away left me something in her will."

Dave raised an eyebrow. The boss of number-crunching was very intrigued.

"I probably hadn't mentioned this before," I continued, "But Justin and I had always dreamed of travelling to the South Pacific. The friend who passed away was a mutual friend of ours. She also happened to be very wealthy. Anyway, she left me money to take my family on a vacation to Bora Bora. I was hoping to go on my son's Christmas break. I know it's short notice—"

"Done," Dave interrupted.

He hadn't even mulled it over, or considered who'd do my work while I was gone. He'd just granted my request, like a magic genie.

"Are you sure?" I asked. "Do you need me to put in some extra hours before I go?"

"Nope," he said. "Just book it. Have an amazing time… and don't worry about a thing."

I couldn't believe my good fortune was continuing. The luck of the Irish, as Justin would say.

Dave began again, "My wife and I have always wanted to go to the South Pacific," he said. "It's always someday, though. That day never seems to come. You'll be the first person I know who's gone."

I grinned. "Me. It's crazy, right?"

"It couldn't have happened to a more deserving person," he said.

I nodded, accepting his praise, then walked out of the office and shut the door. I didn't try to hide the thrill I was feeling. And of course Fatima and Barb—the notorious eavesdroppers—had heard everything.

I walked back to my desk with a spring in my step. If I were any lighter, I'd float away. Once I sat down, I turned to face my friends. Their eyes were as wide as saucers.

"You're finally going, kiddo," Barb said, while doing a little seated dance.

"For real?" Fatima asked.

I shook my head yes.

"Kick ass!" she blurted out.

"I know," I agreed.

The rest of the day was a breeze. Everything fell into place at just the right time. I made no punching errors, and everything balanced.

Life was good.

Chapter 21

The following day, Tyler and I went to the post office to get our passports. I had to pay extra to have them processed in a rush. Afterward, I dropped him off at school and went to work, where I experienced another easy day. They were all feeling that way now, with the bigger picture—Mt. Otemanu, to be specific—on the horizon.

In the evening, I folded laundry, and delivered Tyler's to his room. His Bora Bora painting was proudly displayed on the wall. I smiled. Josephine had helped him come a long way. When he walked in, he saw me admiring it.

"Won't be long," he said. "I told Dad about it the other night. You know, when I talk to him."

A familiar pain gripped my heart. Not because Tyler was talking about him. I was used to that. But because Justin was the one who really wanted to go to the South Pacific. It was his big dream, and we all got caught up in it.

"That's good, honey. I know your dad would be so happy for us."

Tyler nodded, and he took some socks out of my hand and began putting them away in his dresser.

We filled the weekend shopping for summery clothes. No easy task since they weren't in season. On Sunday, I told Mom and Tyler I needed some time to myself to get a present. I took a drive and stopped at Northbrook Court, where I'd met Sabrina. I found Red Door Spa and bought my mom a gift certificate. A full day of pampering. I knew she'd love coming here, rather than spending a day at home with products from under the sink.

Before we knew it, our passports came in. Our trip was booked and the date was approaching fast. I used some of the money from Sabrina to buy Josephine a little something for the holidays. I'd even gotten a tiny gift for Fatima, Barb, and Dave. It felt great to be able to treat them for a change.

Two weeks before Christmas, I received a confirmation email from Expedia, with my full itinerary update.

Before logging off, I saw another email. The subject read: *Feliz Navidad*. I was hesitant to click on it, thinking it could be a computer virus, but part of me knew it was from Miguel. I almost sent it to the trash bin, but I knew that would have been rude. So I opened it instead.

It was as I suspected, a holiday greeting from Miguel. "Amy, It's Miguel. Just wanted to say Happy Holidays to you, and to say I hope you enjoyed your trip, wherever it is you may have gone. Work is slow this month, and my nephew is in town. He helped me create this YouTube video I think you might like. He says it may go viral, whatever that means. Maybe we can get together soon for coffee? Starbucks has the peppermint latte now."

I giggled. Who in their right mind ends an email pitching the coffee of the season? This man had a knack for disarming me, for making something scary seem downright okay. I knew it was his job to be convincing, but it never felt like I was being manipulated. He seemed genuine. He *was* genuine. It was me… I was the one who thought too much, the one who had a hard time letting go.

I clicked on the attachment and it opened in a new window. Miguel was wearing a Santa hat while holding an acoustic guitar. His familiar sidekick, Gordito, wore antler ears and sat beside him.

The strumming began and sure enough, it was "Feliz Navidad." As Miguel sang and played, the cat meowed loudly in all the wrong places. They both looked so serious and professional and that made it even more hilarious. I could tell it was heavily rehearsed.

Laughter would've been appropriate. I think that was the whole point, but I couldn't giggle. Instead as I listened, I watched and wondered. How could a person be so unafraid? To set it all out there, not just for me, but for everyone to see?

When the song ended, I closed the window and re-read the original email. I admired Miguel for his courage. That was a quality I never got a chance to develop. Or maybe I just never really tried.

I clicked the reply button and typed a response. "Miguel, Nice to hear from you. What a video. It was really great. No kidding. I haven't gone on vacation yet. I leave in one week. Regarding getting together for coffee, why don't I give you a call when I come back? I still have your card, Amy."

After I hit send, I wondered if I'd made a mistake. I wasn't even sure I'd said the right things. I didn't know how to talk to men or be charming. With Justin, all I ever had to be was myself. He loved me just how I was.

I decided to stop stressing. I honestly didn't care how things turned out. The man kept asking to see me, so I would meet him and have a cup of coffee. End of story.

Wednesday night, I accompanied Tyler to his art class. Josephine looked especially beautiful, and I thought maybe she'd done something different. Then I noticed what it was. Her hair was smooth and pin straight. I told her she looked nice.

"I have a little something for you," I said while reaching into my purse. I handed her a wrapped gift.

"Thank you. That's so kind," Josephine said. Then she added, "Hey. I heard the Universe delivered big time."

"Come again?" I asked.

She realized I didn't speak hippie and clarified. "Your trip to the South Pacific, I mean."

I smiled. I understood what she meant now. "Yes. We're really excited. We can't wait until next week."

I waved goodbye to Josephine and went to run an errand. On my way around town, I thought about Tyler. I loved him so much and was glad we were taking this trip together. Mom was right. It was a good idea.

Later in the week, as I walked past Tyler's room, I saw him organizing his summer clothing, planning what he'd wear on vacation, grouping items into piles. I didn't interrupt him. I just shook my head in disbelief. Tyler wasn't a normal kid. He was my kid. He was the best.

That night I lay in bed, thinking of the possible coffee date with Miguel, wondering if I would really call. I wished it would happen later, down the road more. I still wasn't ready to start dating.

I thought about what Justin had confided in Sabrina before he died, that he hoped I would find someone else to share my life with… It seemed so strange to think of now. When I'd first heard it, I didn't believe it was true. Then, the more I thought of it, I realized that sounded exactly like Justin. Even while he was leaving this world, he was still thinking of me.

Justin could never be replaced—ever. I felt frightened as I even considered it. The faint glow of the night light nearby was the only thing that calmed me, made me feel safe. It lit up my bonsai tree ever so slightly, throwing soft shadows across the room. I stared at my tree, admiring its quiet beauty and felt my muscles relax. No one would be able to replace Justin. Miguel wasn't trying to. He was just doing what came natural to him... being himself. Wasn't that what I said I liked about my relationship before? That I could just be me?

I decided I wouldn't worry about it anymore. I'd focus on my vacation. That was what Sabrina had wanted me to do.

Chapter 22

The days passed quickly, and before we knew it, Tyler and I were leaving for the South Pacific.

On my last day at work, Fatima came to say goodbye to me. "I hate you right now," she joked.

I responded with a smile and a big hug. "I won't think of you, here at your desk, while I'm bathing in the French Polynesian sun."

She play-punched me in the arm.

"Ouch." But we were both smiling.

Barb came and said farewell. "Relax, and have a good time."

I grinned. "I assure you, I will."

Dave came out of his office and shut the door. He winked, and said, "Enjoy the trip. We'll see you in a week."

I felt like a super-star right then. I'd had nothing but positive send offs all day. People seemed genuinely happy for me, and I made a mental note to socialize with them more when I got back.

I punched out and stepped outside. It was raining. I didn't care about cold, rainy, gray, though. We were leaving tonight. That was all that mattered.

When I got home, I noticed a pizza box on the counter. Mom said she wanted to get us something to eat before dropping us off at the airport. I felt sad that she wasn't coming along, but she had repeatedly assured me it was what she wanted. And Moose couldn't ask for a better babysitter.

We inhaled our food and guzzled our drinks. Tyler had created a checklist for us the night before, so he could make sure we had everything we needed. We gathered our luggage, and then double-checked our passports, IDs, and tickets. Everything was in order.

Moose stood next to me, wagging his tail. "I'll miss you. Be good for Grandma," I said in a baby voice.

Tyler leaned down to hug and kiss Moose, and then we climbed into the car. My mom insisted on driving to the airport. "Chauffer service," she'd said.

After arriving at O'Hare, we parked and Mom walked with us to the departure area. She leaned down to Tyler, "You have a good time," she said, while giving him a big hug and a kiss.

They said their goodbyes and Mom approached me. We didn't have to say a word. She hugged me tight. "Relax and enjoy," she said.

I hugged her back. "I will."

Mom walked back to her car, and I looked down at Tyler. "You all set?"

"Yes, ma'am," he said. He grabbed hold of the suitcase handle and started walking up the ramp.

Tyler and I strode side by side, through the sliding glass doors, and it felt like a scene from a movie. This couldn't be my life, I thought. But it was, and soon the ticket agent was there, showing us how to check in on the computer. Before we knew it, we were seated on the plane.

Chapter 23

I woke up to the sound of the captain saying we'd be landing in Papeete, Tahiti. Weather conditions? Eighty-five degrees.

Tyler and I looked at each other and grinned. We were giddy.

We pushed our tray tables up and adjusted our seats, returning them to their upright position.

An older lady had the window seat, but I didn't mind. I'd heard this wasn't the spectacular part. Landing in Bora Bora was what the hype was all about.

"Almost there," I said, rubbing the top of my son's head.

When we got off the plane, we were greeted by the warm, humid smell of the tropics. I'd never been a fan of humidity, but on vacation it was different. It was something I looked forward to.

I had overheard a couple fellow travelers saying they were connecting to Bora Bora, so we followed them to the next gate. This time, after boarding, Tyler got the window seat and I was right next to him. We'd lucked out. We were even on the left side of the plane, something I read was ideal to catch the best view.

The flight was only forty-five minutes long. A blink compared to the many hours we'd already endured. We were tired but found new wells of energy for this final leg of the trip.

Within a short time, we were descending. And as promised, the view blew our minds. I gasped as I caught the first glimpse. Tyler's jaw dropped open.

It was Heaven.

Green jagged peaks stretched high into the sky, surrounded by electric blue turquoise water enclosed in a protective lagoon.

"My God," I whispered.

"Yeah," Tyler agreed.

After landing, we were able to get off right away. We walked over to a welcome desk for our hotel. An American-looking woman waited for us.

"Welcome to Bora Bora," she said in an Australian accent.

She took our names and we climbed aboard a boat that would transfer us to our hotel. As we stepped in, one of the staff members put leis around our necks. These weren't the plastic leis you find in party supply stores. They were made of real flowers. Then they handed us bottled water and chilled damp white towels.

Tyler looked over at me. "I could get used to this."

"Me, too."

We completed hotel check-in on the boat on the way to the resort. While I quickly went through the forms, I was at the same time aware of the dazzling scenery all around me. Tyler stood at the front of the boat, taking it all in. In a few moments, I joined him.

On the ride to our hotel, which was on the surrounding motu instead of the main island, we stared in awe at Mt. Otemanu. It was breathtaking.

I lifted my sunglasses to take a look at Tyler. Sun

bathed his fair skin and the ocean breeze tousled his blonde hair. There we were... in Bora Bora, on our way to the Four Seasons.

The boat stopped and we were greeted by a new set of staff members who gave us a tour of the resort, then showed us to our room. Like magic, our bags had arrived before we did.

Did I call it a room? It was an overwater villa with its own sundeck and plunge pool. I checked out the bathroom. It had a deep tub with sliding glass doors that opened to a view of the lagoon. Everything was perfect and unbelievable.

I came onto the deck and found Tyler admiring his surroundings, completely in awe. I stood beside him, and we both were still.

I'd never seen water so blue and clear. It was like a million turquoise gemstones had melted into a never-ending sea. It was one of the best moments of my life.

"Are you hungry yet?" I asked Tyler, interrupting the silence.

"No. I'm good. I'm too excited to eat. How about you?"

"I can wait until later," I replied. "It's hot, though. What do you say we jump into our very own pool?"

"Okay," Tyler said, so enthusiastic he could hardly contain himself. "I'll go put on my suit."

We both changed and found our way back to the deck at the same time. Instead of testing the water temperature with our feet, we jumped in, crazed with happiness, and began splashing each other back and forth.

I behaved like a child, like him, and it was pure bliss.

We swam for a bit, and then I got out and climbed onto one of the cushy lounge chairs. I was so jet-lagged, I could've fallen asleep right there. But I didn't want to close my eyes. I didn't want to miss anything.

Tyler couldn't sit still and lay in the sun. He opened his luggage and got out his colored pencils and blank sketchpad. He said he wanted to begin drawing at once. He had the perfect view of Mt. Otemanu and wanted to capture it.

Once I saw him seated and working, I reluctantly closed my eyes. Later, as I rolled onto my other side, I was groggy and disoriented. A distinctly familiar smell had wafted my way. Justin's cologne.

I inhaled again, this time deeper, and it woke me. I sat up and looked around, half expecting to see him.

But no one was there.

I let out a heavy sigh. In my heart, I knew he was with us.

I squinted to get a better look at Tyler. He was drawing and looking very serious with his baseball cap on. He wouldn't wear sunglasses because he said they'd alter his view.

I got up off the chaise and yawned.

"Hey, T.," I called out. "Getting hungry yet?"

"Yeah. I'm starved," he said.

"Okay. I'm going to get changed first."

I dressed in a casual sundress, flip flops, and put my hair in a ponytail. Just for fun, I added some pink lip gloss too.

When I got back on the deck, Tyler had finished his first sketch.

"It's beautiful, honey."

"Thanks, Mom."

Tyler closed his pad and gathered his pencils. Then he went inside to change. Within five minutes, he was ready.

We walked the pier, with its over-water villas jutting out on both sides, and headed to the main restaurant. There was no bad table in the whole place, but I was convinced we got the best one.

"I'm going to order seafood," I announced.

Tyler looked confused. "I thought you didn't like it?"

"I don't usually, but I'm sure I will here. And," I joked, "If I don't love it I will order something else."

"Well, excuse me, Madame," Tyler replied in a fake French accent.

We both giggled, but not too loud. We were at a five star resort after all.

The food arrived and we feasted. Everything tasted delicious. I ordered myself a tropical drink. Then the manager stopped by with a non-alcoholic tropical drink for Tyler. They knew how to take care of their guests.

We were too full to eat dessert, so we decided we'd have some tomorrow night. Instead, we walked around the grounds.

"Do you wanna walk on the beach?" Tyler asked.

I smiled. "Sure. It could count as our family workout."

Tyler grinned back, and we headed for the sand.

The sun was beginning to set. And we both sat there watching it. For the next hour we hardly spoke. We just stared in awe at a sky ablaze with slow-moving orange and purple streaks. The water color shifted from light to progressively darker shades of blue.

"Wow," Tyler whispered.

"Yeah." I was mesmerized by Mother Nature's show.

Afterward, we both got up and brushed the sand off our butts. We walked the pier back to our villa, and once we got back in, Tyler grabbed his pencils and sketchpad again. I'd never seen him so motivated.

I decided to unpack our things and spend time putting away toiletries and hanging our clothes. When Tyler was finished drawing, he called me over to see his creation.

"Another masterpiece, Gauguin," I said and winked.

Tyler puffed up with pride. I hadn't used his nickname in a while.

"Hey. Do you want to walk on the beach at night? I'll bet it will be amazing," I asked.

"I think I will do it tomorrow," he said. "I'm starting to get so tired. Plus, I want to watch TV."

I sighed. I wanted to do it tonight. Tyler picked up on it and said, "Mom. I'll be right here in the room. Why don't you go?"

At first, I wasn't sure it was a good idea. Then I decided it would be safe. I made sure I heard him lock the door after I left with my own room key.

I wouldn't go far. Just from the pier to the beach. I strolled barefoot, on the powdery white moonlit sand. No one else was around.

The air smelled fresh, filled with the scent of exotic flowers. It was warm outside, but a slight ocean breeze cooled me.

I looked up. The night sky was pitch black, with a canopy of twinkling stars overhead.

Just then, a thought crossed my mind. *Sabrina... my odd, unusual friend... I miss you.*

As if in response, a shooting star whizzed past, then fizzled out, disappearing into the heavens.

I smiled and heard Tyler's voice in my head. "The Universe is speaking to you."

Indeed. It definitely was.

Thanks for reading *A Widow Redefined*.
I hope you enjoyed it.

Your FREE book is waiting.

The Rescue is the heartwarming story of the dog that cheated death and transformed a woman's life.

Get your free copy at the link below.

To get your free copy, just join my readers' group here:

kimcano.com/the-rescue-giveaway-lp

Books by Kim Cano

Novels:

A Widow Redefined

On The Inside

Eighty and Out

His Secret Life

When the Time Is Right

Novelette:

The Rescue

Short Story Collection:

For Animal Lovers

About the Author

Kim Cano is the author of five women's fiction novels: *A Widow Redefined*, *On The Inside*, *Eighty and Out*, *His Secret Life*, and *When the Time Is Right*. Kim has also written a short story collection called *For Animal Lovers*. 10% of the sale price of that book is donated to the ASPCA® to help homeless pets.

Kim wrote a contemporary romance called *My Dream Man* under the pen name Marie Solka.

Kim lives in the Chicago suburbs with her husband and cat.

Visit her website for a free book and learn of new releases: www.kimcano.com

Find Kim Online:

Website: www.kimcano.com

On Twitter: twitter.com/KimCano2

Facebook Fan Page:
facebook.com/pages/Kim-Cano/401511463198088

Goodreads:
goodreads.com/author/show/5895829.Kim_Cano

Made in the USA
Middletown, DE
05 July 2024

56867117R00165